Constance VERITY SAVES THE WORLD

A. LEE MARTINEZ

— BOOK TWO —

SAGA PRESS

LONDON SYDNEY **NEW YORK** TORONTO NEW DELHI

SAGA ⟩⟩ PRESS

AN IMPRINT OF SIMON & SCHUSTER, INC.

1230 AVENUE OF THE AMERICAS, NEW YORK, NEW YORK 10020

• Text copyright © 2018 by Alex Martinez • Jacket illustration copyright © 2018 by Jon Picacio •
For information address Saga Press Subsidiary Rights Department, 1230 Avenue of the Americas, New York, NY 10020 • SAGA PRESS and colophon are trademarks of Simon & Schuster, Inc. • For information about special discounts for bulk purchases, please contact Simon & Schuster Special Sales at 1-866-506-1949 or business@simonandschuster.com. • The Simon & Schuster Speakers Bureau can bring authors to your live event. For more information or to book an event, contact the Simon & Schuster Speakers Bureau at 1-866-248-3049 or visit our website at www.simonspeakers.com. • Also available in a Saga Press paperback edition • The text for this book was set in Goudy Old Style BT. • Manufactured in the United States of America • First Saga Press hardcover edition July 2018 • 10 9 8 7 6 5 4 3 2 1 • CIP data for this book is available from the Library of Congress. • ISBN 978-1-4814-4354-8 (hardcover) • ISBN 978-1-4814-4355-5 (pbk) • ISBN 978-1-4814-4356-2 (eBook)

To Mom,
To the DFW Writers' Workshop,
To Sally,
And to Edgar Rice Burroughs

CONSTANCE VERITY
SAVES THE WORLD

I t was date night, and Constance Verity was wrestling an alligator woman in her underwear. How the alligator woman ended up wearing Connie's underwear was a mystery she never solved.

Connie herself currently wore a towel, rolling around on the floor with her opponent. She'd wrestled people and alligators, but not a combination of both at once. It was trickier than she expected. Several times, Connie had the alligator woman locked down, only for the woman to use her tail for leverage or almost bite Connie's face off, forcing a withdrawal.

She did not have time for this. Byron would be there in a few minutes. He would be on time. He was always on time. Usually early. It was one of the things she admired about him, but it also meant she couldn't spend all night subduing her opponent.

She hadn't even picked out her outfit yet.

Connie wrapped her legs around the alligator woman, choked her out with a full nelson. It took precious minutes for the alligator woman to lose consciousness. The moment she went limp, Connie rolled her over, grabbed some rope she kept in her sock drawer, and hogtied the intruder. In Connie's life, it often paid to have some spare rope lying around.

The alligator woman rolled around on the floor. She growled and hissed and snapped her toothy jaws.

Six minutes to get ready.

Connie made a call. She didn't wait for the person on the other end to say anything.

"I've got an alligator woman in my apartment, and I need her picked up now."

There was a pause.

"Who is this?" asked Agent Ellington.

"You know damn well who this is," said Connie.

"I'm afraid you've made a mistake," said Ellington. "I am a government liaison. Not your personal valet."

Connie adjusted her towel, checked herself in the mirror. There weren't any fresh scrapes or bruises, aside from a small scratch on her shoulder. "I'm calling in a favor."

"We don't owe you any favors."

"Don't you? Two weeks ago, I kept the supervolcano under Yellowstone from erupting."

"So?"

"So, that's a pretty big favor."

"Constance, you do things of that nature all the time. Are we supposed to keep a running tally?"

"Isn't that your job?"

Ellington sighed. "Yes, I suppose it is. But I don't work for you."

Five minutes and counting.

"I don't ask for much," said Connie. "But I have a date tonight, and after dinner, we'll be coming back here. If we end up in my bedroom with an alligator woman bound at the foot of my bed, it'll probably ruin the mood."

"He might be into it."

"Is Agent Harrison ever coming back?" asked Connie.

"Now you're just trying to hurt my feelings," replied Ellington. "All right, Constance. One pickup. But this isn't going to become a regular thing."

"Great. Wait twenty minutes and then let yourself in. And, Ellington, thanks."

"You're welcome."

Connie ended the call. Four minutes. She grabbed something easy out of her closet. She'd never been a high-fashion kind of lady. When many little girls were planning their wedding, she'd been exploring the seventh dimension and escaping robots. Comfort was preferred over style in such situations. She was able to get dressed in twenty seconds flat, a skill she'd picked up along the way.

She brushed her teeth and ran a comb through her hair. She'd been toying with the idea of makeup, but that was another thing she didn't have much experience with. She could disarm fourteen kinds of bombs, but she still tended to overdo the rouge.

Three minutes. Plenty of time.

The alligator woman rolled to one side, bumping into a

chest of drawers, knocking a lamp off the top. Connie's reflexes sprang into action. She caught the lamp, set it down safely.

"If you don't stop squirming around, I'm going to have to knock you out again," she said.

The alligator woman growled.

"Have it your way, but I'm unfamiliar with your physiology, so don't complain to me if you wake up with a killer headache."

Connie knelt down and pressed her thumb on the alligator woman's throat. The press itself was less important than the channeling of inner chi to stifle the flow of vitality. The woman passed out.

There was a knock on the door.

Byron was early. Connie hopped over the woman and shut the bedroom door behind her.

He wore a gray suit. He must've come straight from work. His necktie was crooked. He couldn't get it right to save his life. It was one of the things she found endearing about him. One of many things.

He leaned in and kissed her. He ran his finger across a scrape on her forehead. One several days old.

"Trouble in the Congo?" he asked.

"Antarctica," she corrected. "And nothing I couldn't handle." She took his hand and pulled him out of the apartment.

He pulled back. "I was hoping to use the bathroom first."

"Yeah, sure. No problem."

She heard the edge in her voice, but hopefully, Byron wouldn't notice.

"Something wrong?" he asked. Okay, so maybe he would.

She smiled. "No, I'm just hungry."

She didn't like lying to him. She didn't do it often. She didn't need to. He knew all about the other half of her life, but Byron wasn't part of that. Just like she didn't know a lot about his accounting job.

"I know you," he said. "Something's wrong."

"We'll talk about it at the restaurant," she replied, although she had no such intention.

"Connie . . ."

She pushed him into the bathroom and checked on the alligator woman—still thankfully unconscious. Byron came out a few minutes later.

"Connie . . ."

"We'll talk on the way." She maneuvered him out the door. Once in the hall, she breathed easier.

The alligator woman howled.

"Neighbor got a new dog," said Connie as she led Byron down the hall.

At dinner, her attempts to change the subject met with resistance.

"All right, Connie. I'm not an idiot," he said. "What was going on?"

"Nothing," she replied. "Nothing important, anyway."

He stabbed his fork into his pasta and shook his head. "I hate when you do that."

"Do what?"

"Hide things from me."

"What?"

"Don't act like you don't do it," he said.

"I didn't think you were interested in that part of my life."

"Connie, that part of your life is important."

"Can we not talk about this tonight?" she asked.

"When will we talk about it?"

She reached across the table and took his hand. "Later."

He squeezed her hand. "All right, but we *will* talk about it later. You can't compartmentalize your life."

Sure, she could. She could do anything.

Back at her place, she checked her bedroom. The alligator woman was gone, but a strange red fog was spilling out from her closet door.

Byron came up behind her and put his arms around her. He kissed her neck.

She shut the bedroom door and led him toward the couch. He didn't question. They made out for a few minutes until he stopped.

"Okay, something is definitely wrong," he said. "You're distracted."

"What? No. I'm totally into this." She grabbed his head and planted a deep, passionate kiss on him. His concerns melted away as she ran her hands up his chest and curled her fingers through his hair. She was unbuttoning his shirt when she noticed the wisps of red mist creeping from the edges of her bedroom door. This problem wasn't going away. Her problems rarely did.

"Do you mind if we call it a night?" she asked.

"Now?" His hands were resting on her ass as she straddled him. "Okay, so you're definitely distracted."

She slid off him. "I'm just really beat."

"We don't have to do anything," he said. "We could just cuddle."

Cuddling sounded great. More than cuddling sounded even better. But worlds were colliding, and she needed to avert that.

She shoved Byron out the front door. He put up surprisingly little resistance, which was helpful but bothered her a little.

"Connie, we need to talk," he said.

She cringed. They *needed* to talk.

Across infinite dimensions, endless time, and boundless space, nothing good ever came of *needing* to talk.

"Sure. Next time. We'll talk and talk and talk." She filled the air with words, not leaving him space to reply. "Just next time, all right?"

He opened his mouth.

"Great. Next time." She shut the door and waited for him to knock.

He didn't.

Again, she was both relieved and disappointed.

Her bedroom door burst open and more fog spilled forth. A massive warrior wearing a loincloth snorted at her. He narrowed his cruel, red eyes and snorted.

"Relationships. Right?" asked Connie.

The warrior threw an axe at her head. She ducked aside and the weapon buried itself in her door. She wrenched it free and swung it over her head. The balance was off, but she could work with it.

Relationships were complicated, but this was easy.

The warrior hurled himself forward, and she rushed to meet him.

The next day, she met Tia over drinks and shared her aborted date night.

"Wait," said Tia. "Where did the barbarian come from?"

"Dimensional rift in my closet," replied Connie. "I thought I'd had them all cleared, but either I missed this one or the clearing needs refreshing. I'll have to give the place the once-over again."

"Meanwhile, warriors from other realities will just be stepping through your closet?"

"I closed this one. It should stay closed."

"How'd Byron take it?"

Connie mumbled something. Even she wasn't sure what it was.

"He freaked?" asked Tia.

"No."

"Great. I didn't think he was the freaking type, from what you've told me."

"I kicked him out before he could see anything," said Connie. "For his own safety, of course."

"Of course." Tia fixed Connie with a quiet stare. "Bet that pissed him off."

"Maybe a little," said Connie. "He said we *needed* to talk."

"Shit."

"Yeah. Shit."

"You can't exactly blame the guy," said Tia. "You've been stringing him along for a while now."

Connie said, "What the hell does that mean?"

Tia shook her head. "Never mind. You don't want to know what I think."

"Yes, I do."

"No, you don't."

"Yes, I do."

"No . . . Fine, but don't take this the wrong way."

Connie forced a smile. "Why would I?"

"I'm only saying this because I'm your friend, but if you're going to make this work, you're going to have to share more of your life with Byron."

"I share plenty of my life."

"Then how come I haven't met him yet?"

"Do you want to meet him?"

"He's your boyfriend. Yes, I want to meet him."

"We'll schedule something, then," said Connie.

"Saturday," said Tia. "You can come over to my place. We'll have dinner. You and Byron, me and Hiro, some other people."

"Who?"

"Coworkers."

"They don't like me."

"Oh, they like you fine."

Connie was certain they didn't. She'd never done anything to them. She'd only exchanged a few words with most of them, but she always sensed an aura of hostility. It must've been simply a lifestyle clash. She was an adventurer. They were in the insurance game. Like oil and water, but with the oil also being on fire and wrestling bears and getting in gunfights and stuff that any rational insurance adjustor wisely avoided.

"You're making excuses," said Tia.

Connie didn't like the idea of Byron meeting her ninja ex-boyfriend. She wasn't too keen on Byron meeting Tia, either. Tia was a normal person, but by virtue of being Connie's oldest friend, Tia had also accumulated her share of unusual experiences. The thought of the four of them sitting at a table filled Connie with dread.

"It'll be fun," said Tia.

"Sure. Fun."

"At some point, you're going to have to decide if you're serious or not with this guy."

"I am serious," said Connie. "Just not serious serious."

Tia chuckled. "You're really bad at this normal stuff."

"Can we not use that word. *Normal.* Like what I do is abnormal. And I'm not bad at normal stuff. I'm just not great at it. It's only noteworthy because I'm great at so many things."

Tia ordered another mai tai. "So, if you're not serious serious, then what are you?"

"I don't know. I like Byron. A lot. But sometimes, I think— and I know how terrible this sounds—he's a bit vulnerable. He's so normal."

She sucked a deep breath through her gritted teeth.

"He's not special."

Connie's hands fell to her side, and she stared in exasperation at the ceiling. The kitschy bric-a-brac hanging over her head, especially an old-timey bicycle, irritated her for some reason. Just by being there. Just because it was so obviously there to be kitschy.

"He's vulnerable," she said. "So far, I've managed to keep him out of the line of fire, but one of these days, he's bound to end up in the middle of something. You know how I am with . . ." She struggled with a good word, but only one kept popping into her damned brain. ". . . normal guys."

"I know," said Tia.

Connie's normal romantic relationships never ended well. She was usually too busy to be bothered by the breakups, but the guys who were eaten by monsters still haunted her now and then.

"You're paranoid," said Tia. "It makes sense. But you're not the same person you were. You fixed that caretaker thing, didn't you. You're not entirely normal, but you're more normal than you were."

Since removing most of the magical blessing that had defined Connie's life, she'd still been drawn into adventures, but it was more in her control now. She could even ignore them, and they'd sometimes go away on their own. She had something resembling a quieter life now. Quieter than it had ever been before.

"Look at it this way," said Tia. "If you keep dating Byron, worlds are bound to collide sooner or later. But if there's one place in this world where nothing weird or exciting is going to happen, with a complete absence of international intrigue and/ or fiendish plots, it'll be at a party with a bunch of insurance adjustors and actuaries."

"You can't guarantee that."

"No, I can't, since you'll be there, but you're my best friend." Tia grinned. "I have to invite you."

Byron's sister, Dana, lived across the hall from Connie. She was nice, if a little too ready with life advice. It wasn't that her advice was bad. It just didn't usually apply to Connie.

"You should hire a maid," said Dana. "Or you could just give me a key. I wouldn't mind stepping in to dust the place when you're away on your missions." She ran her finger across Connie's television. "That's what they're called, right? Missions?"

"Adventures," replied Connie. "Although sometimes, they're also missions."

"What's the difference?" asked Dana.

"All missions are adventures, but not all adventures are missions."

Dana nodded, but she wasn't listening. She had a tendency to focus on her own thoughts. It might have been annoying, but Connie liked having someone around who didn't think too much of her. Aside from Tia, there weren't many people who could handle hanging out with Constance Verity. Dana was just self-involved enough to not be starstruck.

"I wouldn't even charge you," she said. "Just a favor."

"It's cool, but I do appreciate the offer."

Dana reached for an idol on a shelf. "Shouldn't this be in a museum?"

"It's only a reproduction," said Connie. "And it's cursed."

"A cursed reproduction? Who does that?"

"You'd be surprised. If you're trying to forge a cursed artifact, you have to curse it yourself. Otherwise, it's a dead giveaway."

"That makes a surprising amount of sense, though I would think you'd get rid of it. Just to be safe."

"I've tried. It keeps coming back."

The bug-eyed idol stared at Dana. "Can I at least turn it around?"

"Be my guest."

Dana turned the hideous thing the other direction. A tremor shook the building. The rumble grew in intensity. Connie grabbed her glass as it rattled its way to the edge of the coffee table.

"All right, already." Dana turned the idol back around, and the tremors ceased. "Temperamental, isn't it?" She glanced across the shelves. "Are all these things cursed?"

"About a third. Another third are enchanted."

"There's a difference?"

"Excalibur makes you King of England," she said. "The cursed Muramasa blade makes you an invincible warrior but demands you take a life a day."

Dana pulled her hand away from the ancient Japanese sword on Connie's shelf. "Oh."

"I should probably organize them better," admitted Connie.

"You're going to run out of room," said Dana.

"I give most of them away eventually or put them in storage."

"You shouldn't be living in an apartment, anyway," said Dana. "You should get a house. You're rich. Why not move into a manor? Or a penthouse condo?"

"I like having a small place," replied Connie.

"That's great for you," said Dana, "but what about later?"

The word *later* hung in the air. Dana was Byron's sister, but there were times she was more like his mother. It might've been because their actual mother had died years before or because Dana had fixed Connie and Byron up in the first place. Or Dana was a busybody who knew what was best for everybody, even if she was subtler than most busybodies. Connie had learned to ignore it, and Dana was usually polite enough to allow it. Usually.

"You can't raise a family in this place," said Dana. "You can't childproof a room full of cursed artifacts."

"I grew up around stuff like this."

"But you're you. You're designated to deal with it, aren't you? I'm talking about normal children."

Connie didn't want to have this conversation. She checked the time. Byron wasn't due for another half hour.

"I should really get ready." She had no official plans, but maybe Dana would catch the hint.

She sat on the couch. "I love my brother, Connie. And I like you. But have you thought about where this is going?"

"No."

Connie hoped the brusque reply would deter Dana, but she was a juggernaut of sisterly concern and friendly advice. Once she got going, the only option was to step aside or get run over.

"The life you live, it's complicated. What about kids? If you and Byron settle down and decide to have children, how do you hope to manage that, living like you do? Hard to be a mom when you're off visiting the moons of Atlantis or busting ghosts."

"No offense, Dana, but I don't think that's any of your business."

"Byron is my business. I just want to make sure you're doing right by him."

"That's up to Byron, isn't it?"

Dana chuckled with a touch of condescension. "My brother doesn't always know what's best for him. That's why I have to watch out for him. And I'm hoping you do too."

"Do you want us to break up?" asked Connie.

"I never said that. I like you two together, and it's obvious Byron likes you a lot. But there are things he wants that I worry you won't be able to give him."

"Has he said anything?"

"Oh, no. He doesn't like to talk to me about stuff like that. I don't know why."

Maybe because Dana always knew better. She was confident

in her opinions of how everyone should live their lives.

But it didn't mean she was wrong this time.

Dana said, "Well, I have to get going. Theater tickets."

"You're not dressed for the theater."

"Underground theater," replied Dana, using her fingers as quotation marks. "Whatever the hell that means."

Dana's hipster artist boyfriend wasn't the type of guy Connie would imagine Dana belonged with, but somehow, they made it work.

"God, I hope it's not a one-man show," said Dana.

"You don't know?"

"I didn't have the courage to ask. Wish me luck."

"Can do. I have a feeling you'll need it."

Dana left, and Connie took a shower while waiting for Byron.

She pondered her limits. She was capable of so much, but she tried envisioning herself with a husband and kids, a house in the suburbs, a dog that barked too much, waging a never-ending battle with the homeowners' association over the color of her mailbox. Off-white was close enough to eggshell that they should mind their own goddamn business.

The absurdity of such a simple thing being out of her reach almost amused her.

When she was younger, she'd thought about having children. At twenty-six, there'd been a king who had wanted to make her his queen. She'd almost taken him up on it, but then the grand vizier had betrayed the kingdom, killing the king in an attempt to steal the throne. Connie had killed the vizier, restoring justice and claiming her revenge, but that had been the day she'd decided certain choices just weren't hers to make.

She couldn't scale mountains or fight mutants while pregnant, and she doubted the universe would be kind enough to give her a nine-month adventuring sabbatical. She could always adopt, but how many moments would she miss while out there saving the world? First steps, birthdays, and school plays.

"Sorry, honey, Mommy couldn't make your graduation, because she was keeping serpent men from bringing forth their mad snake god. Have a card and a hundred bucks instead."

She'd made the cosmic forces that controlled her life more manageable, but they were still a factor. She'd made peace with certain sacrifices, and she'd never considered certain choices. She wasn't even sure she wanted kids, but it wasn't only about her now. It was also about Byron. They hadn't talked about it yet. Weird. They'd been together long enough for the topic to come up unless they were both avoiding it.

They were going to have to talk about it at some point. That and other things that made her uncomfortable, a dozen conversational minefields where one wrong step could cause the entire relationship to self-destruct.

She stepped out of the shower, slipped on her shirt while drying her hair. She heard Byron rustling around in the kitchen. He was early.

She heard a dish break. Then another. Then something slam and some gruff voices.

It wasn't Byron.

She did not have time for this tonight.

She stepped out of the hall to see a muscular goon in a tight suit rifling through her kitchen cabinets. She cleared her throat.

"Something I can maybe help you with?"

The snarling muscle shoved her into the living room. A mobster in an Armani suit sat in one of her chairs. He removed his hat and ran his fingers along the brim. "Please, have a seat."

"I'll stand, thanks." Connie toweled her hair. The goon put a hand on her shoulder, but his boss shook his head.

"As you wish."

The goon grunted, folding his thick arms across his chest. She had trouble telling what regular people found scary. Blood-thirsty hopping vampires and giant robots were obvious. Tough guys who relied on scowls and attitudes were a little more nebulous. This one probably assumed she felt exposed, having just stepped out of the shower and not wearing pants.

"What do you want?" she asked.

The boss smiled. "To the point. I like that. I'd like to think we can handle this with civility. Nobody needs to get hurt as long as we understand—"

"Oh, Christ," she said. "You're one of those verbose, *civilized* gangsters, aren't you? The kind that loves his own voice and likes to talk around his actual threats."

The boss frowned. "I don't think you understand—"

"No, you don't understand." She tossed her towel across

a chair and considered taking out the goon. She didn't need the hassle. "I have company coming over. So, just tell me what you want so we can get this over with."

The mobster and his goon exchanged glances.

"You don't know who I am, do you?" she asked.

"Sure, I do," said the boss. "You're the lady who has my diamonds."

"Diamonds, huh. Let me guess. Through circumstances too complicated to get into, you hid a fortune in stolen diamonds in something I just happened to pick up somewhere."

"Yes, my men were fleeing from the authorities and—"

"Don't care. Don't need to know. Under normal circumstances, I'd see that you were all foiled and brought to justice, but this will probably be faster if I just give you what you want."

The gangsters had hidden the precious gems in a velvet purse. Not hers. She didn't own a purse. She didn't ponder how this one had come, unknown, into her possession and under her sink. Things like this fell into her lap regularly. She'd gotten into the habit of checking her grocery bags for loose relics and other bric-a-brac.

She checked the velvet bag, full of diamonds.

"If you would be so kind . . . ," said the gangster boss.

Connie offered the bag but didn't drop it in the goon's callused palm.

She said, "I do have to ask. These are just diamonds, right? They're not cursed or something weird like that? You're not planning on using them to power a doomsday machine? You just want them for their monetary value?"

The boss said, "What other value is there?"

She tried and failed to assess his trustworthiness. He was a bad guy, but a greedy bad guy wasn't that big a deal. If he was working for an evil sorcerer or mad scientist or something else like that, she might as well nip this in the bud now.

Not all of the adventures her destiny sent her way were life-or-death. She saved the world too often, but she didn't save it every week. Sometimes, she just foiled petty crimes and million-dollar jewel heists. Sometimes, she simply happened to be in the right place at the right time to give a lost extraterrestrial directions to the other side of the galaxy.

The goon grabbed her wrist and squeezed painfully. She dropped the bag into his hand as he grinned menacingly. She should've knocked him out, but she was still hoping to resolve this quickly.

"You have what you came for," she said. "You can feel free to leave now."

The goon tossed the bag to his boss, who inspected them again. "Your cooperation has been greatly appreciated. Unfortunately, you know too much."

She sighed. "You don't want to do this."

He unbuttoned his jacket and withdrew a revolver. "It's nothing personal."

"Funny," she replied. "I was about to say the same thing."

She twisted, using her knowledge of the secrets of the

Shaolin masters to pull the goon in front of her. The boss's bullets struck the goon in the chest, and Connie shoved him into his boss. They toppled backward over the chair. While the boss struggled to free himself from his thug, Connie disarmed him. She sat, pointing the weapon at the boss.

"You just had to be an asshole," she said. "I mean, I would've tracked you down eventually and taken the diamonds back, but you had to force the issue."

"We can make a deal," he said from the floor, underneath his dying goon.

"No deals. I'm calling an ambulance. Then I'm calling the cops. And that's that. My whole evening, gone up in smoke because you didn't take the time to do an Internet search. I'm not exactly a household name, but I have a goddamn Wikipedia page. One thug? I'd be insulted, except that you're obviously not very bright."

She called the authorities and checked the thug's wounds. They were bloody, but with some first aid and basic acupuncture she'd picked up somewhere (she'd actually forgotten where), she was able to stop the bleeding. He'd live.

While inserting a needle into a nerve cluster and holding her gun on the boss with her other hand, she cradled the phone between her cheek and neck and waited for Byron to pick up.

"What's up?" he asked.

"Would you be terribly upset if we rescheduled tonight?" she said.

"Is something wrong?"

"Nothing's wrong," she replied. "Just something came up. You know how it is."

"Do you need to leave town?"

The boss thought to take her out while her back was turned. She coldcocked him with a spinning kick to the nose. He knocked over a lamp, but she caught it just before it hit the floor.

"Is everything all right?" asked Byron.

She should've just told him, but she didn't. She didn't know why.

"I'm just tired," she said. "You know how it is."

"I know," he said, but there was a tone she didn't like.

"You're not mad, are you?" she asked.

"Why should I be mad? I'm ten minutes from your place, and you're canceling on me. Again."

"I don't cancel that often," she said. "It never bothered you before."

She waited for him to say something. He didn't. The silence across the phone felt like a gulf she couldn't cross. Worse, it told her it had bothered him before. He just hadn't said anything, and she hadn't noticed. Some master detective she was.

God, she was stupid. Byron had every right to be mad. She *was* stringing him along.

She should've just told him about the mobsters and the diamonds. He'd understand. He knew how her life worked.

"Tia is having this party Saturday," said Connie. "She invited us. You and me. Other people too, of course."

Why was she still talking? Probably because he hadn't

said anything. She didn't need to say anything else. Just give him time to talk.

"It's a dinner party or something. Dress casual, I think," she said. "Nothing fancy or anything."

Thirty-six was too goddamn old to start trying to date like a regular person. If only she'd met Byron on a jewel heist in Morocco or fighting ghost pirates in the Bermuda Triangle. Someplace where their lives had been in danger, where things were as basic as staying alive and saving the day.

It would've simplified things, but it also would've led her down the same path. Crazy, passionate flings that didn't go anywhere. They were fun, but she wanted more now. She wanted something other than wild sex in steamy jungles while waiting for rabid gorillas to strike.

The boss stood and grabbed a sword off her wall. She did not need this right now, either.

"Uh, one second, Byron." She muted the phone, waved her gun at the mobster. "You're kidding, right?"

"Most broads don't have the guts to shoot a man in the face."

Connie groaned. "You did not just call me a broad. What decade are you from? Anyway, I don't have to shoot you. Don't think I wouldn't, but that's one of my cursed swords you're holding. I'd put it back where you found it if I were you."

He raised the sword and ran at her. His foot caught the end table. He fell, cracking his head against her coffee table. The sword sailed through the air. She caught it in one hand and checked him. He was still conscious.

"Warned you. Now just lay down and try not to fall asleep. The ambulance should be here shortly."

She unmuted the phone. "Sorry about that. So, did you want to go to the party?"

"Yes. If you want me to go."

"Of course I do." She was a good liar, but even she had trouble believing herself this time. "I'll see you Saturday, then?"

"Yes, Saturday."

"Great."

She ended the call abruptly before anything could go wrong. Worlds were bound to collide, but not tonight.

The sirens in the distance grew louder.

3

Connie had a history of bad ideas. They came with her life. When most people would run from kaiju attacks or cursed temples, she went forward. It worked out okay. Most of the time.

But this was a bad idea.

Byron buttoned up his shirt and straightened his collar. "Are you getting dressed?"

She sat on the bed, in her underwear. "In a minute."

He smiled at her. "You're stalling."

"No, I'm not. I just don't know what I'm wearing."

"Wear your red dress. You always look good in red."

"Little ostentatious, isn't it?"

"Then a simple top and some pants," he said.

"I don't want to be underdressed."

He shook his head and chuckled. "Sure. Take your time. I don't suppose it will matter if we're fashionably late."

She rose from the bed and hugged him from behind. "Or

we could stay home and entertain ourselves."

"You're stooping to bribing me with sex. You must be more nervous than I realized."

She backed away. "Maybe a little."

"As tempting as an offer as it is, I think we should at least drop by." He put a hand on her cheek. "And if I am your boyfriend—"

"You are," she said.

"Then we have to do this. It's boyfriend stuff."

"Does it really matter? I'm not going to know many of the people there. It's mostly Tia's friends."

"Yes, but it's Tia. She is your best friend, right? It's about time I met her."

Connie shrugged. "She said the same thing."

"So we'll go. We don't have to stay long."

"Promise?"

He picked her blue top out of her closet and held it out to her. "Cross my heart."

She chose some jeans and the top. Nothing fancy. She had a ball gown, but she'd only worn that once while impersonating a princess who just happened to be her physical twin. And she had a formal suit she wore when attending any political affair of note. But this was just a party. No need to overthink it.

They drove to the party. She didn't say much. She'd faced down armies of mutants with less dread. He filled the car with a little small talk, but mostly, he held her hand. It made her feel like everything was going to be all right.

The party was a dozen people. Most of them were Tia's friends, people from the ordinary parts of her life. Connie didn't know many of them aside from their names and faces. They were nice, normal people with nice, normal lives. Connie didn't have much in common with them, but she knew how to fake it.

Tia greeted Connie and Byron at the door. She hugged Connie then Byron.

"So nice to finally meet you," said Tia. "Connie's told me a lot about you."

"Really?" he replied. "She hasn't told me much about you, actually."

"Oh, we should change that, then. Do you mind if I borrow him for a bit? Help yourself to some cheese while we talk."

She took Byron's arm and guided him away before Connie could object.

Connie found the table, loaded with appetizers and a hefty cheese plate. She grabbed herself a pig in a blanket and a beer. The crowd milled about. She exchanged a few pleasantries with anyone who wandered nearby, but no conversations started. Connie scanned the party for Hiro. She was surprised he wasn't there.

"Hello, Connie," Hiro said from beside her.

She didn't jump, but only because she had a lot of practice at *not* jumping.

"Christ, you love doing that, don't you?" she asked.

"One must stay in practice," he replied. "Byron seems nice."

"He is nice," said Connie. "Have you talked to him yet?"

"Not yet, but he's an organ donor and an NPR supporter as well. Good for him."

"You stole his wallet?"

"I'm offended. I don't steal small. I borrowed his wallet. And his keys. And forty-one cents in change from his pockets. Just to get a sense of him. Well, the change was just for the hell of it."

Connie glared.

"I'll return everything before he even notices they're gone," said Hiro. "Heaven forbid he lose his Subway sandwich reward card. He's three punches away from a free six-inch."

"Hiro, if you ruin this for me . . ."

But of course he was gone again. It would've been infuriating if she wasn't used to it by now. Now it was only annoying.

Byron and Tia chatted across the room. Connie deliberately avoided reading their lips. It was a conversation. Nothing more. Tia and Byron were the two most important people in Connie's life. They should meet. They should talk. She'd give them a few more minutes before joining them. Four or five minutes. Three.

Three would be enough.

They laughed. That was a good thing. It had to be a good thing.

She was less concerned with Tia than with Hiro. Tia was at least a regular person. A ninja ex-boyfriend was more troublesome.

Millie came forward and nodded to Connie. "Oh, hello."

Connie pushed forward her most diplomatic smile. Millie was the closest thing to an archenemy Connie had in her ordinary life. She had plenty of archenemies in her adventure life. Too many. It stretched the definition of the word. But on the ordinary side of things, Millie was Connie's biggest foe.

Millie had been Tia's friend for years now. Her ordinary friend. They did ordinary things together and dealt with ordinary problems. Connie tried to be there for Tia, but there were times when adventure conflicted. Millie was there to pick up the slack. It should've been a good thing. There was plenty of Tia to go around.

But there was a weird conflict between Connie and Millie. A friendship tug-of-war, a struggle for best-friend status. Millie didn't have much of a chance in the battle because Connie and Tia had been friends for nearly thirty years. But it was obvious she wanted the title and resented Connie for having it.

It was all a bit silly, but Connie was competitive enough that she found herself invested in the contest more than she should have.

"Try the Roquefort yet?" asked Millie. "I don't usually like it, but this is delicious."

She cut a thick slice and put it on a tiny cracker before taking a big bite.

"So, that's Byron?" asked Millie, her mouth full, implying something with her tone. Something Connie couldn't decipher.

"Yes."

"He seems . . . nice."

"He is nice," replied Connie pleasantly, forcing a lilt in her reply.

"Not what I expected from you."

Connie swallowed her irritation. If she could ignore the thinly veiled insults of the King of the Mummies, she could ignore this.

"Doesn't really seem your type," said Millie, cutting another hunk of the Roquefort, not even bothering with the cracker this time.

"What type is that?" asked Connie before she could stop herself.

"Oh, nice and stable and, well, a little boring."

Connie could jab Millie in a pressure point on her torso that would go unnoticed but would cause her to drop dead in six months. Untraceable. No one could prove anything.

"He's a good guy," said Connie.

"I'm sure he is.

"So, did Tia tell you about her promotion yet?" asked Millie.

"No."

Millie grinned. Little bits of white and blue stuck in her teeth. "Oh, I'm sure she was planning on it soon. You've just been busy . . . doing whatever it is you do."

"Saving the world," said Connie.

"Yes. That."

Untraceable.

"I'm sure it's important stuff," said Millie. "Tia was planning on getting around to telling you eventually."

Sometimes, Connie hated civilized society. She'd discovered a lost tribe in Asia who settled all interpersonal conflicts with hatchet fights. Bloody, sure, but definitive.

"Uh-huh," said Connie, grabbing a bunch of crackers and walking away. Some battles weren't worth fighting. Millie had been a distraction, and Connie had lost track of Tia and Byron. Connie drifted through the party, acting casual, hunting for them.

"They're in the backyard," said Hiro from beside her.

She didn't jump. She'd been expecting him. She hadn't detected him, but his timing was predictable.

She reached for a cracker in her plate, but they were all gone. His plate was filled, though.

"Goddamn it," she said.

"Practice." He bit into a cracker and offered her some of his.

"I thought you told Tia you were going straight."

"Doesn't mean I have to be boring. Speaking of boring, are you sure this guy is right for you?"

"Yes, I'm sure. Boring is what I need."

"So, you admit it, then. He is boring."

"Poor choice of words," said Connie. "He's normal."

"*Normal* is just a nice way of saying *boring*."

"No, *normal* is a nice way of saying he won't disappear on me the moment things get serious. Normal means he's not a cyborg from the future or an alien or a barbarian warlord or a secret agent or whatever."

"If that's what you want . . ."

She stopped him. "It is. I like this guy a lot, and if you screw this up for me, master ninja or not, I will find you and I will kill you. There isn't a hole deep enough for even you to hide in. I'll track you to the ends of the universe. That's a promise."

Hiro said, "That's not a very normal thing to say."

"We're not very normal people," she replied. "But Byron is, so let's smile and act like we're the same."

"You forget. I'm a ninja. Trained in the art of blending in. I've mastered the ninjaly art of inane small talk. I can put a man to sleep just by talking about the weather. This will be no problem for me. I'm more concerned for you. Can you really manage this? Hiding half of your life from him? It isn't necessarily fair to you or him. And it's a lot of strain to put on a relationship."

"I don't hide it from him. I don't dwell on it."

"Still, it's a balancing act I don't envy. I can't imagine how Tia and I would manage if I had to act as if I didn't steal things for a living."

"Don't you mean *used to steal things?*"

Hiro forced a laugh. "Oh, yes, yes. Of course. Used to steal things. No stealing for me now. I'm a good boy."

Connie replied with silence.

"There might be some incidental stealing," he said. "Nothing big. Just a little contract now and then. Tia and I have an unspoken understanding."

"And she knows about this?"

"I assume. It's not like we've talked about it. That's what

makes it unspoken." He waved his hands. "How did we end up talking about my relationship? This is about you and Byron. And I like him. I do. But I don't see it going the distance with you two."

"I didn't ask your opinion."

"Let me finish. I'd like to think of us as friends, and I will do what I can to help you make this work. But, as your friend and as a ninja dating a normal woman, I can tell you finding that balance is key. We are who we are. We can't change that. Now, let's go check up on our significant others and act like you aren't a regular visitor to the center of the Earth or that I didn't steal the Mona Lisa last weekend."

"Hiro . . ."

"Unspoken," he said with a smile as he pushed her outside.

They found Tia and Byron sitting at a table on the patio. Tia was a regular person. Mostly. She'd been, willingly and unwillingly, on a significant number of Connie's adventures. Tia had her war stories. But she surely knew enough not to share many of those stories with Byron. Connie, who had met gods, knew better than to pray for their aid, but Hachiman, god of war, archery, and agriculture, did owe her a favor. She wasn't above cashing it in now, but he'd probably reply by shooting Byron with an arrow or making it rain. Neither would be very helpful.

Connie and Hiro had a seat, catching Tia and Byron in the middle of a chuckle. They shared knowing smiles.

"Having fun?" Connie asked.

"She really is nervous about this, isn't she?" said Byron.

"Yes, weird, considering her past experience," said Tia.

"All right," said Connie. "You've got me. I'm better with saving the world than this."

"Connie, you can relax," said Tia. "I like him. He passes."

"That's a relief," said Byron. "I was honestly a little nervous myself. I know you're Connie's normal friend, but I also know you've done some stuff. Thought I might come across as boring."

"*Stable* is not the same thing as *boring*," said Tia.

The weight lifted from Connie's shoulders. It must've been visible to the rest of the table.

"I get the feeling she would've broken up with me if you hadn't approved," he said.

She didn't deny it. She wasn't sure herself. But it didn't matter. It was a non-problem, and all the time she'd spent worrying about it had been a waste of time.

"Now, now," said Hiro. "Our Connie isn't quite so wishy-washy as that."

Except he didn't just say it. He said it in that winking, smirking way of his. And he put a little extra oomph on the *Our*. It was only a matter of time before Byron figured out Hiro and Connie's past. She should've just told him. Why hadn't she just told him?

Connie was trapped between Scylla and Charybdis. Figuratively. She'd been trapped there once literally, and it'd been easier. She should do something to defuse the situation.

She took the coward's way out.

"Excuse me. I have to use the bathroom."

She beat a hasty retreat. It wasn't her finest moment, but she could take only so much social intrigue. She'd been part of diplomatic conferences that made her less edgy, but in those situations, the most that was at stake was a war or two.

Tia's guest bathroom was occupied, so Connie used the master. She took her time. Every minute, she wondered if Hiro would spill his secret or if Byron would figure it out. It wasn't a big deal. People had exes. Her exes just happened to be ninjas, barbarians, and the Prince of the Mole People.

She was making too much of it. It was her reflex. Byron, Hiro, and Tia were not problems to fix. They were her friends. They weren't out to get her. They'd figure it out on their own. All she had to do was nothing.

It was driving her crazy.

Part of her wished for an alien invasion, a monster attack, a hostage situation. She would've killed for a cadre of gunmen to inexplicably crash the party. That would've been contrary to everything she was trying to have with Byron, but it'd give her someone to punch, something to solve.

Connie sat on the bath mat cross-legged. She cleared her mind with the meditative technique of the Most Perfect and Humble Yogi Atheeva the Exalted. Atheeva's favorite technique was to contemplate her own flawlessness and the paradoxical modesty one attained upon the perfection of flawlessness. Connie had always found it a bit suspicious, but Atheeva could levitate and burn holes into walls simply by staring at them, so who was she to argue?

Someone knocked on the bathroom door, wrecking her state of mindful relaxation. It shouldn't have been enough to disturb her, but it did. The reminder of how far away she was from inner peace only irritated her more, thus ruining the entire point of the exercise.

Grumbling, Connie ceased her pursuit of perfection, though she'd only been aiming for inner chill.

Another knock. More insistent.

"All right, already," said Connie as she got to her feet and opened the door. "It's all yours."

Millie lurched forward. Something shiny flashed in her hand, and Connie's reflexes kept her from being struck across the face. She intercepted Millie's second swing and with a twist, forced her to drop the cheese knife. It clattered against the tile floor.

"What the hell?" asked Connie.

Millie grabbed Connie by the hair. Most people Connie fought relied on martial arts skill, not hair-pulling and biting. It caught her off guard. Millie yanked, taking a few strands with her, clutching them in her fist as she rushed forward with a flurry of punches.

Her technique was sloppy, and Connie blocked and dodged almost on autopilot. When the opening came, she punched Millie in the solar plexus. Gasping, she fell to her knees.

"What the hell is wrong with you?" asked Connie.

Millie glanced up with cold white eyes flecked with spots of blue. She growled and crumbs of cheese fell from her lips. Telltale blue speckles colored her cheeks.

"Oh, hell." She should've seen this coming.

With unexpected energy, Millie hurled herself at Connie. Connie sidestepped, knocked Millie's legs out from under her. Millie hit the floor face-first with a sharp thud.

Connie jumped on Millie's back and tried several pressure points. Any one of them should've rendered Millie unconscious or at least put her in so much discomfort she couldn't move, but she kept struggling.

With an unexpected burst of strength, Millie threw Connie off and rose to her feet. She stumbled, gurgling and hissing. The person she'd been was gone, buried under a cheesy invading fungus. The thing that had been Millie turned toward Connie and snarled. It lurched forward.

"Goddamn Roquefort," said Connie before kicking Millie full in the face.

"So tell me, Byron," said Hiro. "Where do you see Connie and yourself in five years?"

Tia rolled her eyes. "Hiro . . ."

"I'm just asking." He leaned closer. "It's just our Connie has been through a lot of ups and downs, romantically, and we're concerned."

"No, *we* are not," said Tia. "And you aren't either. He's just screwing with you, Byron."

"It's okay," replied Byron. "It's a legitimate question. I don't really know, honestly. I like Connie. A lot. But, if I'm being honest, I don't have a great track record with dating, myself.

And that was with normal people." He frowned. "God, I hate using that phrase. It makes her sound abnormal."

"Well, our Connie certainly isn't ordinary, is she?" said Hiro.

Tia swallowed the last of her drink. "Oh, look, I'm empty. Hiro, honey, it looks like you could use a refill too."

He handed her his glass. "Thanks."

She grabbed him by the arm and pulled him out of his chair. "Perhaps you'd like to join me."

"Of course, honey." He smiled. "We'll be right back, Byron."

She waited until she was in the kitchen before glaring at him. "What are you doing?"

"Just having a conversation, darling." He leaned in to kiss her.

She covered his puckered lips with her hand. "This is why you should never date someone who dated your best friend. Too many complications. Are you over Connie?"

He flashed a playful grin at her. He could get away with so much shit because of that grin. "Yes."

She pushed him away. "God, for a ninja, you are a terrible liar."

Hiro leaned against the counter, shook his head. "Are we going to have this fight again? Here? Now? What do I have to do to prove that I love you?"

"I know you love me," she said. "I just don't know if you love me like you loved her."

"That's hardly fair," he replied. "You're two different people. I love you for entirely different reasons than I love her."

"Love?"

Hiro slouched. "Yes, I love her. I'll always love her. Connie and I have a complicated relationship. But it'd never work between us. Too much baggage."

"Like all the times you tried to kill her?"

"I never tried to kill her. I only occasionally left her in situations where she might be killed."

"You just love semantics, don't you?"

"Oh, damn it, if you want to break up, then let's just break up."

Silence filled the kitchen. Tia took a drink directly out of the wine bottle and handed it to Hiro, who did the same.

"Do you want to break up?" she asked.

"If I wanted to break up, I'd be gone already."

A cloud of smoke erupted at his feet. The cloud dispersed, and he was nowhere to be seen. Tia grabbed a towel to flap at the wisps drifting toward the smoke detector.

Hiro took her by the hand and pulled her close to him. He kissed her, and she pressed herself tight against him.

"I'm still here," he said.

She smiled. "I noticed."

The smoke detector shrieked.

"Damn it," said Tia. "This is why I ask you not to pull that ninja-vanish bullshit in the house."

Connie stepped into the kitchen. Her hair was a mess, and she sported a bruise on her face. She said nothing and quickly checked their eyes.

"The Roquefort? You didn't eat any, did you?"

"I'm lactose intolerant," said Hiro.

"I hate blue cheese," said Tia. "I only bought it because it was on sale."

"Good." Connie opened the refrigerator. "Tell me you have pickles."

"Bottom shelf. What's happening now?"

"You might have bought some evil cheese." Connie pulled the half-full jar of pickles from the fridge.

"I'm not a fan, but I didn't know Roquefort could be evil."

"It's not Roquefort. It's a type of sentient fungus that's indistinguishable from Roquefort until it comes into contact with a viable host. It nearly conquered the south of France once. I stopped it. Now it's trying to kill me for that."

"So, all my party guests are going to become cheese zombies?" said Tia.

"Not if you show me where your squeeze water bottles are."

Connie poured the pickle juice into the bottle, screwed on the cap. She walked briskly to the master bathroom with Tia and Hiro following.

Millie, hogtied with several towels, lay twitching in the bathtub. There wasn't much fight left in her at the moment as she neared final assimilation. Connie grabbed Millie by the chin and squeezed a hefty amount of juice down her throat. She coughed and sputtered, vomiting up a glob of rancid white-and-blue slime.

"What the hell?" she asked with equal parts anger and confusion before throwing up some more.

"She'll be okay," said Connie. "I should've spotted the signs right away, but I was too distracted by Byron." She sighed. "Damn it, I forgot about Byron."

Jennifer from accounting, not Jennifer from customer service, shuffled through the doorway. Blue speckles spotted her flesh, and cheesy drool dripped from her lips. Connie knocked Jennifer off her feet and squirted the antidote into her mouth. Not having eaten as much as Millie, she still coughed up a handful of the rancid cheese.

"Call an ambulance," said Connie. "I'll take care of everything else."

Tia already had her phone out. "On it."

Most of the party guests were in various stages of infection. Many lay convulsing on the floor. Several others stood around in a stupor. The few that hadn't eaten the cheese huddled in a corner, confused by this turn of events. Jennifer from customer service made a clumsy attempt at attack. Connie pinned her to the wall and force-fed her the antidote. She took care of the room before moving on to Byron. One problem at a time.

"Connie?" asked Byron from over her shoulder.

She held down a spitting, howling old man, struggling to open his snapping jaws long enough to cure him, but she paused long enough to see Byron was okay. He must not have been a fan of Roquefort either. Thank heaven for small miracles.

"Give me one second," she said with a relieved smile. "This guy is being really stubborn about this."

She finally gave up on his mouth and squirted the juice

up one of his nostrils. He curled up on the floor and threw up. Connie patted him on the back. "There, there. All better now."

She gave everyone else another quick check for infection, ending with Byron. His eyes were clear and his skin unspeckled.

Worlds had finally collided, and she wasn't sure what to do about it. Byron hadn't said much of anything yet, and she wasn't sure what to say either. So, they both said nothing.

Tia broke the silence. "Ambulance is on its way. I also called Agent Ellington."

"Didn't know you had her number," said Connie.

"She gave it to me. Said I might need it."

"Very considerate of her. Everyone should be okay now with some follow-up care."

Tia helped one of her guests up. "Guess the party's over."

The ambulances and government operatives arrived. The infected guests were taken away for treatment to ensure the last of the fungal infection was cleared. Agent Ellington took statements, but Connie cut it short. It wasn't as if Ellington didn't know where to find Connie. She wanted to get home, get Byron away from this stuff.

He drove, not saying much, and she relished the blessed silence. It couldn't last, though.

"I didn't expect it to be so violent," said Byron.

"Why would you?" asked Connie. "It was just supposed to be a party."

"I'm not talking about the party. I'm talking about the fight."

"I live a dangerous life," she said.

Byron sighed. "I knew that. But watching you beat the shit out of people . . . it's not what I expected."

"What did you expect?"

"I didn't expect anything," he said. "You have adventures.

It was fun to think of my girlfriend out there, somewhere, fighting bad guys and discovering lost treasures, saving the day. I knew there was danger, but you're always so capable. You can do everything."

"Not everything," said Connie.

"Close enough."

"Byron, I promise you I'll do my best to see that something like this doesn't ever happen again."

"That's just it. It will happen again. If I'm part of your life, you can't stop it from happening."

She wished she could argue, but there was a radius of weirdness and danger extending to Connie and her immediate friends. It didn't get Mom and Dad often, but even they weren't entirely immune.

"I'm sorry," she said.

"Why?"

"I didn't want you mixed up in this part of my life."

"Connie, I knew who you were on our first date. I could've walked away at any moment. I didn't. It wasn't because I wanted to have an adventure. It was because I liked you. I'm not an idiot. I was expecting something like this sooner or later."

"You were?"

He pulled a fleck of evil cheese from his hair. "Not this exactly. But something. It's unsettling. Violent. I don't really like it."

"You can drop me off at my place," she said.

"Damn it, Connie, will you let me finish? We all have our

baggage. Yours is just more colorful than mine. But, damn it, I love you."

It was the first time either of them had said it. They'd been dating a year now, but they'd been hedging their bets by avoiding the word. And now he'd gone and raised the stakes.

"I'm not sure I can protect you," she said.

"Sure, you can. You've protected Tia all these years."

"That's different. Tia has practice with this. She's almost as experienced as I am. She knows when to keep her head down."

"I'll learn. I've signed up for some self-defense classes. And I bought a Swiss army knife."

"Problem solved, then. If you're serious, you have no idea what you're in for. Do you want some time to think about it?"

"I've thought about it." He took her hand. "I'm willing to take a few lumps. I dated a woman who broke out in baby talk all the time. This is a lot less irritating. And if I get into trouble, you'll rescue me."

"Most guys wouldn't take being the damsel in distress so happily."

"I'm a modern man." Byron leaned over and kissed her cheek. "And most guys aren't lucky enough to be dating Constance Verity."

She laughed. "For a regular guy, you're pretty special."

"That's why we work so well together."

Sighing, she shook her head.

"What's wrong?" he asked.

"Nothing," she replied. "I just realized I love you too."

There were henchagents waiting outside of Larry's apartment. Neither of them acknowledged him as he approached the door. Their skull-shaped helmets covered their faces, and their red jumpsuits covered everything else, even their hands. They didn't move, making it easy to mistake them for statues.

He slipped his key into the lock. "Evening, fellas. Um . . . ladies." It could've gone either way. It didn't really matter.

He entered his apartment and tossed his keys into the bowl by the table. A tall, dark silhouette stood framed by the fading light coming through the half-closed blinds.

"Hi, Mom," he said. "To what do I owe the pleasure of your visit?"

The woman stepped forward. She wasn't his mother. She was taller, about his age, wearing a gray suit with a black tie. Unlike the henchagents, she wasn't wearing a helmet. She was striking, which didn't surprise him. The elite minions tended toward extremes, either scarred and hideous with metal teeth or supermodel good looks.

"You're new," he said.

The woman adjusted her black-rimmed glasses, pulling them to the end of her nose before pushing them back up. It felt like being eyed by a predator. Without malice but with a cold calculation of whether he was worth killing.

"Lord Peril, your mother sent us," she said.

"Tell her I'm not interested," he replied. "I'm out of the evil-genius game. I've made my peace with that."

The woman glided toward him, and he was struck by how much taller she was. Really, it was only a few inches, but it seemed more. "You were never meant to be an office manager. You were groomed for greater things."

Larry walked past her. He was aware of his own plodding, clumsy steps. Her presence alone put him in mind of a three-legged antelope loping pathetically.

"We all know how that worked out," he said as he grabbed an apple juice from the fridge. "Mom will just have to look elsewhere for her successor. Not that I expect she'll ever need one. The old lady will probably live forever."

"Lady Peril is dead."

He would've laughed, but it was no longer funny. "Right. Just like the last time. And the time before that." He put the juice back and grabbed a beer. He struggled with the twist-off. "Didn't catch your name."

She took the bottle and twisted off the cap. "Apollonia."

He took the beer back, tilted it back, sputtered as a bit of foam went up his nose. He grabbed paper towels to dab at his damp shirt.

"Well, Apollonia, I don't know how long you've been working for Mom, but she dies a lot." He set down the beer and used his fingers for air quotes. "She *dies* a lot. It's kind of hard to give a damn at this point. Did they find a body?"

"No."

"That settles it. No body, no death. Not that a body would prove anything either."

Apollonia eyed him with undisguised disapproval. She and Mom must've gotten along swimmingly.

He said, "I don't know what your deal is, but you can go back to whatever secret headquarters you crawled out of and wait for her to return. Because she'll be back."

He went for his beer, but Apollonia snatched it off the table. She went to his cupboard and looking for a glass. "Don't you have any mugs?"

"I just moved in."

"Three years ago," she said.

"Mom's been keeping an eye on me." It *wasn't* a question. He'd known.

"All in the files." Apollonia settled on a Slurpee cup with a picture of Optimus Prime on it.

"Careful," he said. "That's a collectible."

She poured the beer with a steady hand. "No serious relationships in four years. Two dates with an office temp, leading to one brief, awkward sexual encounter. No call afterward."

"I'm not in the right place for a relationship," he said.

"No known associates or friends."

"I go bowling on Tuesdays."

"Coworkers, not friends," she said. "191 average."

"I'm getting better."

"Actually, your scores have been declining these last three months. No hobbies. A few flirty exchanges with the cashier at the local convenience store. In bed by ten on most nights. Unremarkable job performance."

She handed him the glass. He took a drink. It did taste better, though there was only so much to be done with Pabst Blue Ribbon.

"I'm trying to keep a low profile," he said. "Doing better would lead to a promotion. I'm happy where I'm at right now."

"You should eat something." Apollonia opened the refrigerator and sorted through his provisions. "Do you have anything besides bologna?"

"I like bologna. Beats the hell out of the tasteless nutritional paste I was raised on."

She tossed the lunch meat on the table, grabbed his half-jar of mayonnaise, and found his bread.

"So, you're here to pour my beers and make my sandwiches?" he asked. "Seems like a waste of your talents."

She rinsed a dirty butter knife in the sink. She turned, and he assumed from the look in her eye that she was debating whether to use it on the mayo or him.

"Whether you accept it or not, Lady Peril has appointed you her handpicked successor."

"Now I know you're full of shit. Mom would never trust me with her legacy."

"Nevertheless, she has," said Apollonia.

She made the sandwich, her every move a model of efficiency. She even cut off the crusts, like he liked. They probably had a file on that somewhere.

"I don't know you, Lord Peril—"

"It's Larry." He bit into his sandwich. "Just Larry."

"I don't know you, Larry. From everything I've learned, I see your lack of ambition to be entirely justified."

"Jeez, for a minion, you're not very nice."

"I am not a minion. Those idiots outside your door, they're minions."

"What are you, then?"

"I'm someone Lady Peril entrusted to inform you of this opportunity. I don't give a damn whether you take it or not."

"So, if I say no, you'll go?"

She nodded.

"What happens to Siege Perilous if I say no?" he asked.

"Not your problem, is it?

"I'm no mastermind. I'm not interested in conquering the world. What the hell would I do as head of an international criminal organization?"

"That's up to you," she said. "I'm just the messenger."

She cleaned up her mess, though most of the bread was

moldy, so she threw that away. He sat on his couch and viewed his small, plainly decorated apartment. This was his life now, and it wasn't great, but it could be worse. It'd get better.

Apollonia gave him his TV remote. "You'll want this."

She opened the door, a shadow of possibility, maybe the last sliver of a life he'd never lived walking out of the life he was living, but just barely.

"Hey, wait. I guess it doesn't hurt to take a look, right?" he asked.

She didn't smile as she stepped aside and gestured toward the door. "After you, Lord Peril."

C onnie and Byron arrived ahead of their realtor. They
didn't mind waiting in the lobby, but Annie had left
word that they were to be shown to the condo and wait
for her there. A nice older man named Sven led the way and
offered to give them the tour. Byron accepted, but Connie
elected to wait in the hall. When Annie arrived, they'd have
to do the whole thing over again, and she didn't feel like
paying attention twice.

The door across the hall opened, and a pair of older gentlemen stepped out. Both wore crisp polo shirts and perfectly
creased slacks. They had the bronzed skin and straight white
teeth of catalogue models. She assumed they were off to stand
somewhere nondescript, hands in pockets, smiling and talking
about the virtues of relaxed-fit clothing in solid colors.

"Oh, hello," said the blond one. His voice had the smooth
polish of a radio ad announcer. Not the fun guy who got
the clever dialogue, but the one rattling the legal copy at

the very end. "You must be our new prospective tenant."

"Must be," said Connie, shaking their hands. Their palms were dry and cracked, as were their faces around the neck and ears upon closer inspection. Too much tanning, she told herself, though her experience suggested otherwise.

Vance, the blond one of the two, appraised her. "Have we met before?"

"I just have one of those faces," she said.

They would find out. Eventually. Everyone found out.

She wondered if the condo board would accept their offer. Not everyone saw her colorful history as a bonus. She'd had one apartment burn down and a rental house explode. That would probably reflect badly on her application. Enough money could smooth anything over, and Agent Ellington might be able to put in a good word.

"You'll love it here," said Luke, the dark-haired one. "It's a great building. Everyone is very friendly."

He blinked. Slowly. Not so slowly that someone would notice it if they weren't looking for it, but she was looking.

Their haircuts were identical. Stylishly shaggy, covering the tops of their ears. Ears that were probably pointed.

They smiled. Their skin crinkled, and a bit of dark red showed by their eyes where the flesh pulled away from whatever was underneath.

She didn't need this. Not today.

"We have a great sushi restaurant just a few blocks down," said Luke.

"Okay," said Connie, "I'm just going to come out and ask it. I hope it's not rude, but you're Bluphinites, aren't you?"

They smiled at one another. "What is a Bluphinite?" asked Vance innocently.

"You don't have to lie about it," she said. "I'm just asking. Your disguises are very good. I just know what to look for."

They didn't reply, instead glancing to one another.

"No need for telepathy," she said. "I don't care. Just as long as you aren't here to cause any trouble. Please, tell me you aren't here to conquer the Earth."

"I can assure you, we have no idea what you're talking about," said Luke.

"Have it your way. I shouldn't have said anything. It's just that my boyfriend likes this place, and if I'm going to be living here, I thought it might be better to start out with everything in the open. My mistake. Let's just pretend like this conversation never happened."

"Yes, let's," said Luke as he and Vance turned back toward their apartment.

"Wait," said Connie. "I think I might have screwed up here. I'm cool. We're cool. You're aliens. I know lots of aliens. Some of my best friends are aliens." She shook her head. "Never mind. We'll never talk about this again. Nobody here but us Earthlings, am I right?"

"Yes, if you'll excuse us—" said Vance.

They quickly disappeared back into their condo before she could say anything else.

Connie thought she should knock on the door and straighten things out, but that also might make things worse. Most aliens weren't out to cause trouble. Most were living their lives. Probably best not to poke at it for the moment.

The decision was made when the realtor showed up. She apologized for the delay and led Connie inside. Sven was shoved out the door, and the tour started again.

Annie Stein was a short, plump woman who had a weird obsession with fixtures. It was always the first thing she pointed out when showing them a new place.

"Great fixtures," she said, pointing to the open ceiling dome hanging above their heads.

Connie knew it was an open ceiling dome because Annie had pointed this out multiple times with the other properties they'd seen. In the course of the two weeks since contacting Annie, Connie had become something of an expert on light fixtures. She had a tendency to pick things up fast and remember them on the off chance they might prove useful during an adventure. She didn't imagine knowing the difference between cove and troffer lighting would be vital information, but she couldn't stop herself.

Annie led them through the unfurnished condo, indicating various fixtures as they passed by. "Now, it's a new condo in a nice neighborhood—lovely pendant light there—so demand is high. But the investor of this unit backed out—exquisite sconces here—and they're eager to get it sold. Of course, with your colorful history—never mind the track lighting here, we can always rip it out—there will be some concerns. You might pay a little more, but it's in the neighborhood you—check out this chandelier—wanted, and I'm sure we can make arrangements suitable to the condo board."

They arrived at the master bedroom, and while another realtor might have paused to allow them to enjoy the view, Annie drew the curtains and switched on the lights.

"Beautiful, isn't it?"

"Beautiful." Connie parted the curtains and looked down at the neighborhood. It was all very pristine and carefully arranged. Upper-middle-class people milled around the streets with the faux quaint shops with the faux quaint architecture. Gentrification at work, though even that was faux, as this had never been a downtrodden neighborhood in need of fixing up.

The view was nice, though.

Annie rattled off more details: the square footage, the number of bathrooms, gym access, access to good schools. She always brought up the schools last with a knowing wink. She was further along in their relationship than they were.

Thankfully, she would always return to some other topic with a little prodding.

"What about the low bay lighting in the bathroom?" asked Connie.

Annie's face screwed up as if Connie had suggested they all eat worms for lunch. "Oh, I know, I know. Ghastly. But fixable." She walked out of the bedroom, ostensibly talking to them but more to herself because she kept talking though they didn't follow.

"What do you think?" asked Byron.

"It's nice," said Connie.

"You always say it's nice."

"I travel a lot," she said. "I won't be spending as much time here as you."

"I know, but whatever place we get, it'll still be ours. Though this place is a bit pricey."

"We can afford it."

"No, you can afford it. The doorman would've probably shot me in the foyer if I'd dared enter alone."

"We can find a cheaper place."

He laughed. "That wasn't my point. I'm glad you have money. It makes this easier. And this is a really nice place, and it could be our place."

She took his hand. "You should just pick, then. I'm good with anywhere. Just as long as you're there whenever I get back from wherever."

"Then let's do it. Here's as good as any."

"Annie will be overjoyed."

"Good," he said. "I live to make Annie happy."

They joined their realtor in the spacious living room. She was chatting with the walls about the virtues of the mid-grade marble flooring and the natural light from the north-facing windows. Byron informed her of their desire to purchase, and she smiled.

She never smiled. They'd assumed she was some manner of real estate–selling cyborg.

"Wonderful, wonderful," said Annie as she shook Byron's hand. She started going on about paperwork and calls, and Connie stopped listening.

She hugged Byron. "Our new place."

He grinned. "I like the sound of that."

So did she. She needed this. Worlds might collide now and then, but they'd make it work. She wasn't worried. Much.

A boxy silver robot with four arms burst through the wall.

The robot stomped forward. Vance and Luke stepped through the hole left in its wake. Both were clad in battlesuits as polished and catalogue-fresh as their previous outfits. The manner in which they held their blaster rifles indicated they didn't have much experience with the weapons.

"Oh, goddamn it," grumbled Connie. "I think this is all a big mistake."

"You made the mistake, bounty hunter," said Luke, sounding about as threatening as a country club member upset that someone screwed up his sandwich order. "Now prepare to meet your Sytusk masters in the Fourth Ellipse of Kurturkar."

He pointed his rifle at her, but it only buzzed as he pulled the trigger.

"You've got the safety on," said Vance.

He helped Luke fiddle with the various knobs and switches on the weapon.

"Oh, the hell with it," said Luke. "Robot, destroy her!"

The robot raised the spiked ball on the end of its third arm and the whirring rotating blade on its second. It took a clumsy swing. She threw herself at Byron, shoving them both out of the way as the ball cracked the flooring and the blade gouged a hole clean through.

"Hey, now, just one minute!" said Annie, outraged by the damage to the marble tile.

The robot turned its visor toward Connie as it powered up the ray gun on its first arm.

"Don't suppose we can just talk about this?" she asked.

"Destroy. Destroy," said the robot.

They laughed about it afterward.

Luke and Vance's security robot lay in a shorted-out heap on the floor.

"Well, this is embarrassing," said Luke, removing his helmet.

"I warned you we might be overreacting," said Vance.

"No, you didn't."

Annie stood to one side. The battle was barely over before she'd started making calls. She didn't ask if anyone was okay, and she didn't seem fazed in the slightest that a robot had nearly thrown her out a window in the scuffle. Not while appointments needed to be rescheduled and her assistant rushed her a new jacket. This one had robot smudges on it.

"It's my fault," said Connie. "I shouldn't have said anything."

"Nonsense," said Vance. "You were very clear. It is we who jumped the gun. We just assumed you were a bounty hunter, though why a bounty hunter would go to the trouble of announcing herself is a question we probably should've asked before unleashing our robot."

The broken automaton sparked and twitched.

"Sorry about your robot," said Connie.

"No need to apologize. It's still under warranty," said Vance. "We're just glad no one was hurt."

"Byron, honey," said Connie. "This is Vance and Luke, our potential new neighbors."

"Oh, and now we've failed to introduce ourselves," said Luke. "How unforgivable."

"Don't worry about it," said Byron. "No harm, no foul."

The hanging light fixture broke off its chain and crashed to the floor. Several of the windows had been shattered in the struggle, and scorch marks seared a wall.

"Say, this might be a rude question," said Luke, "but you aren't the Snurkab, by chance?"

"I am."

"The Legendary Snurkab?" he asked.

Vance elbowed him. "What other Snurkab is there? My mothers will freak."

"Honestly, we feel just terrible about this," said Luke. "We know it's a terrible first impression, but we'll put in a good word with the condo board by way of apology. And we insist on paying for the repairs."

"It's the least we can do," said Vance.

Annie, detecting real estate opportunities, closed in for

the kill. "Perhaps we could do something about the bathroom lighting while we're at it," she said as she led them away.

"What's a Snurkab?" asked Byron.

"Long story."

He rubbed his elbow.

"Are you okay?" asked Connie.

"Just banged it when you threw me to the floor the second time. All things considered, it beats being zapped by a robot from outer space. I guess this is a thing that's going to happen from time to time now that we're living together?"

"Probably. You're free to back out now if you've come to your senses."

"Every relationship has its problems, Connie. I once dated a woman who liked to pee with the door open. If I can deal with that, I can deal with this. And those guys seem like they'll be good neighbors. Never lived next door to aliens before. Should be a new experience."

Annie reappeared, still holding her phone to her ear, talking half to them and half to her assistant on the other end.

"Great news. It turns out your neighbors have a lot of pull with the board. We can get you in here in two weeks. Yes, I'll have a tuna on toast and some mineral water. I'll put a rush on the paperwork, but it'll take a few days to get all the repairs done. No, no mayo. I hate mayo. Will you be providing your own furnishings or should I contact my decorator? You'll love him. He has a great sense of color. Rye."

She ended the call.

"So, what do you say, you two? It's a great little fixer-upper."

Byron nodded.

Connie plunged heedlessly into yet another adventure, this one weirder and more exhilarating than any before.

"We'll take it."

7

Tia came home from work to find Hiro sitting on the couch, watching TV. Again.

"How was your day?" he asked.

A few months ago, she would've told him. He had no interest in her job. She barely had any interest in it lately. But it was something to talk about, and he'd feign some passing curiosity toward the inter-office politics and breakroom-fridge conflicts. Now, as she leaned in to kiss him, he didn't even take his eyes off the television and his rerun of *The Beverly Hillbillies*.

"Oh, the usual," she said.

He nodded and grunted.

"How was yours?" she asked.

"Good," he said.

It was all he ever said. Most days, he lounged around the house, sleeping in, watching TV, goofing off on the Internet, working out, whatever. She was fine with it. Really, she was. He had more than enough money squirreled away that he didn't need to work another day in his life. Though he still worked now and then.

He didn't talk about his work. She didn't ask.

While hanging up her coat, she noticed an old statue tucked behind the shoeboxes. For a master ninja and thief, Hiro was lousy at hiding things. She'd found *Portrait of a Young Man* by Raphael under their bed once, not even covered up. Usually neither of them remarked upon these discoveries, though he had once tried to pass off an ancient Greek kylix as a gravy boat, which then led to him lying about having to return it to the store next day because he decided it clashed with JCPenney's china.

He wasn't a great liar.

She grabbed herself a wine cooler.

"Could you get me one while you're up?" he asked from the other room.

She plopped down on the couch beside him, handed him his cooler. He put his hand on her knee and kissed her cheek. "Thanks, babe. You're the best."

"What do you want to do tonight?" she asked.

Hiro shrugged. "I don't know. What do you want to do?"

"We could go out to eat."

"We could. Any place in mind?"

It was her turn to shrug. "That new pizza place opened up down the street."

"Don't know if I feel like pizza," he said. "We could go to Huang's, get some Chinese."

"We got Chinese Monday. You still have leftovers in the fridge."

"Oh, yeah."

He focused his attention on the television, on an episode he must've seen six or seven times before. She didn't speak, waiting for him to carry on the conversation. Five minutes passed in silence.

"There's the Lebanese joint," she finally said.

He frowned, still not taking his eyes off the TV, even though it was only a commercial. "I don't know if I'm in the mood for ethnic food."

"Chinese food is ethnic food," she said, sensing an edge in her voice she couldn't tamp down.

"Not really. Not for me."

"You're Japanese."

"Yeah."

"Japan and China are two different ethnic groups."

"Yeah."

"Therefore, Chinese food is ethnic food for you."

Hiro had mastered the art of ninjaly intuition. He could hear someone walking up to their door twenty seconds before they knocked and had the uncanny ability to find the exact spot in any room, no matter how crowded, where no one was looking. But he remained clueless about her smoldering annoyance.

"I'm not in the mood for Chinese," he said.

"So, what are you in the mood for?" she asked, praying

he'd stop this conversation before it reached its inevitable conclusion.

"Oh, I don't care, babe. Whatever."

Tia closed her eyes. She wouldn't get mad. They wouldn't fight. They wouldn't have *this fight* again. He'd figure it out *this time*, and if he didn't, she wouldn't take the bait. Not *this time*.

"We could always get pizza," he said.

She jumped off the couch. "Are you fucking serious? Pizza? Did you just say pizza?"

He feigned innocence. As if he didn't know exactly what the hell he did. "I thought you liked pizza."

"I do like pizza," she said, trying to remain calm even as she felt her heart pump harder. "I said let's get pizza. And you said you didn't want fucking pizza."

"I did?"

"Yes. Like three minutes ago."

He scratched his chin. "Yes, now that I think about it, I don't really want pizza."

She thought about opening the closet, retrieving the artifact they both pretended wasn't in there, and smashing it to bits. Antiquity be damned. It was probably the only way to get his attention.

"What about that Lebanese place?" he said. "You said you wanted to try that the other day."

She expected to explode at that moment. Instead, all her rage abandoned her, draining away as she realized she didn't really give a shit anymore. She walked into the bedroom, fell into bed, and stared at the ceiling. Hiro came in a moment later and joined her. He ran his hand down her cheek and along her neck. He still had that, whatever that was. He could still do things to her without having to *do* anything to her.

She grabbed his hand. "What are we doing?"

"Ordering in?" he said as he moved closer.

He wasn't getting out of this so easily. She pushed him away and rolled off the bed.

"Not that. I mean, what are we doing? Is this it? The same conversations, the same fights? The same pizza?"

He put his hand on her shoulder, but not in a way that made her tingle. Not much anyway. "Do you want to talk about what's really bothering you?"

"This is bothering me," she said.

"Is it?"

"Yes. It is."

He smiled, and she wanted to smack him. Or kiss him. Or both.

"Is it?" he asked. "Because I think there's something else that's bothering you."

She didn't want to have this conversation, but it was different than their usual one, so she plunged forward. "And what is that?"

"I think you're getting a little antsy. You haven't been on an adventure in a while."

"I don't have adventures," she said.

"Sure, you do. Maybe they're Connie's adventures and

you're along for the ride, but you're still there for some of them. And I've noticed you get edgy when you haven't been kidnapped in a while. And it has been a while."

She dismissed the idea.

She did have a history of getting kidnapped. From the ages of twelve to twenty-one, she'd averaged six abductions a year. They were always incidental. Connie had adventures, and sometimes, the easiest way for those adventures to get started was for the universe to use Tia's safety as motivation. Not that Tia often felt in danger. Not with the knowledge that Connie was on the case.

Tia still remembered the first time. She'd been eight and stumbled across a gangster on the lam in her backyard. He'd taken her as hostage, dragging her to some forsaken cabin in the middle of nowhere. She'd thought for sure she would wind up dead. Until Connie, following a series of clues, led the police to the gangster's hideout.

The ordeal had been terrifying, but looking back on it now, it was almost quaint.

"We all have our fetishes," said Hiro. "If you like, I can pretend to be an alien come to steal you to ensure the genetic survival of my species."

"Maybe later."

"If you want my opinion—" he started.

"I don't."

"—I think it's not the abductions you miss. It's having something to come along and break up your day now and then. Connie might be the adventurer, but you've done some amazing things, seen some amazing places."

"Not really," she said. "I'm usually blindfolded."

"You're sidestepping." He took her hand. "When's the last time you and Connie did something thrilling and heroic? Not counting the cheese zombies?"

"I don't know. Month or two ago. We broke up an exotic animal smuggling ring. Saved a rare tiger. Might have been magic. I was never really clear on that."

"I remember the day you came back from Sumatra." He pulled her close and kissed her. "I remember that night even more."

She smiled, despite herself. "You're incorrigible."

"I'm right. You always get grumpy when it's been too long. I get the same way when I don't do my thing. Not that I do it anymore."

She pulled away from him and opened the drawer on his bedside table. The Hope Diamond lay there with his mints and Daniel Steele novel.

"How did that get there?" he said, and she was almost convinced he was innocent.

"Uh-hmm." She closed the drawer and sat next to him on the bed.

"You're bored," he said. "And you're missing your friend. You two are closer than most anyone could be, but now there's Byron, and he's taking up a lot of Connie's time."

"That's normal."

"Normal, sure, but it's still hard on you. You've had Connie to yourself, more or less, for a long time. She might have gone off to save the world without you regularly, and every so often with you, but when she was here, she didn't have much to get in the way of hanging out."

"Okay. So, maybe you're onto something."

"I am. And the best part is I even know how to fix your problem."

"Oh, do you?"

"Call her," he said. "Tell her you want to go with her on whatever strange adventure she goes on next."

"That's not how it works."

"Didn't you make her take her with you when you destroyed the Great Engine?"

"That was the exception."

"Make another exception. You'll be glad you did, and I bet Connie would love to have you along."

Tia said, "I see what you're doing. You think if I go off on some wild adventure, I'll come back not annoyed at you."

"I'll admit it sounds nice."

"And while I'm away, you're free to do your thing."

"Seems only fair. You must admit, we do avoid these types of evenings when we're allowed our indulgences."

"I don't approve of stealing."

"Nor should you. Distasteful business, really. But I console myself by being terribly good at it."

He winked, and she went for her cell, but it wasn't in her pocket.

"Looking for this?" asked Hiro, holding the cell in his hand.

She reached for it, and he pulled it away.

"It was your idea to call Connie," she said.

"Yes, but not right this minute." He lifted her up in his arms and had her on the bed in one graceful sweep. "Unless, of course, you'd rather get something to eat first."

Laughing, she grabbed him by the shirt and pulled him close.

I t was Byron's idea to throw a housewarming party and invite the neighbors. Connie hadn't spent much time at home in the past. She'd never had much reason, but now that adventures were more infrequent and she was in a relationship, she planned on being there more often. It couldn't hurt to get to know the other condo residents. If she made a good impression, they might overlook the occasional incident that was bound to happen.

She never would've thought of it herself, but that was why life with Byron was an adventure. It wasn't simply getting a chance to do normal things. It was having someone in her life who knew how to do them.

While Byron prepared the snacks, Connie did a final check. They'd unpacked, mostly. Some boxes were shoved into a closet and an out-of-the-way corner. They'd used half of her furniture and half of his. It didn't match, but her furniture rarely did. They'd gathered a dozen folding chairs.

Among them, she spotted an old stoop chair antique.

"Byron, did you put the cursed Busby chair out?" she asked.

"No. I thought we put that in basement storage," he said.

She picked up the haunted chair and shoved it in a closet. "Nice try. Now stay."

The cursed chair sat there innocently as she closed the door on it.

Someone knocked on the front door.

"Can you get that, honey?" shouted Byron from the kitchen.

"Sure thing," she shouted back, feeling very domestic at that moment. It was weird but welcome.

She opened the door. Doctor Malady and his robot bride Automatica stood in the hall. The evil genius smirked at her. "Ah, Miss Verity, so good to—"

Connie seized Malady by the collar, pulled him inside, and threw him against the wall. She pinned his arms behind his back while searching him for nefarious devices.

"I saw you die, Doctor," she said.

"Oh, that. I got better."

"I don't know why you're here," said Connie, "but I'm only going to tell you once. Byron is off-limits. If you want revenge, you won't start anything here. Am I being clear?"

Doctor Malady nodded. His monocle fell. "Very, though I'm not here for vengeance."

"Then why are you here?"

"The housewarming," he said. "We brought cookies."

Automatica, the Doctor's robot bride, stepped forward and uncovered a platter of cookies. "They're sugar."

Connie released Malady and sniffed a cookie suspiciously.

Automatica, her face an unchanging metal smile, said, "I do hope they are satisfactory. An analysis showed sweetness variance within acceptable parameters."

"Don't be so modest, my dear. Your baking skills are second to none."

The seven-foot-tall robotic woman tittered. "Oh, you. Excessive flattery will increase my self-esteem matrix to inadvisable settings."

He winked, reset his monocle, and had a cookie.

"You're not here for revenge?" asked Connie.

"Heavens, no," said Doctor Malady. "Revenge is a sucker's game. I'm honestly glad you foiled me the last time we met. A man has time to think about his life choices as he's plummeting into a volcano for the second time. Puts things in perspective."

"What's your scheme?"

"No scheme. We're retired. Aren't we, sweetie?"

Automatica beeped an affirmative. "Current mission objective: wedded bliss."

She leaned downward to allow the short evil genius to kiss her cheek.

"I suppose it was unfair to spring ourselves on you like this," said Doctor Malady. "When I'd heard you were moving into the building, I suspected this would be an issue."

Byron stepped out of the kitchen. "Oh, friends of yours, honey?"

"I'm afraid calling ourselves friends might be a bit of an overstep," said Malady. "More like respected rivals. Though who can know what the future might hold? You must be Byron. A pleasure to meet you."

Automatica curtsied. "We brought cookies."

"You can set them on the kitchen table," said Byron.

The Doctor and Automatica wandered into the kitchen.

"Should I be concerned?" asked Byron.

"I'll let you know," replied Connie.

They followed their guests into the other room.

"Don't tell me we're the first ones. This is your fault, y'know," Doctor Malady said to Automatica.

"Punctuality is among my higher directives," admitted Automatica.

"It's just as well," said the Doctor. "It gives us a chance to clear things up. I don't blame you for being suspicious, Constance, but I can assure you that my villainy days are well behind me. I don't expect you to trust me. Not right away. But we do hope we can put our past behind us. I'd like us to be good neighbors."

"You live in the building?" asked Byron.

"Unit 2A. You should drop by sometime. Automatica and I do love company."

"I don't believe you," said Connie. "You're up to something."

Doctor Malady chuckled, a soft rasp that scraped its way

out of his throat. "Perhaps I am. If so, then I can think of nothing better for this world than having Constance Verity three floors up, keeping an eye on me. If I can be honest, I have had the old megalomaniacal itch, but now that you're here, I know it would all be pointless. You're my own little reminder that all my previous world-conquest attempts haven't fared very well."

"Shall I prioritize disassembly of the subjugatitron, then, dear?" asked Automatica.

"Oh, not just yet. Haven't the heart to tear it apart. A memento of a different man. Perfectly harmless so long as its power core isn't replaced."

"Shall I cancel the delivery of the new power core, then?" asked Automatica.

"Now, now, dear. No need to bore our hosts with the trifles of our daily lives." Doctor Malady smiled sheepishly at Connie. "Love what you've done with the place."

"Thanks," said Byron. "Would you care for a tour?"

"As a matter of fact, Automatica was hoping to see how you've remodeled the bathroom. She isn't happy with ours."

"Its spatial dimensions are a barrier to efficient functionality," said Automatica.

"I hear that," said Byron. "We installed a whole new sink. Really opens up the room."

"Color us intrigued," said the Doctor as Byron led them away.

Connie stayed in the kitchen. She didn't buy that Malady

was retired, but this wasn't the time nor place for that confrontation. Malady wasn't likely to start something there. He was an evil genius, but he always did have a sense of decorum.

The next guest arrived. The elderly couple, named Jim and Nim, lived on the second floor. They brought a fruit tart. Connie showed them in as Byron returned with Malady and Automatica.

"Jim, Nim, how lovely to see you," said Doctor Malady. "And is this your famous fruit tart I see before me? You must share the recipe one day."

"Oh, I don't think so," said Nim with a coy titter.

"Now, Nim, don't make me dig my old hypno-ray out of storage."

Jim and Nim and Malady and Automatica all laughed. Byron offered them something to drink as another knock came. Connie answered it and was greeted by a tall, pale gentleman in a dark suit.

"Hello," he said. "Welcome to the building."

His accent was vaguely European, and his bloodshot eyes pierced her soul. Her soul had been pierced on multiple occasions, and most creatures that could do that tended to be impressed by what they saw.

He smiled. "Are you going to invite me in?"

"Vampire, right?" she said.

He nodded. "That's not going to be a problem, is it? The invite made no mention of excluding the undead."

"No, I guess not. Please, come in." She stepped aside.

"Though if you have an invitation, you didn't have to ask to enter."

He floated through the doorway. An unnatural fog swirled around his ankles. "It is still a matter of politeness, is it not?"

"And I appreciate it. So, you live here too?"

"Unit 1B. Got a great deal on it because it has terrible sun exposure. Welcome to the building." He smoothed back his slick, black hair and produced a bottle of wine from under his opera cloak. "A delightful vintage, I'm told. I don't drink the stuff, myself."

She pointed him toward the kitchen.

The guests arrived in a steady stream. Most of them were normal people. People with names like Nathan or Pepper or Craig and normal jobs like accountant or lawyer or auto mechanic. But mingled among them came the occasional alien or scientist-adventurer or derring-doer. Things were going fine, though Duke Warlock, vampire, and Baron Solaris, vampire hunter, were giving each other a wide berth. Doctor Malady wasn't too keen on Automatica making time with Luke and Vance's security robot, but so far, it was little more than a few unhappy glances on his part.

Tia and Hiro were the last to arrive.

"Sorry we're late," said Tia. "Somebody had to change three times."

"You might dislike the wait," said Hiro as he smoothed his lapel, "but I think we can both agree with the results."

Tia scanned the gathering. "A colorful group."

Connie shrugged. "No hijinks yet. Although Byron's sister is talking to a bunch of gnomes in an overcoat. Fortunately, she has a boyfriend, so that's probably not going anywhere."

Byron pulled himself away from a conversation. "Glad you could make it."

"Glad to be invited." Hiro handed Byron a small rectangle wrapped in brown paper. "It's a Vermeer. I do hope you like it."

Hiro and Tia mingled with the crowd.

"We're returning that," said Connie.

"I assumed." Byron kissed her. "Something bothering you?"

"I wanted normal, and here we are with three robots at our housewarming."

"Three? I only count two."

She pointed to Lucy from 4C. "Android. She may not know."

"Okay, so we have some robots and a mad scientist and Susan Lash, rogue archeologist, at our party. We also have Jim and Nim, Bart and Vanessa and Yolanda. So, we have a few eccentric neighbors. Everybody's getting along. Automatica does make a mean cookie, and Warlock has excellent taste in wine. I think it's going great."

"You're not worried about living next door to fugitive aliens and a vampire one floor down?"

"They seem like perfectly nice neighbors, and nobody in the building seems put off by them. I think you're just put off by not being the most interesting person in the room."

"Did I ever tell you about the time I used a Rubik's cube

to prevent Zorthlokart the All-Devouring from consuming the galaxy?" she asked.

"All right, the most *obviously* interesting person in the room," he corrected. "But look at it this way. With neighbors like these, we probably don't have to worry about complaints when something does happen."

He made sense, but she was still on edge. She was so used to trouble, it was impossible for her to imagine all these elements mixing together without repercussions. Her own adventure-drawing presence might just be the catalyst to throw the delicate balance out of whack.

The front door burst open and a quartet of masked gunmen entered the condo. They waved their machine guns around the room as their leader stepped forward.

"Your attention, ladies and gentlemen. Follow instructions and this will all go smoothly. We don't want any trouble. It is in your interest as well as ours that this is over as quickly and quietly as possible."

Connie pushed Byron behind her and grabbed a pig in a blanket. She ate the hors d'oeuvre and clutched the toothpick between two fingers, waiting for the nearest thug to draw a few steps closer.

The leader droned on. "The previous tenant of this condominium left an object of some value that we are here to recover. It shall take us only a few minutes at most to—"

Doctor Malady zapped the leader with a transmogrifier ray, and the petrified statue stood in mid-sentence.

A gunman attempted to fire on Malady, but Automatica snatched away his gun and bent it into a useless lump. Max Jackhammer, Crimebuster, coldcocked two others. The final gunman paused, thought better of the whole situation, dropped his weapon, and bolted out the front door.

The party resumed.

Doctor Malady pocketed his ray gun and tapped his knuckles on the petrified gangster. "Don't worry. The effect is temporary. I think. 90 percent certain it should wear off in a decade or two. Century at the most."

Connie tossed her toothpick on the tray. "Maybe this is the right place for us after all."

Byron smiled. "Told ya."

A ringing phone in the middle of the night was never a good sign.

Connie rolled over in bed and cuddled Byron.

The phone kept ringing.

"Are you going to answer that?" he asked.

"No," she said.

"What if it's important?"

"It isn't."

She kissed his shoulder and closed her eyes.

The phone kept ringing.

"We should answer it," he said.

"We shouldn't."

"What if somebody we know is in trouble?"

"Somebody I know is always in trouble," she replied.

"What if it's not somebody you know? What if it's some-body I know?"

"It isn't. Go to sleep."

He sat up and switched on the lamp. "Why does it keep ringing if it's not an emergency?"

Sighing, she turned her back to the light. "It's always an emergency, but I don't always have to answer the call."

"What if you don't?" Byron asked. "What if it's some alien-fighting guy and he needs your help to fight aliens and you don't take the call and tomorrow, the Earth is enslaved?"

"Then I'll take care of it." She pulled the blankets over her head. "Tomorrow."

The phone stopped ringing.

"There?" She lowered the blanket. "See?"

It started ringing again.

"I'm going to answer it." He reached for the phone, but Connie put her arms around him, pulling him away.

"You could do that, or . . ." She kissed his neck.

"You can't just distract me with sex," he said.

"Who's distracting? I'm just offering alternatives."

She kissed him. His hand slid down her back. The phone stopped ringing, and she was undoing the string on his pajama bottoms when it started again.

"I have to answer it!" yelled Byron, lunging over her.

She could've stopped him, but she was mildly curious herself at this point.

"Hello?" he said. "Uh-huh. Yes." He put the phone to his chest with an apologetic half-smile. "It's for you."

She mimed a surprised expression before taking the phone.

Byron shuffled out of the room for a glass of water.

"This is Verity," she said. "What do you want?"

She didn't recognize the voice. "We need your help with a most urgent—"

"It's late. Get to it. I'd like to get back to sleep."

The voice gave her an address, and she hung up.

Byron returned and joined her on the bed. He hugged her. "Sorry. I should've listened."

"It's fine."

"So, what was it about? Aliens? Space robots? Mutants?"

"Didn't say," she said. "Didn't ask."

"But it's a mysterious phone call," he said. "Aren't you curious? Don't you want to be prepared?"

"Not really. Whatever it is, I'll deal with it in the morning." She undid the pajama string.

"So, you really weren't trying to distract me?"

"I was, but now that we're both up, might as well make the most of it." She ran her fingers through his hair and kissed him. "I'll deal with it in the morning."

In the morning, Byron got dressed for work while Connie lay in bed.

"Are you sure it's smart to go alone?" asked Byron.

"It's nothing to worry about," said Connie. "I do this all the time."

"It's still weird to me that you're going at all."

"It's not that weird. Think of it like this. Do you have meetings at your job? And do a lot of those meetings seem pointless or vaguely purposed?"

"Sure."

"And do you sometimes wish you could just not go to those meetings, but you go anyway because you know not going will just make everything more of a hassle around the office?"

"Sure."

"Same thing for me. It's better to go and get it over with rather than try to avoid it."

"I still think you should take some backup," said Byron. "Call Agent Ellington."

"She's a government agent. Not a personal valet. I can't call her every time some little annoyance pops up."

"What about Tia?"

"She has a job. Trust me, I know how to handle this. It's not my first rodeo."

He shrugged. "You know your business."

"I'll text if anything goes wrong. Promise. By the way, isn't Wednesday your day to pick up the donuts for work?"

"Damn it." He fumbled with his tie. "I'm going to be late. You do not want to be late with the donuts. Welker will spend half the day whining about it."

Connie sat up and waved him over. She helped him with his tie and handed him his briefcase. She kissed him. "Go get 'em, tiger. Those debits aren't going to credit themselves."

"That's not how it works," he said.

"Accounting is one of the few things I know nothing about," she replied. "Now, don't you have donuts to pick up?"

He gave her a peck. "Love you."

"Love you."

He rushed out the door, and she took a moment to enjoy the domesticity.

A pair of intimidating goons in matching black suits guarded the manor. The guards barely acknowledged her, but the security camera over the door swiveled in her direction. The doors swung open automatically.

Connie made a show of glancing at her wrist. She didn't wear a watch, and she didn't have any pressing engagements. But it'd hopefully remind whoever was watching that she had better things to do with her time.

"One question: this isn't one of those fiendish-death-trap manors?" she asked a guard.

"No," he said, though he hesitated and didn't sound convincing.

She could either turn around or plunge headlong into unknown dangers. Her life tended to go askew when she refused adventure, and she could usually beat death-trap manors in a few hours. Better to get it over with, she decided.

She stepped across the threshold, and the doors closed behind her with an ominous click. She inspected the marble floors for telltale signs of trapdoors or land mines. The place was mostly empty, but a shiny lion statue in the center of the room might be a robot. And the sconces might conceal flamethrowers or machine guns.

A tall, serious man in a butler's uniform stood at the top of the stairs. "This way, ma'am."

Connie climbed the stairs. She spotted the hidden gears that could turn the stairs into a slide with a flip of a switch, leading to a pit of whirring blades or something equally inconvenient, but she reached the top. The butler was a foot taller than Connie, and his well-tailored uniform did nothing to hide his muscular frame. He moved with the self-assurance of a rhino.

They walked down a long hallway. The butler's polished shoes clicked against the tile, echoing off the walls. Busts of scholars, artists, captains of industry, and a dictator or two lined both sides. They might shoot lasers or poison darts out of their mouths, but nothing triggered.

They entered a windowless, undecorated room. A monitor was bolted to the wall. The butler gestured toward a plush leather recliner that could conceal retractable manacles. "Please, have a seat, Ms. Verity."

"I'll stand. Thanks."

"As you wish."

"So, we're not going to fight?" asked Connie.

He smiled slightly as if amused by something unspecific. Maybe an old joke that had popped unbidden into his head. "Not unless you want to."

"No, I'm good."

The monitor switched on and the image of a man from the neck down appeared. He wore a polo shirt. There was a single golden ring on his finger with a familiar insignia of a sword atop a pyramid. Connie recognized it but couldn't place the exact organization. After a few decades, all the secret societies and hidden conspiracies blended together.

The man spoke, and his voice was tinny and digitized. "Hello, Connie. Great to see you again. Can I get you something? Maybe a drink or a scone?"

"No, thanks."

"I'm sorry I couldn't be there in person," said the man, "but I had pressing matters here." A pair of hands appeared and set some papers before him. He quickly signed them and handed them back.

"Join the club," she said.

"Right. I'm just glad you could find the time. I know how crazy your schedule gets."

"Siege Perilous," interrupted Connie, placing the ring's insignia. "Larry Peril, is that you?"

"Yes, of course it's me." Peril pressed his hands together. "Oh, for the love of . . . Georgia, where did you learn to operate a camera?"

Someone chattered lightly off-camera.

"It's not that hard. Look through that end and make sure it's pointed— Wait. Is the voice thing on too? Oh, hell, why did you do that?" Larry Peril bent down into frame, tilting his head sideways. "Give me a second, Connie."

She sat in the recliner. "I'll take that scone now."

The butler nodded and walked away.

"And some earl grey if you got it," she called before he left the room.

The audio became static as he removed the microphone pinned to his shirt and set it down on the desk, and moved out of camera. Little snippets of audio were audible.

"No, you look through this here," said Larry. "Well, if I'd known you were going to have this much trouble, I would've hired someone from the union."

The camera raised. He took his seat back at the desk, reattached the mic. It'd been at least fifteen years since she'd seen Larry Peril. He had his mother's piercing black eyes. He smiled. As a kid, he'd had a sweet smile, and he'd never lost it.

"Well, damn." He sighed. "Turn off the voice thing already, Georgia." His digital voice snapped to his normal tone. "Thank you. Much better. This must appear all very sinister to you."

"You mean the mysterious calls in the middle of the night, the death mansion, the henchagents? No, it doesn't look good."

"Wait. They called you in the middle of the night? Why would they do that?"

Georgia mumbled off-camera.

"Yes, I said it was urgent, but have some decorum. I knew I should've made the call myself. And I specifically said not to use the death mansion."

Georgia mumbled something.

"What about the bungalow?" he said.

Mumble mumble.

"How long does it take to decommission a mutant piranha tank, anyway?"

Mumble mumble.

"Whose idea was it to make them flying if we don't have a way of ensuring they stay in the water?"

Mumble mumble.

"No, do it right. If those things get out and start breeding, it'll defeat the whole purpose. I know you're doing your best, but it's frustrating sometimes."

He turned his attention back to Connie. "Sorry. There's just a certain way people are used to doing things around here. I should've done this personally, but I'm fairly overwhelmed. I don't know how Mom did it."

"How is your mother? I'd heard Lady Peril had died trying to activate the ancient doomsday device in the Great Pyramids."

"She did. At least, as far as anyone can tell. Who knows for sure? But if she isn't dead, she's faking it more than usual. I inherited the controlling interest in Siege Perilous. You're looking at the Mastermind Interim."

"I didn't think you had any interest in the family business."

"I don't, but I figured if I didn't do it, somebody else would. I've been trying to change things around here, but it's an uphill battle."

"So, you're not evil?"

"You're kidding, right?"

"You wouldn't be the first mastermind's kid to take up his parent's mantle after their death."

His smile dropped. "Maybe it sounds terrible, but I'm not upset by her death. I stopped going to funerals when I was twelve."

Connie said, "Sorry. That was out of line."

"No, it wasn't. I know I was always a disappointment to Mom. I was never what she wanted in a son. Remember when I wore that stupid cape, just to please her?"

"I remember, Lord Peril," she recalled with a chuckle before catching herself.

He covered his face and laughed. She joined him, and they laughed for a good thirty seconds.

He wiped his eyes. "Goddamn. Stupid kids, right?"

Larry said, "Jeez, Connie, I missed you. You're looking really great, by the way. Adventuring must agree with you."

"Thanks," she said. The butler returned with her scone and tea on a platter. She helped herself, blowing on the tea.

"So what's this all about?" she asked Larry. "I don't think you went to all this trouble just for a reunion."

"You're right." He leaned forward and smiled. "I need you to help save the world."

She sipped her tea. "I'm listening."

I t wasn't the first hydra Connie had fought. Or the largest. But it was certainly the most stubborn. It just kept coming, no matter how many of its heads she cut off. Sticky, acidic blood splattered across her face and shirt as she decapitated a fourth. It stung her cheek and burned holes in her clothes.

The stump bubbled as a new pair started to grow.

"I'm on it," said Tia as she stabbed the road flare into the monster's regenerating wound. Its other head squealed as its rage grew.

The last hydra head struck out at Tia, but Connie deflected the venomous strike with an old, rusted shield she'd found lying around on the temple floor. She stabbed the creature through its throat, and it hissed and wheezed as it flopped around on the dusty stone floors.

Connie took an ancient battle axe from the skeletal hands of a long-dead Viking who had been unfortunate enough to stumble onto the hydra's lair several hundred years before.

She pinned the monster's head with her foot and finished it off. It took several strokes from the dull blade. More blood splattered on her hands and arms. Tia took shelter behind Connie to avoid the splash zone, though she rushed forward to sear shut the final wound.

Connie sat on the floor, leaned against a crumbling column, and caught her breath.

Tia offered Connie a towel. "You've got a little something there. On your cheek. And chin. And a little under your eye. And in your hair." Tia made a sweeping gesture at Connie's body. "Well, you get the idea."

"Thanks." Connie wiped the warm blood from her cheeks as the headless hydra squirmed limply.

"How long will it take to die?" asked Tia.

"It won't. Not unless we kill it. The fire slows the process, but it'll still regenerate, given enough time. We'll be gone by then." Connie rifled through her backpack. "Shit, I can't find it."

"I got it." Tia produced the steel box from her own backpack. "Noticed you dropped it when we were running from that tiger, though what the hell is a wild tiger doing in Africa?"

"The mysteries of a life of adventure." Connie took the box and opened it. The yellow flower inside didn't look like much, but she'd once saved the universe with a handful of change in her pockets, so she didn't judge by appearance. "You're a lifesaver."

"Don't mention it." Tia sat beside Connie on the stone stairs. "Just part of the sidekick service."

The air around the ancient altar crackled with mystical forces as the planar alignment approached. The earth rumbled as alien evils slumbering in a realm outside of time and space stirred. The opening in the ceiling showed a sky full of holes into other worlds, other times. Most were harmless. Alternate realities and nameless dimensions. But in some of those dimensions, things waited. Unknowable things that ate universes with casual indifference as they passed through to other dimensions.

The hundred eyes on the dozen statues surrounding the altar glowed red.

"Almost time," said Connie.

They waited for the proper moment, watching reality itself ripple, dissolve, and reform like a broken television trying to tune to every station at once.

"Have you decided to take Larry up on his job offer yet?" asked Tia.

"It's a favor, not a job. And I think so. Siege Perilous's rating among secret societies was hovering around an eight last time I checked the Global Peril Index."

"Who the heck is in charge of making that list?"

"They have computers or something that do it," said Connie. "Or they used to. I think the computer went rogue and tried to use satellites to make killer tornadoes. The only reason it failed was because the computer rated itself a nine. Now it's a bunch of number crunchers somewhere. I've been there once. It's a nice building. Great cafeteria. They tried explaining all the informational matrices and statistical sifting, but I stopped paying attention after a while. Regardless of how it works, their accuracy is solid. They predicted Ragnarok a week before anyone else suspected a thing. So, if they give Siege Perilous an eight, I have to take it seriously."

"But Larry's in charge now. Shouldn't that defuse the situation?"

Connie shook her head. "Doesn't work like that. When someone puts together a massive secret operation bent on acquiring wealth and power through any means necessary, that organization doesn't just dissolve because the leader disappears. It's only a matter of time before Larry's deposed or . . ."

"Or?"

Connie leaned in and whispered. Not because she was worried about anyone overhearing, but because she felt bad about what she was about to say.

"Or Larry becomes a mastermind himself."

Tia laughed. "You're kidding, right?"

Connie shrugged.

"This is Larry we're talking about," said Tia. "He's never been very good at megalomania."

"True, but he is his mother's son, and he does have a sinister worldwide secret society at his bidding."

"Yes, but . . . it's Larry."

"It's Larry," said Connie noncommittally.

"Larry can't be evil," said Tia.

"Wouldn't be the first to be corrupted by all that power,"

said Connie. "I'm not saying he'd be great as a mastermind, but a lot of these so-called masterminds aren't all that capable or bright. The Scorpion Society is run by a brain in a jar with the exact level of intelligence you would expect from a brain in a jar, but that didn't stop it from nearly launching Chicago into the sun."

"Wait. When did that happen?"

"Nine or ten months ago."

"And you didn't tell me? My Mom lives in Chicago."

"I didn't know about it until after the fact. Had nothing to do with it. I foil a lot of evil schemes, but it's a small percentage overall. The government kept a lockdown on public knowledge. They usually do."

Tia frowned. As Connie's friend, she knew about the many hidden dangers lurking around the world. It had bothered her for years until she'd accepted that people were on the job, keeping such impossible threats under control. Honestly, she'd never quite accepted it so much as resigned herself to the fact.

"Do you think it's a bad idea?" asked Connie. "You think it's a bad idea," she added before Tia could reply.

"I didn't say that."

"You didn't have to. I know you. I know that face. That's your bad-idea face."

"No, it's my *undecided* face. This sort of thing is out of your wheelhouse, isn't it? I get that you're always foiling evil schemes, but this doesn't seem very foil-y." Tia tapped her finger against her chin, searching for a better word. "Foil-ish? Foil-ic?"

"That was Larry's exact point. I'm always putting out fires. Here's a chance to stop a fire before it starts. Hundreds of fires."

"It does make sense when you put it like that, but it can't be as easy as that."

Connie said, "I don't imagine it will be. If it was, Larry wouldn't need me."

"And we're certain this isn't some elaborate scheme to lure you into a deathtrap?"

"He already had me in a deathtrap, and he didn't spring it."

Tia said, "Yes, but it could be a bigger scheme than that. Or maybe he's trying to win over your trust before destroying you."

"Do I need to keep reminding you we're talking about Larry here?"

"Larry Peril, son of Lady Peril, the seventh or eighth most dangerous mind in the world," reminded Tia.

"Eleventh," said Connie. "I checked. I get your suspicions, Tia. I share some of them, but I also think it's a chance worth taking."

The holes in the sky grew darker and sharper. Horrible things growled and shrieked from beyond. They attempted to shove their way into this universe, only to clog the portal trying to be the first one in.

Connie and Tia approached the altar. Whispering shadows slinked through the temple, but Connie and Tia ignored the distraction.

"And how's Byron feel about this?" asked Tia.

"He's fine. Why wouldn't he be?"

"He's not worried about you working in close quarters with your first boyfriend?"

"Larry was never my boyfriend," said Connie. "We were just kids, thrown together by hormones and circumstances. Larry and I were never a thing."

Tia paused. "Whatever you say."

"What does that mean?"

"It means I remember you two. You always had chemistry. Not hard to understand why. You have a lot in common. Larry's an ordinary guy from an extraordinary background, and you're an extraordinary girl from an ordinary background. There are sparks there. Or there were. Don't act like you didn't almost lose your virginity to him when we were racing Siege Perilous across the globe, gathering bones of Theseus."

"Eurystheus," corrected Connie.

"Whatever. Why did we have to do that again? Never mind. The point is that when a seventeen-year-old girl and boy are off on a globetrotting adventure together, stuff is going to happen. And don't pretend like there wasn't something exciting about teaming up with the son of your archenemy."

"Lady Peril was never—"

"It has a real Romeo-and-Juliet vibe to it. I know something happened between you two when we were visiting the Hidden Library of Alexandria. Don't deny it."

Connie looked away and mumbled.

"What was that?" asked Tia.

"Second base," said Connie. "It wasn't the first time."

"Aha!" exclaimed Tia as if cracking the case.

"We never went any further than that," said Connie. "We haven't seen each other in at least ten years."

"Uh-huh."

"You aren't seriously suggesting that this is all a ploy Larry's using to get close to me?"

Tia's face dropped. "No, I wasn't. But now I'm thinking I am."

"That's even stupider than your betrayal-and-deathtrap theory. For all we know, Larry is happily married with kids and doesn't think about me like that at all anymore."

"Did you see a wedding ring?" asked Tia.

"I didn't notice."

"Not buying it, master detective."

"I wouldn't say *master*."

Tia leaned forward with a knowing smile.

"No wedding ring," said Connie, "but not everyone wears one."

"Tell me this, then," said Tia. "Did he comment on your appearance?"

The interdimensional alignment fell into place. Horrors from beyond crawled their way into this universe. Connie dropped the flower on the altar. It flashed with a blinding brilliance as the unnamable things roared their displeasure. She smashed the flower with the box, and the sacrifice sent a shockwave rippling through time and space. Connie and Tia were thrown from the altar as the sky closed. The horrible things wailed as they were hurled back to their dimension of origin, to be bottled away for an age or two.

"Goddamn." Tia sat up, rubbing her back. "I landed on a rock."

Connie helped Tia up. They left the hydra behind to regenerate as they left the temple. The faint hint of stars twinkled in the twilight. They took a moment to appreciate it. It was easy to miss this stuff while saving the world.

"Please tell me we don't have to hike fifty miles back to civilization," said Tia.

"Helicopter should be coming by soon," replied Connie.

"Thank God."

Tia unslung her backpack and removed a pair of candy bars. They sat there, enjoying the quiet.

"Larry said I looked good," said Connie.

"Good?"

"He might have said *great*."

"Just *great* or did he add a *really* or two?"

"There might have been one *really*," admitted Connie. "That doesn't mean anything, though. It's just something people say."

"How did he say it?" Tia adopted a polite lilt. "Jeez, Connie, you're looking really *great*." She narrowed her eyes, smiled coyly, and lowered her voice. "Connie, you're looking *really* great."

Connie closed her eyes. "This might be the stupidest conversation we've ever had."

"What about that time you spent twenty minutes trying to teach me the difference between a replicant and a replicoid?"

"You'll thank me for that if you ever end up stranded in the future."

"Noted. So, if you don't think your history with Larry is important, then why haven't you told Byron?"

"It's not relevant. Anyway, if you're so concerned about me and ex-boyfriends, why are you still with Hiro?"

"Hiro's different. We all know where we stand there."

"Am I supposed to tell Byron anytime I run into anyone I have any romantic history with? No matter how long ago? No matter how irrelevant?"

"I never said that."

"What are you saying?"

Tia considered the question. "I'm not really sure anymore."

"Are you *not* really sure? Or not *really* sure? So, I should turn down Larry's offer to make the world a safer place because he might still have a lingering crush on me?"

"Does sound dumb when you put it like that," agreed Tia. "There's just something about this situation that I don't like. It feels . . . tricky, but I think you're right. We should do it."

"We?"

"I've been thinking about it. I'd like to apply for full-time sidekick status."

Connie said, "It's about time."

"You're cool with the idea, then? I thought maybe you'd be concerned about dragging around a liability."

"You've never been a liability, Tia."

"Not even when I've been dangling over bottomless pits while some sinister genius uses me as a hostage?"

"Not even then," said Connie, "but you've grown into a capable sidekick over the past few years. I've been wondering when you'd finally ask."

"You could've let me know the position was available."

"I didn't want to pressure you, but it's easier to save the world with reliable backup."

"I'll drink to that."

They tapped their canteens together. They heard a distant thumping sound as the lights of a helicopter appeared on the horizon.

11

A few days later, Connie stood before a sleek, black private jet in its very own hangar.

The pilot, a stocky woman in a matching black uniform, asked, "Is there a problem, Ms. Verity?"

"No. No problem. I just assumed I'd be flying commercial."

The pilot laughed. "Lord Peril was very insistent you be treated well. We're just running a few checks, and we should be leaving on schedule. If you'll give your bags to me, I'll be happy to see they're loaded on board for you."

"Yeah, sure." Connie handed the pilot her bag.

The pilot glanced behind Connie. "Is this it?"

Connie usually flew commercial and, like most skills required for her lifestyle, she'd mastered the techniques required. She could pack a carry-on like a Sherpa, control the armrest like Sun Tzu, and tune out the world with the meditative abilities of a warrior monk. She'd never gained enlightenment, but she'd survived a sixteen-hour flight beside a screaming toddler on one side and a yapping shih tzu without succumbing to madness. She still considered it one of her greatest triumphs in a life full of impossible escapes.

Connie said, "I travel light."

"I see. Well, if you'd like to have a seat while we finish up final preparations . . ." The pilot gestured to a table and chair where a server in a red vest and crisp black pants stood at attention. A full kitchen had been assembled behind him, where a round chef also waited.

"Yeah, sure," said Connie again.

She sat, and the server handed her a menu. "Given the timetable, I'm afraid the soufflé is out of the question," he said, "but the chef does have an excellent German chocolate cake ready to go, if you would like."

"I'm good," she said. "German chocolate, huh?"

He bowed at the waist like a precision mechanical man. "Yes, madam. We were told it was your favorite."

"Oh, it is. I'll just take a water."

His impeccable mustache twitched. "Is that all, madam? We have a wonderful selection of beverages and libations. If we might make a suggestion, we have a delightful cabernet sauvignon that pairs beautifully with the cake."

"Water. No cake."

"A soda, perhaps?" He swallowed his disgust with a facile smile. "Many people do seem to enjoy a preflight Coca-Cola or Dr. Pepper."

She didn't feel like fighting his offended sense of decorum, but she dug in despite herself. "Water."

"Very good, madam."

She caught his sleeve as he turned to fetch the drink. "Tap."

She expected him to faint, but after a small stagger, he nodded. "Yes, madam."

Connie pulled out her phone and called Tia.

"What's up?" asked Tia.

"Not bothering you, am I?" asked Connie.

"No, I'm at lunch."

"If I'm bothering you, I can always call back later."

"It's cool."

"I'll call later."

"Connie, what is it?" asked Tia.

Connie exhaled. "I think I screwed up. You were right. Larry has a thing for me."

"Well, no shit," said Tia. "Do you want me to act surprised now? I can make a surprised face if you want, though you won't be able to see it on the phone."

"He's flying me by private jet," said Connie.

"That doesn't necessarily mean anything."

"He had German chocolate cake prepared for me."

"Well, shit. That's not good."

"It's not, is it?"

"Maybe he's just showing his appreciation. You are helping him out."

The server returned with a glass on a tray. He handled the glass as if it contained radioactive slime and set it before her. "Shall there be anything else, madam?"

"No, thank you."

"Very good." He stood to one side, staring ahead as if he'd been switched into standby mode.

Connie took a drink of the water, and a trace of a frown crossed his thin lips.

"Maybe I'm reading too much into it," she said to Tia. "If he's in charge of Siege Perilous, he probably has a dozen private jets."

"Probably," agreed Tia. "And Larry knows you're not the kind of lady to fall for the wine-and-dine routine."

Connie put the phone to her chest. "Are you just going to stand there?" she asked the server.

"Would you prefer we remain in the kitchen?" he asked.

She nodded.

"Very good, madam. How is your . . . water?"

"Delicious, thank you." She took a sip, and he raised an eyebrow in rampant disgust. She was certain he must've had the nerves in his face deadened to prevent him from accidentally displaying an untoward emotion.

"If you need us, madam, simply ring the bell."

He retreated to the kitchen area, never once making eye contact with the chef. They stood there, beside each other, silently.

Connie turned her back to them. "This is weird. Are you

sure you can't make it? I'm sure I can get them to delay the flight."

"Can't do it," said Tia. "I've managed to do this job despite sidekicking, but I'm swamped right now."

"You can always blow them off."

"Considering how often they've looked the other way for me, it wouldn't feel right. I've given them my two weeks' notice. You don't need me for this. Just tell Larry you're in a relationship."

"I do not want to have that conversation. Not after flying on his jet and eating his cake."

"You ate the cake?"

"Not yet, but I will," said Connie.

"So, don't go."

"Then what do I tell him? *I'm sorry, but I can't help you make the world a safer place because I'm afraid you might have feelings for me and I'd rather not deal with that?*"

"Who says you have to be honest? Just tell him you've changed your mind. Tell him you're busy. Tell him you have to fight space vampires from dimension X. You shouldn't have a hard time coming up with believable excuses, considering your choices of what is believable for you."

"Doesn't seem right," said Connie.

"Then go. Tell him the truth."

"What if it gets weird? This is Larry. I don't want to hurt him."

Tia sighed. "I don't know what to tell you, Connie."

"You should," said Connie.

The pilot approached. "We are ready for takeoff, Ms. Verity."

"Sounds like you're off," said Tia. "Good luck."

Connie disconnected. She boarded, taking a slice of cake to go, despite her better judgment. She'd spent most of her life ignoring it, so why start now? The flight was quiet and smooth. She ate her cake and tried not to think about what she'd do after landing.

She hoped she wouldn't have to do anything, but if Larry had something more in mind than neutralizing the forces of evil, she'd politely correct him on that. And Larry would be fine with it. Why wouldn't he be? He wasn't a real mastermind. He wasn't likely to turn evil at her rejection and take his vengeance out on the world.

He was the son of a supervillain, though. Dangerous territory. The children of evil geniuses tended to either become evil geniuses or dedicate their lives to disrupting evil geniuses. It came with the territory. Guys like Larry Peril were the exception, not the rule.

Except Larry was now in charge of Siege Perilous.

She tried to imagine Larry in a cape or with a metal gauntlet. She couldn't do it. She tried something simpler like merely sitting in a chair, stroking a Persian cat sitting on his lap, briefing his underlings on their latest nefarious scheme. He'd express disappointment with one of them and push a button that would send them to their doom.

She couldn't see that either, but Larry could've changed. It'd been a long time since she'd seen him.

When the plane landed, she decided she'd put all her cards on the table. Whether Larry was a mastermind or a guy nursing a decades-long crush or simply what he seemed to be, she'd figure it out the best way she could. By just being honest with him.

The plane set down in a nondescript hangar in a small airport in the middle of nowhere. She surveyed the rolling hills spread in all directions as she disembarked. Her blood ran cold.

"Don't tell me I'm in Kansas," she asked the pilot.

"I'm afraid I can't disclose that information," he replied.

She studied the landscape, the bluestem grass, the bur oak trees, the fringe-leaf ruellia. She knew it like she knew the sinister laugh of her greatest enemies.

"Kansas. Shit."

Connie thought about turning around and telling the pilot to fly her home. Kansas had always been her kryptonite, the place where the universe loved to screw with her. But she'd come this far.

A limo waited for her. The driver carried a sign with her name on it, as if anyone else would be here in this three-hangar, one-runway stop. He opened the door for her, and she sat in back. The jet-black windows offered no view. She leaned back, closed her eyes, and thought about nothing until the car came to a stop again forty-five minutes later.

A statuesque brunette in horn-rimmed glasses opened the door. She stood a good foot taller than Connie. Her gray suit was impeccably tailored and wrinkle-free. Connie scanned for any signs of weapons, a slight bulge under the jacket, a hidden knife up a sleeve. She spotted nothing, and that only made her nervous. The unarmed ones were the ones to watch out for.

Connie stepped out of the car and surveyed the Spanish villa before her. She hadn't known what to expect. Supervillain lairs came in a hundred different varieties. This one was beautiful but unassuming. Aside from the fact that it sat in the middle of Nowhere, Kansas, it didn't stand out. Guards in matching black jumpsuits were stationed at the gates and along the walls. A black helicopter passed overhead.

"Ms. Verity, I'm Lord Peril's personal valet, Apollonia. If you should need anything during your stay here, please do let us know."

"Uh-huh."

Connie measured Apollonia. She was a tower of a woman, not just tall but solidly built. She turned and strode toward the villa with a sturdy grace, like a big cat that knew you were only alive because she hadn't found a reason to eat you yet.

"Someone will fetch your bags. This way, Ms. Verity."

"Uh-huh," said Connie.

She wondered if she should say something witty, but nothing came to mind. There should've been some clever line about villas in Kansas, but damned if she could find it. She was off her game. Once she cleared the air with Larry, she'd be better.

Better at what? This was only a consultation. She hadn't agreed to anything yet. She could always change her mind.

They passed through the house, and she was too distracted

to pay much attention to the tasteful furnishings. Larry sat at a table ringed by a giant swimming pool. Connie and Apollonia crossed the bridge as the bull shark swam in slow circles below the pristine waters.

Larry looked up from a stack of papers he was reading and smiled. "Connie! You made it." He set the papers aside and shook her hand. It felt weird.

"That feels weird," he said.

"Yes," she agreed.

They hugged. Awkwardly at first, but within a second or two, it all came back to them.

"It's been too long," he said. "We're so glad you chose to help us. Aren't we, Apollonia?"

"Yes," Apollonia replied flatly. "Very happy, Lord Peril."

They had a seat, and he started rifling through his papers again.

"Larry, I think we should—" started Connie.

"Are you hungry?" he asked. "Apollonia, have the chef make something. What would you like, Connie?"

"I'm fine," she replied.

"Something to drink?"

"I could use a beer," she admitted.

"What kind? We're fully stocked."

"Doesn't matter," said Connie.

He smiled. "Oh, right. You're not picky. Guess you can't afford to be when you never know where you'll be. Jeez, I missed you, Connie. You're looking great. How long has it been?"

"Ten years," she said. "Larry—"

"Don't just stand there, Apollonia. Get that beer."

Apollonia nodded. "Yes, Lord Peril."

She glided away, and the shark in the pool submerged deeper to avoid swimming too close to her as she crossed the bridge.

"Lord Peril?" asked Connie.

"Oh, that." He shrugged. "She's just a bit traditional. She's great, actually. Very loyal. Very efficient. A little stolid, but that comes with the job, I think. All the good henchagents, er, women, uh, henchagents are like that." He frowned. "That's what they prefer to be called now. Henchagents. Doesn't exactly roll off the tongue, does it?

"Larry, I just—"

"I'll admit that this *Lord Peril* stuff does make me sound like a guy with an eyepatch and a robot army. I thought about *Mr. Peril*, but that doesn't sound much better, and I can't get them to call me Larry. Old habits." He set down the papers again. "Damn, listen to me. Going on and on. I'm just so excited you're here. I've missed you, Connie."

"Yes, you said that already."

"So, what's been going on in your life? Still having those crazy adventures? Still saving the day?"

"Yes, but before we—"

"I bet." He laughed. "Do you want to know something? I almost didn't call you because I was afraid you'd think I was some sort of evil genius. And then we had that disastrous first call, and I thought for sure you'd assume I'd taken after Mom."

"Never crossed my mind."

"It's okay. You don't have to lie about it. There were days I thought for sure I was set on the mastermind path, myself. Seems unavoidable at times. I might have even done it if I was any good at masterminding, but I'm a month into this and already in way over my head. It's why I'm so glad you're here."

Apollonia returned. She opened a can of Pabst Blue Ribbon and set it before Connie.

"I'm happy to help, Larry," said Connie, "but you should know—"

"How's Tia?" he asked. "Do you two still keep in touch?"

"We're still friends. She's my sidekick now. Officially."

"That's great. I remember that time Mom threw her into that nest of cobras, and you jumped right in after her. Mom never did figure out how you managed to survive that one. You don't know how many family dinners I had to listen to her complaining about it."

"Cobras aren't that dangerous if you know how to handle them," she said.

"That's what I finally told her. I said, 'Mom, they're just goddamn snakes. Connie can deal with some goddamn snakes.' Didn't talk to me for a week. Made some excuses about having to supervise a doomsday device, but I knew she was just mad because I was right. And she always sort of hated you. Can't hardly blame her. Nobody likes having their plans for world domination foiled by a twelve-year-old."

"I was fourteen with the cobra thing," said Connie. "I was twelve when I stopped her from freezing the Earth."

She realized, as she occasionally did, that she'd been doing this a long time. Kids shouldn't be responsible for saving the world, but at the time, it'd been a grand adventure.

"We were just dumb kids then." He held up his wine glass. "To dumb kids and old times."

"Old times."

She smiled, tapped his glass with her can, and took a drink of the warm beer as Apollonia glowered down at her. They were going to fight at some point. Connie had a bad history with henchagents, and it was bound to happen.

"I am sorry about your mom," said Connie. "She wasn't a good person, and she's probably not really dead. But she was your mom and if she is, I'm sorry."

"Thanks. Means a lot."

"And before I agree to anything, I think it's important to set some—"

Something exploded just on the other side of the villa. The black helicopter came plummeting into view, spewing flames and smoke as it wobbled out of control. It crashed into a marble fountain.

"They're here," said Apollonia.

The sounds of gunfire being exchanged echoed from nearby.

"Who's here?" asked Connie.

Apollonia took Larry by the arm and dragged him toward the villa. "We need to get you to the safe room, Lord Peril."

Connie ran after them. "Who is here?"

"Funny story," said Larry. "Remember when I mentioned being worried about some people in Siege Perilous not being interested in my new policies? Turns out some people in Siege Perilous are not that interested in my new policies."

They entered the house. Apollonia threw a hidden switch or pushed a secret button or something and armor plating fell across all the windows. Outside, a war raged. She pushed another secret switch somewhere and the fireplace opened, revealing an elevator. "This way, sir."

Apollonia blocked Connie from entering the elevator. "You're not authorized."

Connie craned her head back to stare down the Amazon. "Like hell I'm not."

"We were safe until you showed up. You're a security risk."

Connie poked Apollonia in the chest. It was like poking a granite pillar. A granite pillar that didn't care for you very much and might do something about it.

"I'd love to beat the shit out of you right now, but we have more important things to worry about."

Apollonia sneered. "I have the time. How long could it take, short stack?"

"I'm average height," said Connie, realizing it wasn't a great rebuttal but too late to retract now.

"Yes. *Average* would best sum you up."

Larry put his hand on Apollonia's shoulder. "It's all right. She's cool."

His henchagent wasn't happy about it, but she followed orders. Connie boarded the elevator, which descended into the hidden recesses under the house. Apollonia positioned herself between Connie and Larry.

"It's really no big deal," said Larry. "Everything's under control. It's only one division that's having the issue."

"What division is that?" asked Connie against her better judgment.

"Assassinations." He tried to sound relaxed about it. "We'll be fine. Just so long as they didn't send Scimitar."

The elevator doors opened and a woman in glasses greeted them. "Scimitar has been identified leading the assault," she said.

Larry tried to wave away Connie's concerns. "It'll be fine. It'll be fine. Just so long as Hardcastle isn't here too."

"Lord Peril . . ." The woman held up a photo of a giant of a man, like a shaved bigfoot on mutant growth hormone.

"It'll be fine," said Larry as Apollonia led him into the control center. "This facility is built to withstand a bomb blast. We already have reinforcements on the way. We only need to hold them off for half an hour. Forty-five minutes, tops."

"Uh . . . sir, there are reports of preemptive strikes against—"

"Fine. It'll be fine."

They sat in the control bunker while explosions rocked the outside. On the monitors, a confusing battle raged. It was difficult to tell who was winning when everyone wore the same uniforms and used the same equipment. Larry reassured Connie that this eventuality had been considered and that, while inconvenient, it was nothing to worry about. Not as long as the outer doors held. When those fell, he explained that this is what the secondary doors were for. When those gave way, he admitted that it might be a problem, but all the final security doors had to do was hold out for another ten minutes before help arrived.

They fell off their hinges two minutes later. Smoke and dust billowed into the bunker as Connie and Apollonia pushed Larry behind them. A squad of elite soldiers poured into the room silently. They pointed their assault rifles at Larry's outnumbered security forces.

Hardcastle and Scimitar strolled in behind their troops. Hardcastle was bigger and more powerful in person. Tall and thin, Scimitar was the Laurel to Hardcastle's Hardy.

Hardcastle carried a custom machine gun designed to mow down tanks. He held it against his hip while chewing on a half-smoked cigar.

Scimitar, dressed all in black with a meticulous vandyke, playfully traced the air with his sword.

"This is treason," said Apollonia. "You swore an oath of loyalty."

Hardcastle guffawed, but Scimitar raised a hand to silence his partner.

"My oath was to Lady Peril, not this dimwit. And I'm an assassin. Anyone who relies on my loyalty is bound to be disappointed." He held up his sword in preparation to give the fire command but paused, leering at Connie.

"Hang on. What have we here? Is it really Constance Verity I see before me?" He bowed. "It is indeed a pleasure to make your acquaintance. We studied under the same teachers, I believe. I was told repeatedly, you were among the best. Master Chaput said he'd trained none better."

"He flatters me," said Connie.

"Flattered." Scimitar half-smiled. "I'm afraid the Master is no longer with us. I killed him. It was necessary to test my steel against his. When I found him beneath me, I spared him continued embarrassment by killing him. It was the least I could do. I suppose you'll want to avenge him now."

"We're wasting time," grumbled Hardcastle.

"Won't take a moment, dear boy."

Scimitar nodded to a henchagent, who threw Connie a sword. Connie and Scimitar met in the space between the two factions. They touched swords. He immediately lunged, which she parried and countered with a forward recovery. He met her blade with a riposte headed right to her heart. She pushed the attack aside, but he managed to slice her shoulder. The cut was shallow, but he stepped back and laughed.

"It's been years since it's taken me this long to draw blood. You're quite good."

She should've replied. Something to challenge his ego. Something to keep him talking, to buy time for reinforcements to get there. But she didn't like Scimitar, and she wanted to beat him.

She held up her sword, and he launched into another

attack. This time, he gave her no quarter, relentlessly swinging and striking. His form was flawless, and she could only parry the flurry, waiting for an opening. It never came. He stopped and stepped away.

Her cheek felt wet, and she wiped a trickle of blood away. She'd seen the strike, but only barely. He could've taken her eye. He'd just chosen not to.

Scimitar lowered his sword and stroked his mustache. "Indeed, you're good, but I'm better. A pity. I was hoping—"

She wasn't in the mood for this. She advanced, thrusting with every bit of skill she had. He parried with more effort than his bored expression might indicate, but not much more.

"Really, now you're just being sloppy," he said. "Best to end it now, I suppose."

He stabbed for her heart again. She met the strike and pushed it slightly aside. Enough to avoid an immediately fatal blow. She followed her half-defense with a thrust of her own. Scimitar, in his arrogance, wasn't ready for the blade between his ribs.

Scimitar stared at the sword in his chest. "Very good, Constance." Grinning, he fell over. His sword tip pulled from her side, and she grabbed the wound. Blood soaked through her shirt. It looked worse than it was, but it hurt like hell.

The floor lurched under her feet. She fell over. It shouldn't have been this bad, but everything grew fuzzy. Her hazy vision saw minions from both sides collapsing. Apollonia had Hardcastle on the floor, punching him repeatedly.

Larry, a portable gas mask clamped over his mouth and nose, stood over Connie.

"Oh, god," he said. "You're hurt."

Her side stung as he touched it. His hands came up covered in red.

"Fucking Kansas," grumbled Connie before succumbing to unconsciousness.

12

Tia met Connie at the airport.

Connie tried to convince Tia otherwise.

"I'll catch a cab," said Connie over the phone. "Don't trouble yourself."

"It's okay. Your plane is landing during my lunch. Should be able to squeeze it in."

"What about your job?"

"They're used to me taking long absences," said Tia. "They won't mind."

"It's fine. I'll be tired as hell when I land. Won't be much fun to talk to."

"Connie, I'm your sidekick. Airport pickups are just part of the service."

"You're really taking this new position seriously," said Connie.

"How do you think I managed to hold down a job while being semi-regularly kidnapped by aliens and gangsters and alien gangsters? By making myself indispensable, that's how.

You'll wonder how you ever got along without me."

There was no talking Tia out of it. That'd be fine normally. But Connie's last adventure had left a nasty gash in her side and a bad taste in her mouth, and she didn't want to talk about it.

Standing on the curb, she focused, calling on ancient techniques of biomanipulation to override the pain in her gut. It was only pain. Pain was an illusion, a feedback response from nerve endings, transmitted to the brain. The brain couldn't feel pain. The brain could only report pain from other parts of the body. Pain wasn't real. Pain was just nerves doing their job. Pain was only a matter of perception.

She drew in a deep breath, and the ache dulled. She still felt it, but only in a vague way. She smiled at her triumph over her own flawed biology. The *sōhei* warrior monks would be proud of the way she stood without the slightest hint of injury. A soldier needs only strength enough to stand and hold a sword to perform her duty.

A woman brushed hastily by Connie with barely a muttered "Excuse me."

Connie winced and dropped her bag. "Goddamn it."

Tia's car pulled up to the curb. Connie groaned, tossed her bag in the backseat, and climbed in. She grunted involuntarily as she sat.

"Everything okay?" asked Tia. She didn't ask specifically about the Band-Aid on Connie's cheek. Coming back from an adventure with a fresh bruise or two wasn't really worth commenting on.

"Peachy." Connie stared straight ahead, fearing that turning her head might lead to some incidental torso-twisting. "Had a little trouble in Kansas, but nothing I couldn't handle."

Tia pulled into traffic. "Kansas, huh? Surprised you went."

"Didn't know it was Kansas until I got there," said Connie.

"So, how'd it go?"

"Good," said Connie. "Saved Larry from an assassination attempt."

"That's good. And what about the other thing?"

Tia changed lanes. The sudden shift popped in Connie's side. She frowned, stifled a grimace.

"I don't think that other thing is a thing," she said. "I think he really just wants my help."

"Did you talk to him about it?"

"It didn't come up."

"Connie . . ."

"Things got crazy faster than I expected. I didn't think it was the right time to talk about feelings."

"You never think it's the right time," said Tia.

"He was attacked," said Connie. "I think it confirmed he had valid reasons for wanting me around."

"Hey, if you don't want to deal with it like a mature adult, who am I to make you?"

"Exactly."

Tia smirked. "But you should."

"If it comes up, I'll talk about it," replied Connie.

They drove a while in silence. She managed her pain,

not as well as she would've liked, but well enough.

"Are we going to talk about that?" asked Tia.

Connie feigned innocence. "Talk about what?"

"That way you're holding your side there. Did you get hurt?"

"I've been hurt before," said Connie. "Comes with the job."

"Then why are you trying to hide it?"

"Why are you so interested?"

"Why are you so defensive?"

"When did you become so nosy?"

"My best friend is a master detective," replied Tia. "Maybe she's rubbing off on me."

Connie sank in the seat. The seatbelt applied pressure to her wound, and she swore. "I might have gotten stabbed. Just a little."

"Knife?"

"Sword."

"How little?"

"Larry's docs were able to clean the wound and stitch it up. I'm taking antibiotics."

"Stitches? That's serious."

"I've had stitches before," said Connie.

"Can I see it?" asked Tia.

"It's just a stab wound."

"Can I see it?"

Connie lifted her shirt to show the puffy, swollen flesh around the stitched-closed wound. The bruised blue-and-yellow skin made it look worse than it was.

Tia glanced from the road and back again. "Wow. That's ugly."

"I'll be fine. I have a nanotechnology kit somewhere at home. Slap on a bandage and six hours later, good as new. Not even a scar." She covered up the bruise.

"I should've been there," said Tia. "This wouldn't have happened if I'd been there. I'd have done something to distract the bad guy. *Hey, jerk, don't do that!*"

Connie smiled skeptically.

"I work better under pressure," said Tia with a frown.

"It's fine. I'll live, and even if you are officially my sidekick now, you are not responsible every time I'm a little slow and get stabbed or punched or thrown into a pit."

Tia asked to see the wound again, and Connie reluctantly obliged.

"Have you thought about what you're going to tell Byron?" asked Tia.

"The truth," said Connie. "He knows about how things work."

"Yes, he does," said Tia.

She didn't say what Connie already knew. She'd come home with bruises and scrapes before, but nothing quite like this raw slash emblazoned below her ribs. This day was inevitable, but she could only hope he took it in stride.

Byron didn't take it well. To his credit, he tried to fake it.

"Does it hurt?" he asked after she showed it to him.

"Yes," she said, "but I've had worse."

"Oh."

The way he said that bothered her. Like he was realizing things. Things he probably should've realized a while before but was only now seeing.

"It's not a big deal." She took his hand. "I wasn't in any real danger."

"But you said it was a swordfight with a deadly assassin."

"If the world's most dangerous swordsman could kill me, I'd be dead a long time ago," said Connie with a laugh.

He didn't laugh. He managed a slight smile.

"This doesn't have to be a big deal," she said as she put her hand on his cheek. The move caused her side to sting, but she hid the pain. "I thought you knew to expect this sort of thing."

"I did. I do. It's just . . . It's like that thing with the cheese zombies. I know intellectually what you do, but seeing it up close is a different thing. This is up close."

"I'll be okay."

"I know. I guess it's just dumb, but I always imagined you living a charmed life. Close calls and narrow escapes, but in the end, you never get hurt. And now . . . this. It's my problem. Not yours. I'll get used to it. It's like your dad told me. Worrying is just part of having Connie in your life."

"My parents haven't worried about me since I was ten."

"Connie, you do know your parents worry about you, right?" asked Byron.

She laughed. "Why would they worry about me? I can handle things."

"You were a little girl off fighting criminals and solving mysteries. Of course they worried about you."

"Okay, maybe then. But not once I grew up."

Byron said, "Wait. You don't think your parents worry about you, even now? Connie, you're their daughter. They're going to worry."

She thought of all the times she'd disappear for hours or days or weeks at a time. Then she'd show up out of the blue, and Dad would make her favorite waffles while Mom would talk about the neighbor's dog digging up the rosebushes or some other unimportant thing. They'd both adjusted. They'd accepted the path Connie had taken.

Hadn't they?

"What did Dad say, exactly?" she asked.

"That it wasn't always easy, and how I'd have to just accept certain things."

"That's out of line," she said.

"They were just being honest."

"They? Mom was part of this conversation?"

He looked away as if unable to look her in the eyes while confessing. "She might have been in the room."

"Fan-fucking-tastic."

"It's not . . . They were just . . ."

"Just what? Just screwing with the only good relationship

I've ever had by trying to scare you away? Just sticking their noses where they don't belong?"

"That's not fair," he said.

"I cannot have this conversation," she said. "I was almost killed barely a day ago."

"So, you were almost killed."

"*Almost* doesn't count," she said.

"That hole in your gut says differently."

She searched for a rebuttal. The best she could do was redirect the conversation.

"I'm not crazy about my parents and my boyfriend, the most important people in my life, conspiring about me."

"Goddamn it, Connie," said Byron. "Maybe it's not about you."

He sounded mad.

He never sounded mad.

He said, "They weren't trying to scare me. They were just preparing me. It's like what Tia told me—"

"Oh, Tia is in on this too. Wonderful."

"Jesus, Connie, all of us love you. That's what matters."

"Yeah, yeah." She stamped down her irritation. "Dad said there were things about living with me. What sort of things?"

Byron hesitated. "I'm not sure I should say anything else. It was a private conversation."

"A private conversation between my father and my boyfriend. About me."

"I shouldn't have said anything."

"But you did."

She stalked her way to the bathroom. She rifled through the medicine cabinet. "Have you seen a little white box?" she shouted, aware of the edge in her voice.

"Haven't seen it," he said from behind her, making her feel stupid for yelling.

She closed the cabinet and glared at his reflection in the mirror. "It has a little caduceus on it."

He shrugged.

Connie went to the corner of the bedroom where they'd thrown the boxes she hadn't unpacked yet. She knelt down and groaned as her side ached. Byron hung back by the door as she searched through the boxes.

"I know it's here," she said.

"He said that you're away a lot," said Byron.

Connie paused. She looked over her shoulder at him. He stared down at his crossed arms.

"I said I knew that," he continued. "But he said it wasn't just that you'd be away. I'd have to accept that you had this whole huge part of your life that I could never be a part of, that I'd never understand, no matter how hard I wanted to. I said I knew that, too."

She thought she should say something. She returned to looking through the boxes.

"We're just a small part of your life, Connie," said Byron quietly.

She was irritated. She didn't know if that was because of her stinging side or him.

"That's not true, Byron."

"Yes, it is. It's true. True for most everyone. The difference is that your life is full of danger and intrigue, and it's really hard to relate to sometimes. And sometimes, a lot of times, it's even a little bit scary."

She found the medkit and sat on the bed. "You said you understood."

"I understand. Doesn't always make it easy."

"I knew I should've had a secret identity."

He sat on the bed beside her. "You can't expect us not to worry about you."

She held the box over her wound. It scanned the damage and beeped, spitting out a bandage. She slapped it on the scar, and a tingle ran through her as the nanites went to work.

"I know," she said.

Thirty-two hours later, another call from Larry had Connie and Tia aboard one of three experimental jets soaring over the Ténéré Desert. They sat strapped in beside each other, not saying much of anything, surrounded by sixty-eight Siege Perilous commandoes. The silent commandoes stared straight ahead with barely a muscle twitch. The steady roar of the engines was the only sound for the last fifty miles.

Tia adjusted her bulletproof vest and tightened her helmet. "I still think I should have a gun."

"You'd only hurt yourself," said Connie, inspecting her Kalashnikov. She'd done it several times already, but it killed time.

"Why do you have that thing? You never use guns."

"I don't like guns. Doesn't mean I don't know how to use them. It's just a precaution."

"What are we walking into here?" asked Tia.

"Siege Perilous lost contact with this research lab a month

ago. Dispatched an inspection team to check on it. Didn't hear anything from them. Sent another team in a week after that. No word."

"And now it's our turn," said Tia. "Could I get a handgun maybe? Some pepper spray? A knife?"

"You won't need it," said Connie. "Just stick close."

"I didn't think sidekicking meant I had to be unarmed. Even Robin gets batarangs. Robin-rangs?"

Connie unholstered her pistol and handed it to Tia. "Don't shoot anybody, especially not yourself. That's the safety. Aim before pulling the trigger. Don't pull the trigger, though."

"I know how to operate a weapon," said Tia. "What the hell is up with you, anyway?"

Connie didn't reply, hoping Tia would assume the loud, steady engine thrum swallowed the question.

"You've been weird since we started this mission," said Tia. "Is this about Byron and Larry?"

"This isn't the time to talk about this," said Connie.

"You always do that," said Tia. "You're always using adventures as an excuse to avoid having difficult conversations."

Connie smiled humorlessly. "Is that what you told Byron?"

"Is that what this is about?" said Tia. "You're mad because I talked to Byron."

"No, I'm mad that you talked to Byron *about* me." Connie sneered at the commando sitting across from her, though she wasn't aiming at him. She had to sneer somewhere, though, and it was hard not to hit someone. "And I'm not mad."

She turned to Stone, the craggy lieutenant assigned to the mission. "What's ETA to target?"

"Twenty minutes, ma'am."

She imagined herself sitting there for twenty more minutes, not talking to Tia. It could be done, but they'd have to have the conversation eventually. Now was as good a time as any.

"What did you say to Byron?" asked Connie. "And don't try saying it was a private conversation. I have a right to know."

"I told him the truth. It's not always easy to be your friend, but it's usually worth it." Tia frowned at the same commando Connie had earlier scowled at. He didn't seem to mind. "Usually."

"You wanted to come along," said Connie.

"I'm on board with commando missions. I'm talking about your tendency to shut down when you don't like the way things are going."

Connie laughed mockingly, and the soldier across from her who had been scowled and sneered at lowered his head. Whether to hide his hurt feelings or avoid an unpleasant situation remained to be determined.

"Excuse me for finding it irritating that people in my life are all sharing secrets about me."

"We can't always talk about this stuff with you, so we talk to each other. You're telling me you let me know everything about everything."

"No, but that's for your own protection."

"Right, so when you withhold information, you're being noble, but when we do it, we're being sneaky."

"I still don't like it," said Connie.

"Who does? But your family and friends are going to talk about you sometimes. So, what were they researching in this place, anyway?"

"Psychic supersoldiers."

"Telepathy or telekinesis?"

Connie tossed the file to Tia. "Telepathy *and* telekinesis and clairvoyance and everything else. The whole ball of wax."

"We're walking into a nest of supersoldiers that can move things with their minds, read ours, and predict the future? You're right. There are some things I don't want to know."

"I'm immune to mind control, so we should be fine."

"Who said anything about mind control?" Tia flipped through the files. "I don't see anything about mind control."

"Just an assumption on my part," said Connie.

"Just promise me that you won't kill me if I become a psychic thrall," said Tia.

Connie smiled. "We'll see."

The trio of aircraft set down on the compound's landing pads, and as the troops deployed, Connie and Tia surveyed the desert stretching for miles around them. The commandoes secured the area with efficient gusto.

"Should we be nervous that there were no people to greet and/or attack us?" asked Tia.

"It's not a good sign," admitted Connie, "but with some luck, they won't need us to keep a lid on the situation."

The bay doors opened and out stepped an unarmed

scientist in a white lab coat. He approached Lieutenant Stone.

"Hello. Very pleased to have you join us. Won't you please come this way?"

Stone asked, "What's the status of this outpost?"

The scientist smiled, slowly, like an android having been programmed with the expression only an hour before. "All your questions will be answered soon enough."

"Oh, that's not ominous," whispered Tia to Connie.

The scientist turned his head toward Connie. "I can assure you, once you see what we've created here, you will find your fears unfounded."

He turned and walked back into the compound. Once the scientist was out of sight, Stone turned to Connie.

"Ma'am, I've got a bad feeling on this. I suggest we fall back and bomb this place into oblivion."

"I'm with him," said Tia.

"We can't just drop a nuke because we're suspicious," said Connie.

Stone's weathered face creased with what she could only assume was a frown. It was hard to tell. "Yes, ma'am."

"Tell you what," said Connie. "I'll go in with a squad of your eight best. If you don't hear from us in an hour, you have my permission to order a bomb strike."

He might have smiled. Or it might have been gas. He saluted. "Yes, ma'am."

Connie and Tia led the squad deeper into the complex. The scientist greeted them at the bottom of a flight of stairs.

"This way, please," he said mechanically as he led them deeper into the heart of the base.

In the depths of the complex, they passed scientists, technicians, and custodial staff all carrying on with their jobs. All wore the same blank, unfocused stare and moved with mechanical efficiency.

"We agree this is mind control, right?" asked Tia.

"Obviously."

A buzz vibrated between Connie's eyes. She'd had enough experience with telepathy to know when someone was trying to poke around in her mind. Her psychic defenses were formidable, and that made the experience all the more unpleasant. Tia and the soldiers were open books and most likely oblivious to the mental eyes running over their pages. Connie's book was sealed shut, and the prying attempts made her want to ram a wire up her nose just to scratch her frontal lobe.

The scientist stopped before a door and stepped aside. "She's waiting for you."

"Who?" asked Tia.

His mouth smiled. His vacant eyes didn't. "Why, the future master of the world, of course."

"Can't keep her waiting, then, can we?" said Connie.

They stepped into the room, decked out with all the usual secret-science bells and whistles. Dozens of technicians busied themselves with their duties, which seemed to involve staring at monitors and pushing buttons. Six or seven engineers and mechanics worked on a cylindrical machine standing thirty feet high in the center of the room.

"No guards," said Tia.

Someone laughed. It echoed through the room as a giant chair on mechanical spider legs tromped loudly from behind the central machine. "Guards are for lesser intellects."

A bluish woman with a giant head sat in the mobile chair. Her massive head, a veiny mass of throbbing green-and-blue flesh, was secured and supported by a series of elaborate braces designed to keep it from crushing her under its own weight.

"So, they've sent the legendary Constance Verity. I must say, I expected us to meet sooner or later, but I had calculated it at later. I already know who you are, but you can call me . . . Debra." She scowled. "I'm trying to come up with something better, but all the good supervillain names are taken."

"Gets harder every year," agreed Connie. "Mind Mistress?"

Debra shrugged, and her massive brain trembled. "A little on the nose. Oh, you won't need those silly little toys here. Put them down."

The soldiers and Tia dropped their weapons on the floor. Connie's hand loosened on her own rifle, but she didn't let go.

Debra chuckled. "Do you really think you can simply shoot me? As if I would allow you to walk in here if you were any threat to me at all. I am no longer the simple experimentation subject I once was. I now operate—"

"On a level I couldn't possibly understand," interrupted Connie. "You have evolved unto goddesshood. You have already calculated every possibility, and your triumph is inevitable. Only a fool would dare challenge you, and I'm only still alive because it amuses you. Also, I'm perhaps the only person alive who can appreciate your genius, and it'd be a shame if I died before witnessing your inevitable victory."

Debra glowered.

"That was what you were going to say, wasn't it?" asked Connie.

Because she couldn't turn her head, Debra turned her whole chair instead. Its spider legs clomped with clicks and whirs. "Not necessarily."

Connie pointed to the towering machine in the middle of the room. "And this psycho-amplifier will allow you to exert your will over all humans on Earth."

"You have some familiarity with devices of this type, then? Of course you do. And you no doubt know exactly how to shut it down or, even worse, use it against me somehow."

Connie shrugged. She'd need a screwdriver and two seconds to undo all of Debra's plans. She just had to keep the mutant genius talking until the opportunity presented itself.

"Shall I tell you why you won't do whatever you're planning on doing?" asked Debra.

"Please."

"Because I am the only one in this universe who can save you from what's coming. Among my powers is clairvoyance, and I know what is to come."

"That's precognition," said Connie. "Not clairvoyance."

Debra glared with disdain. "Regardless, I have seen your future."

"And let me guess," said Connie. "You don't see any possible future where I can defeat you, so I might as well surrender."

"You are not as smart as you think you are," said Debra. "Do you think you've seen everything, understand everything? Do you think I don't know your reputation, your abilities? The odds of you stopping me are ridiculously small, but those are exactly the kind of odds you enjoy. Yours is a life of the improbable, a reliable succession of statistical absurdity. At this moment, you are in your element. If anyone can foil my brilliant plan, it is you. But you won't, and I'll tell you why.

"How long do you think you can continue to live like this? Even the most fortunate soul has their bad day, and your bad day is coming." Debra gazed off into the distance, as if she could see the future there. "Sooner than you think. And I am the only one who can show you the way to save yourself."

Debra pressed her fingertips together and leered at Connie. "You will join me, or you will die."

"That's it? That's your pitch? It's not very original."

"You misunderstand me. I'm not threatening you. I'm simply presenting a fact. In all the fields of probability before me, I see not one where you survive more than two or three weeks. Four at the outside. Except for the one where you join me. Guided by my understanding of your role in the universe, you and I shall become unstoppable. Defeat me, and you will only be sealing your own inevitable doom."

The psycho-amplifier hummed and rattled as it neared completion. Its lights blinked in colorful patterns as the entire room vibrated. Connie edged closer to the toolbox.

"Tell me, Connie. How many close calls does a single person get? How many have you had this year alone?" asked Debra.

"I don't know," replied Connie. "I don't keep track."

"No, I suppose you don't, but I can promise you that the universe does. Sooner or later, the law of averages catches up to us all. Do you not ponder when that day comes for you?"

"It's bound to eventually," said Connie. "I don't worry about it."

Debra clomped before Connie. "But what if you could do something about it? All your life, you've defied the odds. But there is a day of reckoning coming. I can sense the unraveling fields of probability around you."

Debra placed her hand on her side in the exact spot Connie had been stabbed, and whether through psychic manipulation or the mere power of suggestion, Connie's side twinged.

"It's only the beginning, you know."

"And I'm supposed to just let you take over the world because you can stop it, and look the other way while you conquer the world?"

"Why not? We're not so different, you and I."

"Oh, brother. Not the *we're not so different* speech," said Connie to Tia, who, like every other person in the room, had fallen under Debra's control. Tia didn't reply. Only stared straight ahead. Connie wiped some drool from Tia's lips.

Debra said, "If you think about it, all you do is put a bandage on a disordered world. I'm a more permanent solution. I will bring peace and order to all, and all I ask for in return is absolute obedience. In that way, am I so different from the governments that came before me? The people always look to leaders for answers. I am the answer they have always been waiting for."

"You're just another megalomaniac," said Connie. "I've heard the Join Me and We Shall Rule the Galaxy Together speech a hundred times before."

Debra's eyes narrowed, and the veins on her giant head pulsed. "I take that as a no, then."

"Hell, no."

Connie snatched the screwdriver from the toolbox and dashed around Debra's walking throne. A pair of technicians moved to stop her. She knocked them aside without breaking stride and was a few steps from the psycho-amplifier when her body stiffened against her will. She fell over, a numbness creeping through her limbs.

Debra cackled. "I may not be able to control your mind, but I can certainly access your nervous system. What good is a brain unable to communicate with its body? Not much. The question is how best to dispose of you? Heart attack?"

Connie's chest tightened.

"Suffocation, perhaps?" said Debra.

Connie stopped breathing. She didn't panic. If Debra was

as smart as she claimed, she'd have simply killed Connie out-
right. But she was a mastermind. They loved to gloat. Connie
had time.

"Or I could just play it safe and shoot you." Debra's mobile
throne stepped aside and a commando picked up his weapon
and walked forward. "Good-bye, Connie. You have no one to
blame but yourself."

Connie called upon ancient meditative techniques to
reboot her nervous system under her control. It would take only
a few moments. Moments she didn't have. She tried shouting a
taunt. Something to get Debra talking again. The only thing
that came out was a strangled grunt as Debra clomped away.

A gunshot rang out, but it wasn't rifle fire. The mesmerized commando glanced down at his bleeding shoulder, more
perplexed than anything.

Tia fired her pistol twice more. The shots missed their
target. One ricocheted a few inches from Connie's face.

Connie gained control of her mouth. "Shoot the mutant!"

Tia, her body still stiff from conflicting signals, aimed at
Debra. Tia emptied her gun. It was difficult to not hit the
giant brain directly in front of her. Every bullet found its mark.
Or would have, if Debra hadn't telekinetically snagged them.
They orbited her head like a halo.

"I don't even know who you are," she said. "And after I've
killed you, I'm going to erase the very memory of you from
everyone you've ever met."

Connie stood and punched the commando. Her reflexes were off but up to the task of smacking aside the clumsy lab technicians in her way. Debra hurled several bullets at Connie but stopped as she reached the psycho-amplifier.

"I should've seen this coming." Debra shook her head with a grim acceptance. "And you should've taken my offer."

Connie inserted the screwdriver and adjusted the master control. She pushed the activation button, and a psionic surge blasted out of the machine. For most everyone on Earth, it wouldn't register. For some, it'd be a headache for a few hours. For Debra, it was a massive misfire of mutated, overpowered neurons. She shrieked. Veins on her head burst, and her head sagged like a fluid-filled balloon.

Her mechanized chair stomped wildly out of control. It spun around the room, nearly crushing Connie, crashing into the psycho-amplifier. The tower wobbled, and she thought about getting out of the way. But her head was buzzing and her body didn't respond as the amplifier fell toward her.

Tia yanked Connie out of the way. The amplifier smashed into the floor with a final thud. Connie stared at the several tons of electronics. The static in her brain processed the geometry of the situation.

"Are you all right?" asked Tia.

It was hard to think, but her reflexes would've kicked in, and she would've moved out of the way on her own.

Tia snapped her fingers in front of Connie's eyes, and Connie pushed away the oppressive psychic crackle. Tried to. It skittered in the back of her skull.

"I'm fine," she said.

Debra's thralls stopped working. The commandoes surrounded her, but she only lay in her overturned chair, groaning.

"My God," Tia said. "What happened to your eyes? They're all red."

"Side effect of sabotaging the device." Connie played it cool, but her eyes were itching so badly, she had the urge to scratch them out of her skull. It'd pass. Along with the headache. She wasn't psychic, but being beside the amplifier was bound to have some effect.

She wiped her runny nose. Her hands came away with blood.

"Damn." Tia produced a handkerchief from her pocket and offered it to Connie.

"It's nothing." Connie tucked the cloth under her nostrils. "I'm surprised you were able to resist Debra's telepathic control."

"What can I say? I'm strong-willed. Picked it up from someone. I told you I work better under pressure."

"More likely, she'd overextended her powers and didn't consider you important enough to prioritize."

"Yeah, but that unimportance just saved your ass."

Connie said, "Hey, I didn't say *I* thought it. And, yes, thank you."

"Don't mention it."

Connie's headache worsened, a hot blade scraping at her cortex. She staggered, leaning her weight on Tia.

"We should get you looked at," said Tia.

"I'm fine."

Connie threw up. It was a welcome distraction from her watering eyes, which she would've gladly gouged out otherwise.

With Debra subdued, her operation could be dismantled without Connie and Tia. They caught a flight home, and Connie was in the middle of cooking dinner when Byron opened the door.

"Honey, I'm home!" he shouted from the other room. "Unless you're some sort of chef alien who is here looking for Connie!"

"No alien!" she called back. "Just me."

Byron stepped into the kitchen, set his briefcase on the counter, and came up behind her to give her a hug while she sautéed peppers and steak in a skillet.

"Smells great," he said. "What is it?"

"Just a recipe I picked up in the Lost Incan Empire. I had to improvise a bit. We don't have a huatia, and I didn't have any guinea pig meat."

"Yeah, I've been meaning to talk to you about getting a huatia," he said with a chuckle. "They practically pay for themselves." He loosened his tie and poked through the cupboard, settling on a bag of chocolate chip cookies. "So, how was your trip?"

"Good. Stopped a telepathic superbrain from enslaving humanity. You'll ruin your appetite."

"Maybe, but I'll risk it, since we don't have any genuine guinea pig." He bit into a cookie and offered her one, which she accepted.

He got his first clear look at her face. The worst of the psychic headaches had gone, though an ache still lingered. Her eyes no longer felt like crawling bugs nestled in her face. They were still bloodshot, and the swollen, discolored skin wasn't pretty.

"Jeez, Connie," he said. "What happened?"

"Telepathic feedback." She looked away. "It looks worse than it is."

"Oh."

"It doesn't hurt," she said. Lied. But the lingering pain wasn't a big deal, so it wasn't a lie she felt badly about.

"That's good."

He ate the rest of his cookie, chewing long and slow and thoughtfully, which had all manner of implications she was likely imagining but still didn't care for.

"How was work?" she asked.

"Good. Found an error that could've cost the company fifteen thousand dollars."

"Go you."

She gestured toward a plate of sweet potatoes just out of reach. He slid it closer.

"Why didn't you tell me you'd be coming home?" he asked. "I almost worked late."

"I wanted to surprise you," she said.

"You can't really do that anymore."

She raised an eyebrow. "Oh, really?"

"That is *not* a challenge," he said. "I just meant that I've come to accept the unlimited weirdness you've inserted into my life. In a good way. So, telepathic superbrain?"

"Oh, the usual. Somebody gets psychic powers and suddenly thinks they should rule the universe."

"And they did that to you."

"Not them, but the psycho-amplifier device she was planning on using to take over the world." Connie shrugged. "Not really that interesting."

"Tell me about it anyway."

"I have a better idea," she said. "Pass the chile sauce and tell me about your day."

"Not much to talk about. Not like the fate of the world turns on what I do."

"That's where you're wrong," she said. "The fate of the world depends on everyone. You saved your company money. That's something. That's laudable."

"Yes, because of my hard work, a company made a little more money." He pumped his fist slowly in the air. "Hooray."

"It all adds up," she said.

He glanced away and mumbled into his cookie. "Uh-huh."

She knew he was annoyed, and she knew why. She elected to ignore it as she checked the pasa.

"You know it's all right to talk to me about these things, right?" he said.

"Uh-hmm." She hoped it would be enough.

"Connie, I'm going to worry about you whether we talk about it or not. You can't just pretend like it's not happening because we don't mention it. Especially because it's right there on your face."

"Uh-hmm." She took a drink of beer and focused on mixing the ingredients together as if the fate of worlds depended on getting it just right.

"What happened?" he asked.

"Telepathic superbrain. I already told you. No big thing."

"Why don't you want to talk about it, then?"

"Because I told you. It's boring."

"As opposed to accounting?"

She didn't have a good reply, so she stirred her potatoes and peppers and steak.

He reached out to touch her face. He ran his fingers gently across her swollen cheek. "It looks painful. Are you sure it doesn't hurt?"

"A little," she admitted. "But not much."

She took his hand and pulled it away. She squeezed it. "It's almost ready. Can you set the table?"

Silently, he did so.

Silently, they sat at the table, eating a few bites.

"Why won't you tell me about it?" he asked.

"Why do you want to know?" she replied.

"Something happened," he said, "didn't it?"

"Nothing happened. I didn't die. I had a reaction to some incidental psionic feedback. I don't know why you assume the worst. Why can't you assume the best?" She stabbed her meal with her fork. The metal clinked against the plate. The stress was bringing back her headache. "I'm home. Why can't we just enjoy a nice evening?"

"Connie—"

She groaned, despite herself. "This is supposed to be the place I get away from the bullshit."

"Connie, your nose is bleeding."

Red dots splattered on her plate.

"Goddamn it." She grabbed a napkin and stuck it under her nose.

She closed her eyes and pushed through her annoyance. The night could still be salvaged. She took his hand.

"Nothing happened, Byron. Nothing unusual for me anyway."

She told him about the confrontation with Debra. She left a few details out. Nothing important. Just the prediction of her impending death, which didn't mean much because Connie was always flirting with danger.

It wasn't exactly a lie. It wasn't exactly the truth either, which was just a roundabout way of ignoring that it was a lie. She convinced herself that knowing the whole truth would only cause him to worry more. That wouldn't do either of them any good.

After she finished, she set aside her bloody napkin. She checked for crust on her lip before leaning in to kiss him. "There. Now you know. Better?"

He nodded. "Better."

Guilt crawled into her gut, and she poked at her food. It was all so complicated. She'd navigated the Minoan Labyrinth with less trouble than this relationship. There, the worst that could happen was getting killed by the Minotaur. Here, she could screw everything up with Byron. The stakes felt a hell of a lot higher.

"I love you," she said. It only made her feel worse.

"I love you, too."

That made her feel better. She hadn't earned it, but she didn't give a shit. Saving the world meant making tough decisions sometimes. Keeping this relationship going required the same. She only did it for his own good.

And by the time they'd finished dinner, she'd almost convinced herself of that.

Hiro greeted Tia at the door with takeout from her favorite Chinese place. They watched harmless romantic comedies as they ate. She snuggled up next to him on the couch as he fed her a bite of his General Tso's chicken.

"Good," she said as she offered him some of her sweet-and-sour pork.

On the TV, a young, inoffensively handsome man raced to the wedding of a young, inoffensively beautiful woman.

Hiro said, "If movies were any indication, you'd think the only reason to marry someone would be to spur the love of your life to interrupt the ceremony."

"You're overthinking it."

"Right." He kissed the top of her head. "It's just . . . if this movie wasn't about these two, we'd think they were colossal assholes. Look at all the people at that wedding. I bet some of them flew there, booked a hotel room and everything. Spent hundreds, maybe thousands of dollars. And then, boom, this guy walks in, ruins the ceremony, and everyone's supposed to not be mad about it?

"And this guy, he's kind of an asshole. You're not supposed to notice, because the guy she's marrying is a bigger one, but that raises the question of what issues she has. She didn't end up with the first asshole by accident."

"It's just a movie."

"So, we're just supposed to overlook these two inconsiderate jerks because the movie says they're our heroes? We're just supposed to pretend like they'll walk out of that church, hand in hand, and everything will work out?"

"Yes."

The guy kissed the girl, and, sighing, Hiro got up and left the room. The credits rolled, and Tia poked at her peapods, readying herself for his inevitable return.

"I'll tell you what'll happen next," he said.

She smiled. "Do tell."

"He becomes the next dumb jerk to be used up by this crazy chick, but he only realizes it when some asshole busts in on his wedding. And she runs off with that jerk to start the process all over again. And endless procession of aborted weddings and stupid movie endings."

He turned away from the TV as if repelled by it.

"Sorry. Sorry. I know you like these things."

"It's okay." She paused the movie, and the forgettable pop ballad stopped playing over the credits. She patted the couch beside her, and he sat, visibly annoyed.

He was so cool most of the time. She loved watching him lose that cool. It was why she loved making him watch these movies. It reminded her that, beneath all that suave ninja style, he was still human.

She also was a sucker for *love conquers all* stories, even with all their inherent flaws.

And she loved forgettable pop ballads.

"How was your thing with Connie?" he asked.

"Complicated," she replied.

"I take that to mean more complicated than usual."

"I think she's in danger, and I don't think she's taking it seriously."

"Can you blame her?" asked Hiro. "I'm trying to figure out why you're taking it so seriously."

"It's hard to explain," said Tia. "I know Connie gets out of life-and-death situations all the time. I've seen it hundreds of times myself. But this time, it just felt different. I don't know. Maybe she's right. Maybe I am making too much of this. It's just . . . after getting stabbed like that . . . I don't know. And her face after the psycho-whatchamacallit shorted out. Something feels wrong."

"I would think Connie would have a better sense of that than you."

"That's just it," said Tia. "Would she? I think she's so used to looking death in the face that she can't tell the difference between regular doom and inevitable doom."

"There's a difference?"

"There could be," said Tia, "and if there was, I don't think she'd notice it. Or she'd simply be too stubborn to back down."

Hiro put his arm around her. "That's her call, isn't it? Not much you can do about it."

"I can keep a closer eye on her. I can make sure she has someone to watch her back. Connie's so busy saving everyone else; I'll be the one to save her."

"Honey, you don't think maybe that's putting too much pressure on yourself?"

"You don't think I can do it?"

"I just know Connie and the situations she gets herself into. You're a damned fine sidekick, but you're still not Connie. You can't afford to be as reckless as she is. You have to watch out for yourself."

"If I'm not there to help, why go?"

Hiro took her hand. "Just promise me you'll think twice before doing something stupid to save Connie from something she can probably save herself from."

"I promise."

"Okay, then. I'm sure you're worrying about nothing, but if you need me—"

Tia perked up. "That's it." She poked him in the chest. "I do need you!"

He leaned in to kiss her, and she pushed him back. "Not for that. I mean, yes, for that. But later. But I'm talking about Connie here. You're right that I can't do this by myself. It's too big a job. Why settle for one sidekick when you can have two?"

"Connie would never go for that," said Hiro.

Tia's eyes glinted with brilliant delight. Or it might have been the reflection of the television. Whatever it was, Hiro was uncertain how he felt about it.

"That's the beauty of it," she said. "She'll never know."

The airport buzzed with the usual airport activity as people marched to and fro. Tia and Hiro arrived early, waiting for Connie to show up.

"I think this is a bad idea," said Hiro.

"I think it's a great idea," said Tia. She looked him up and down. "I'm surprised you didn't wear black."

"Rookie mistake. You wear what helps you blend in. A guy wrapped head to toe in black is going to stand out here." He tipped his worn baseball hat. "I'm just a guy on vacation."

"Connie already knows who you are. She's not going to be fooled by a T-shirt and a pair of shorts."

"It's not for her. It's for everyone else. First step to invisibility is to not be noticed by the crowd."

"What's the second step?"

She turned around, but he was gone. She scanned the airport crowd for any sign of him. He couldn't have gotten far. She had specifically memorized the color of his hat and shirt to make him easier to find. After a minute of scanning, she came up with nothing.

"Damn, he's good."

"Yes, I am," Hiro said from beside her.

She jumped with a squeal. The squeal pissed her off. Like a surprised child, not the hardened sidekick she was supposed to be.

"You love that," she said.

"I do indeed."

He was gone again. She didn't bother looking for him. No normal person could find Hiro if he didn't want to be found.

Connie showed up a little later, and Tia expected to be called out immediately. Connie didn't say much as they were escorted to the private jet.

"I thought we were flying commercial," said Tia.

"Larry wanted to send his plane. It's just easier."

And just like that, Tia's plan had fallen apart. She watched the door of the jet close after boarding. Hiro was good, and she didn't expect to spot him. But she thought she might see a shadow or a flitting shape as he zipped inside.

She saw nothing.

It didn't mean anything. Hiro slipped in and out of places all the time. He'd once disappeared for three hours in the house while she was doing some housework, only reappearing once she'd put up the vacuum. But hiding in a private jet with Connie was a tall order. Even for the world's greatest ninja infiltrator.

"Something wrong?" asked Connie. "You seem distracted."

"What?" said Tia. "No. Nothing."

God, this was horrible, a futile waste of effort. Connie was a master detective. She'd figure this out in another minute. Better to just confess now and get it over with.

"Connie—"

"I'm not an idiot," interrupted Connie.

"I just thought—"

"I know it's a bad idea," said Connie.

Tia's carefully worded explanation fell to the wayside. "What idea?"

Connie shook her head. "You don't have to act like you don't know it either. I know that I shouldn't be doing this. It's not my problem, right? I can't save the world all by myself. Not every time, anyway. I don't have to fix everything."

Tia didn't say anything. She thought maybe she should, but she wasn't sure where Connie was going with this.

"You're right that I'm probably just being stubborn about this," said Connie, staring out the window as the plane taxied out of the hangar. "It's a problem I have. When you're ten years old and dangling from a cliff while rabid hyenas circle below, you learn to be stubborn. You can't quit, because quitting isn't an option. You dig your fingernails and pray that root doesn't come loose. And if it does, you plan how best to fend off hyenas when all you have is a Pez dispenser and a priceless diamond in your pocket. I fight. It's what I do. It's how I survive. When people turn and run, I go forward. It's kept me alive so far, but it's skewed how I look at things.

"Somebody tells me I can't do something, I want to do it more. *Want* isn't a strong enough word. I need to do it. Give me that big red button labeled DO NOT PUSH in bright neon letters, and I'll push it every time. Every goddamn time."

Connie cracked her knuckles and gripped her armrest with tight fingers. She closed her eyes. "I think I'm screwing things up with Byron. He wants to be part of my life. Like you. But I keep thinking how often I've fucked up your life."

"You've never fucked up my life," said Tia. "You've complicated it, but that's how every relationship is. For every kidnapping and life-endangering thing I've gone through, you've given me ten more things. Anyway, you need to get over yourself. You don't think I haven't considered how I complicate your life?"

"That's crazy."

"Is it? How many times did some sadistic villain or random booby trap force you to make a choice between saving the day and saving me? You want to talk about hyena moments? I was about to be squashed by a robot while you were fighting your way to rescue me, and I thought, *I'm just getting in the way.* I was just one more thing for you to worry about. You had enough responsibilities. You didn't need another."

"That wasn't your fault."

"No, it wasn't. And it's not your fault that you are an adventurer. And it's not Byron's fault that he worries about you. It's nobody's fault, but it's stuff we all have to learn to live with."

"It's all a load of crap," added Tia. "You're not worried about keeping Byron in your life. You just said it. You just don't like being told you can't do something. Someone tells you you're fated to die if you push that button, you need to push it more. Byron suggests, even merely accidentally, that you could play it a little safer, you get more reckless.

"Relationships aren't adventures to be conquered," said Tia. "Byron is not a villain you need to outsmart. If you don't realize that, you will screw it up."

The jet rumbled down the runway for takeoff. Tia imagined Hiro hanging out in the wheel well. Did private jets have wheel wells big enough for a person to hide in? What the hell was a wheel well, anyway? Could a person freeze or suffocate in one? Did she just send her boyfriend to his death on some half-assed scheme to protect Connie from an imagined threat?

Tia hoped he'd realized how dumb her plan was and was now sitting in the airport bar, grabbing a drink, planning a jewel theft in the south of France. When she returned home, she'd hug him and apologize. If he wasn't dead, his mangled body crumpled against landing gear.

When they were in the air, and after the captain turned off the FASTEN SEAT BELT sign, she excused herself to use the bathroom. She checked each seat as she passed, as if there were any reasonable place for Hiro to hide on this jet. When he didn't appear, she went to the bathroom and closed the door.

"You were right," said Hiro.

She squealed. Again.

"How did you . . . Never mind." She wrapped her arms around him in the tiny bathroom and kissed him.

"What was that for?" he asked.

"For not being dead. You were right. This is stupid."

"No," he replied. "You were right. Connie is in danger. The flight attendant is a trained assassin."

"How do you know that?"

"We went to the same school. She's good. Valedictorian in assassination studies."

"There's ninja school?"

"It was more of a secret monastery where kids are trained from a very young age in the way of shadows. But if you get a bunch of kids together, you're going to have cliques and drama and all the usual popularity problems. Akane was always stuck up. Never had any time for thieves. Always thought she was better than us."

"I better warn Connie."

He didn't move aside. "And what are you going to tell her? A little bird whispered a warning to you?"

"I'll just say . . . something. Like I thought I saw a knife."

"That won't work."

"Well, can't you take Akane out?"

"Unlikely," he said. "She might have been full of herself, but she was top in her class."

"Sneak up on her, use those knockout darts of yours."

"I can't just sneak up on her."

"You can sneak up on anyone."

"I appreciate the vote of confidence, but vanishing isn't the same as stalking. If I make one mistake, Akane will spot me. Did I mention she was valedictorian? She'd kill me in three seconds flat, and that might be a tad generous on my part."

"Then we'll just warn Connie," said Tia. "I'm sure she can handle it."

"She'll want an explanation," he said. "And she'll most likely see through any lie you try to tell her. You'll have to admit I'm following you, and then what? Once she knows I'm here, she'll be harder to follow. And I can't help to keep her out of trouble if I'm busy trying to avoid being noticed by her. I can barely manage it when she isn't looking for me."

"We have to do something. I'm just going to tell her, and if she asks, I'll admit the truth. She can't get mad at us if it saves her life." She squeezed past him and exited the cramped bathroom. "But stay out of sight just in case—"

She went to shut the door, but he was nowhere to be seen. She took a moment to check the bathroom again. She even checked in the small space behind the toilet before giving up and heading back to Connie.

Tia was still busy concocting a story about how she spotted an assassin when the flight attendant stumbled down the aisle. She brandished a dagger in her hand, and Tia reflexively jumped back, her arms raised. She had some self-defense courses, but her only chance in this situation was to hope she could fend of Akane long enough for Connie to rescue her. Tia punched the deadly assassin in the chest. It was a sloppy punch, but it connected. The dreaded ninja gasped and fell flat on the floor. She didn't get up.

A dagger, the same style as the one in her hand, stuck out from between her shoulders.

Connie knelt down and checked the killer. "Don't worry. She's dead."

"What happened?" asked Tia, as if she didn't already know.

"She tried to kill me. Must've been sent by someone who doesn't want me to help Larry."

A few slashes tore across Connie's shirt. Most of the cuts were shallow, though the one on her arm was bleeding badly.

"I brought bandages." Tia rifled through her bag. "And antiseptic. Just in case."

"Thanks."

Tia bandaged the wound. "I can't believe I missed the knife fight."

"Probably better that you did. Tight quarters like this, she almost had me. She might have if she'd gotten the drop on me like she intended. But I spotted a Coalition of Assassins tattoo on her wrist when she was handing out peanuts."

"Huh. You'd think assassins would avoid having distinguishing marks like that."

"You'd think. I'm going to check the pilot and copilot. I'm fairly certain they're just people, but it doesn't hurt to take a second look."

The pilot apologized for the inconvenience, but Connie assured them that these things happened, and if the worst that happened was a few cuts and having to get their own drinks, it was nothing to be concerned about.

Larry sent a car to pick them up. The driver said nothing beyond the standard greetings as he drove. Tia thought he might be another assassin. Connie didn't seem concerned, but she rarely did.

"Are you all right?" asked Connie. "You seem on edge."

Tia almost broke. Again. She'd never manage this. It felt wrong lying to her friend. It also felt more and more unnecessary. Connie wasn't worried because she didn't need to worry. A few close calls didn't mean anything.

"I'm fine," said Tia. "Are you certain the driver isn't a hired killer?"

"Certain? No. I'm never certain, but it doesn't seem likely."

The unlikeliness only bothered Tia more. Unlikely things happened more often than not where Connie was concerned, and Tia, who had been Connie's friend for decades, understood it in a way she hadn't ever before.

Tia had assumed since she'd been dragged onto adventures before that she got it, but Connie had adventures constantly, whereas Tia had a mostly normal life disrupted by adventures now and then. She also wasn't responsible for much in those situations other than staying alive until Connie rescued her.

Sidekicking changed all that. She was no longer a passive participant. She was in the game, and her job was to support while Connie did the heavy lifting. Tia wondered if it wasn't getting to her already. Maybe she didn't have Connie's talent for constant intrigue and adventure without falling into paranoia.

The driver didn't try to kill them. He delivered them to Larry's townhouse, an unassuming four-story domicile surrounded by equally unassuming buildings. Apollonia greeted them at the door. The statuesque Amazon appraised Tia with neutrality tinged with disdain, as if deciding whether to step on a tiny spider or let it pass unmolested.

"I wasn't told you'd be bringing company," said Apollonia.

"I'm the sidekick." Tia tried to sound tough, but it was hard to intimidate while craning your head back. "I go where she goes."

To Tia's surprise, Apollonia didn't break her neck. She pursed her lips and nodded. "I'll alert the kitchen staff we have an additional guest." She walked away without so much as a nod to Connie or Tia.

"What's her deal?" asked Tia.

"Oh, her? She's just standard-issue master henchagent. You know the type. All business. No sense of humor. But she's keeping Larry safe, so she's cool. Although I'm fairly certain we're going to have to fight at some point."

"Promise me you'll let me watch when you kick her ass."

"We'll cross that bridge when we get to it."

They were shown their rooms, across the hall from one another. Tia considered asking to be moved to the same room, just to be that much closer in case trouble popped up, but this was probably close enough.

They were taken to the dining room, where Larry waited. He gestured for Connie to sit in the seat beside him. She elected to not read anything into that. Tia sat beside her. Apollonia took the other seat beside Larry, across from Connie. She and Apollonia locked eyes. Cold hostility radiated from Apollonia.

In Connie's experience, aggression came in hot and cold varieties. Hot was the most common kind. She'd seen it on the faces of a thousand foiled villains. Cold came from someone who had no real reason to hate you. It was calculating and dangerous and rare. So rare, she convinced herself she was imagining it.

Connie smiled at Apollonia.

Apollonia didn't smile back.

Connie elected to not read anything into that, either.

The serving staff, all dressed in matching henchagent uniforms—black pants, black shirts, armored vests, helmets with the Siege Perilous logo stenciled on them—brought forth the first course. Their black gloves weren't designed for delicate work, and one of the servers stuck his thumb in Connie's soup. She refrained from mentioning it out of a sense of decorum.

Larry dipped his spoon into the soup. "It's Campbell's chicken and stars." He smiled. "My favorite. The chef hates it, but being Mastermind Interim has its advantages."

He laughed, and there was a hint of something in it. Connie caught it. A glance at Tia, eyebrow raised, confirmed she'd caught it too.

Apollonia sat still. She didn't touch her silverware. She sat across from Connie, blinking just enough to avoid being called out for staring.

"Don't like soup?" asked Connie, blinking at her own stiffly regimented intervals.

"Apollonia doesn't eat," said Larry. "I mean, I've never

seen her eat. I assume she eats at some point. But it's weird to have her just standing around while I'm eating, so she sits at the table while I eat."

Tia took a sip of her soup. "Yes, I'd hate for things to be weird."

Connie and Apollonia continued to not-stare at each other across the table.

"So, Tia, how long has it been?" Larry asked. "You're looking good. I heard you got married."

"I was. I'm divorced."

Larry said, "I'm sorry to hear that."

"It happens. I have a great boyfriend now."

"If you'll excuse me." Apollonia pushed away from the table. "I need to check on the salmon. I shall return shortly."

Somehow, it sounded like a threat.

She left the room, and once she was gone, Connie was free to finally try her own soup.

Tia asked, "What about you, Larry? Anyone special in your life?"

"Who has the time?"

"You must've had a serious girlfriend or two over the years."

"It's not really any of our business," said Connie through gritted teeth.

Tia smiled innocently. "We're just catching up."

"Oh, sure. I've had a few," he said, oblivious to their battle of wills. "There was Linda. We had a good thing going for a few years until I discovered she was a secret bodyguard assigned to protect me by Mom. When I found out, I told her it didn't matter. I loved her anyway. She said it was just a job, and that she didn't actually care for me very much."

He clinked his spoon against his bowl and gazed into the broth as if it held secrets.

"After that, there was Ida. She was cool. So smart. So funny. I was about to ask her to marry me when Mom decided she was too much of a security risk. Had the entire relationship erased from Ida's memory. Last I heard, she'd settled down with some guy in Idaho and has a couple of kids.

"Then there was Patricia. She was great, and Mom really liked her too. Then she left me for a guy she met at the gym. Brad or Bud or Barry. Something with a B. I thought it was just a phase, but Mom had her liquidated before she could get through it.

"Relationships are complicated. Who the hell can figure them out?"

He stood.

"I'll be right back."

He rushed out of the room before they could say anything.

"Poor guy," said Tia.

"What the hell are you doing?" asked Connie.

"Talking. Catching up. Larry's my friend, too."

"That's not what you're doing."

Tia slurped a spoonful of stars. "Oh, then what am I doing?"

Connie said, "You're doing something."

"Oh, something. I'm doing something."

"Yes, you're doing something, and I don't think I like it."

"Well, one of us needs to do something."

"Aha, so you admit you're doing something."

Tia said, "I didn't say that. I said one of us needs to do something. I didn't say it should be me."

They sipped their soup, not taking their eyes off each other until Larry and Apollonia returned together along with the serving staff, who removed the soup bowls and brought the salmon.

"It's funny," said Larry. "I think you might have been my best relationship, Connie. The only girlfriend I could trust who could stand up to Mom."

Larry, Connie, and Tia all laughed. Apollonia half-smiled, which was probably as close to a laugh as she ever came.

Connie took a bite of the salmon, chewing it long and slowly, debating what to say next.

"Something wrong with your fish?" asked Larry. "It's not overcooked, is it?"

"I can have the chef disciplined," said Apollonia.

"We've talked about this," said Larry. "Siege Perilous no longer has a *bad fish requires discipline* policy."

A perplexed expression crossed her face, followed by a slightly disappointed one. "Your mother wouldn't approve of allowing such sloppiness to go uncorrected."

"Mom's not in charge, I am, but if it will make you feel better, you can give the chef a write-up."

"As you command, Lord Peril." Her shoulders slightly slumped as she sighed internally.

"She's just mad we don't use the dungeon anymore," he said. "I'm planning on turning it into a rumpus room."

Connie swallowed her thoroughly chewed food. "There's nothing wrong with the salmon. It's delicious."

"I don't know." Larry poked his serving with his fork. "Could use more basil."

Apollonia perked up.

"Don't get any ideas," he said.

Connie had another bite, eating it with an exaggerated smile and a nod. "You know, Larry, we were never together."

She'd tried to pass it off as natural conversation, but the comment hung over the table.

"I know we weren't *together* together," he said. "But we were sort of together."

"No, we weren't," she said. "We were just kids. We never even went out on a date."

"Yes, we did. You're forgetting about that time we went to the movies. What movie was it? Some weird science fiction thing. Old black-and-white classic. It's on the tip of my tongue. Something something saucer men. Day of the something." He set down his fork and drummed his fingers with nervous energy on the table. "Something conquered something."

"*The Day the Earth Stood Still*," said Apollonia quietly, with noticeable reluctance.

He slammed the table. "That's it! That's the one."

Connie searched her memory and found a fuzzy recollection. "Are you talking about that time we hid in a movie theater from your mother's henchagents?"

"You do remember. That was when we first made out. It was the first time I'd ever kissed anyone."

Now that the memory was unlocked, she recalled the sloppy, awkward kiss between them. It'd only been to blend into the crowded theater.

"First time I touched a boob," he added with a wistful chuckle.

She recalled the groping, pokey fingers now, too. She hadn't had much experience at that point, but she had enough to know Larry was doing it wrong.

Larry said, "Afterward, we went to that Japanese place. Ate sushi hidden in the back while henchagents ransacked the place. Good times, right?"

"Yes," she said. "But it wasn't really a date."

"Oh, sure it was. Closest I'd ever had up to that point, what with Mom always watching me."

He rang the bell for dessert, and the henchstaff cleared the table.

"I fell for you pretty hard that night," said Larry as the strawberry sherbet was brought out. "Had a crush on you for years. Came to a head when we were sixteen and trekking through the jungles of wherever—"

"Kakadu, Lord Peril," said Apollonia, sounding very irritated. She was back to staring at Connie, and Connie deliberately avoided making eye contact, knowing she couldn't help herself by not-staring back if she did.

"That's the one," he said. "It was so wet everywhere that your clothes started sticking to your body, and . . ."

His voice trailed off.

"Shit. This is sort of sounding creepy, isn't it?"

"Not at all," lied Connie.

"Sorry. Just memories." He raised the sherbet to his lips and set it back in the bowl. "That didn't mean anything to you?"

"Of course it did, Larry."

It'd been the right place, the right time. They'd made out under the half moon while helicopters hovered over the jungle. Larry wasn't the first boy she'd kissed, but it had been beautiful at the moment. She might have even lost her virginity to him that night if not for the wild gorilla attack. How gorillas made it to Australia was a mystery she never solved.

"We were just kids, but it meant something."

She reached for his hand, but he pulled it under the table.

"Damn, I'm such an idiot," he said.

A henchagent entered and whispered in his ear.

"Now? Really?"

"Is there a problem?" asked Connie.

"Nothing to worry about. We'll take care of it. Please, finish your dessert."

He and Apollonia stood.

"Connie has a boyfriend," blurted Tia. "His name is Byron, and they live together."

"I see," said Larry. "Good for him?"

The questioning tone might have meant something. Or

it might have just been a side effect of the non sequitur.

"We'll talk later."

They left.

"That was subtle," said Connie.

"Someone had to do something," said Tia.

"Oh, that was something, all right. I don't know what, but something."

"Are you still denying he has a thing for you?"

"What? Those were just memories, a shared history. That's all. You're making too much of it."

"Or you're making not enough of it."

Larry never returned. Connie and Tia finished their dessert before heading back to their room. A henchagent suggested they retire early since they were scheduled for an early-morning departure for their next mission.

"If you need me, just knock," said Connie to Tia.

"Likewise."

They parted ways.

Connie changed into her pajamas. When she stepped out of the bathroom Apollonia was sitting on the bed, lit by a lamp on the bedside table.

"We need to talk," said Apollonia.

Connie rolled the kinks out of her neck. "Are we finally going to fight? Because I don't give a shit if I am in my pajamas, I'll kick your ass whenever you want."

Apollonia removed her glasses and tucked them in her shirt pocket. "Just what are your intentions?"

Connie lowered her fists. "Intentions?"

"Why are you here?"

Connie said, "Larry asked for my help. We aren't going to fight?"

Apollonia shrugged. "Why are you here? Now? In this place?"

"I'm here to help Larry."

"That's not why you're here." Apollonia pointed to the floor under Connie's feet. "You don't need to be here to do that. We could easily give you your assignments through more efficient methods. Why are you here?"

Connie said, "I don't see how that's any of your business."

Apollonia stood, folded her arms across her chest.

Connie folded her arms across her chest.

"What are your intentions toward Larry?" asked Apollonia.

"Intentions?" Connie would've laughed, but she didn't want to drop her guard. She moved her right foot a few inches to the left for a more stable stance.

Apollonia countered by turning her body ever so slightly to get into a stronger position. She had reach, power, flexibility. Connie had a record of beating opponents with all those advantages.

"I don't have intentions," said Connie. "Who has intentions anymore? What decade are you in? And I'm in a relationship."

Apollonia's arms fell to her side. Her right hand balled into a loose fist, and Connie shifted her weight to be ready for a punch. Apollonia noticed the shift and counter-shifted.

"Are we going to fight?" asked Connie.

"I don't want to fight you."

"I don't want to fight you, either," said Connie.

Although she kind of did. Just a little bit.

Apollonia said, "Larry's in a fragile place. He's bothered more by Lady Peril's death than he's willing to admit."

"We both know she's probably not dead," said Connie.

Apollonia frowned, raised an eyebrow.

"Do you know if she's dead or not?" asked Connie.

Apollonia didn't reply.

"Of course you do," said Connie. "You're her chief hench-agent. You probably know all kinds of secrets."

Apollonia remained inscrutable.

"Is she not dead? She's not dead, right? If this is all an elaborate ruse, I'll find out. You might as well tell me now."

Apollonia said, "You're changing the subject."

"So, she is alive," said Connie.

"I didn't say that."

"She's dead, then?" asked Connie.

"I didn't say that, either."

Connie fought the urge to take a swing at Apollonia. She could see Apollonia was struggling against the same instinct.

Apollonia went slack, leaving herself susceptible to a dozen strikes. "Cards on the table. I don't like you, Verity."

"Yeah, well, I don't like you, either," said Connie.

"You killed my brother."

Apollonia said it so casually, it took a moment for Connie to absorb.

"You threw him into a vat of acid while he was working for Freerik van Catastroph."

"Oh, the acid guy," said Connie.

"Don't do that. You don't remember him."

"No, I don't," said Connie. "I try not to kill people. I'm very good at avoiding killing people."

But she had killed. Her body count was low, but it was there. The consequences now here. Standing before her.

"If he was henchagenting for a bad guy, he knew the risks."

"He was a mechanical engineer. Spent three years of his life working on that weather control machine you destroyed in three minutes. The stupid idiot picked up a gun and tried to stop you."

"It was self-defense," said Connie. It did make her feel a little better, though it obviously didn't do much for Apollonia.

"You couldn't have disarmed him? You couldn't have knocked him out?"

"Stuff gets crazy sometimes."

Connie immediately regretted saying it. It was crass, flippant. It was easy to forget that minions had family and friends and lives. The technician building the doomsday device was usually in it for the paycheck, not the glory. They were bad guys, but everybody had to make a living.

"Damn, I'm sorry," said Connie.

Apollonia's body language changed. She was still ready for a fight. She always was. It was a habit Connie understood all too well. But it was a more relaxed readiness.

"People get hurt around you, Verity. I don't want that to happen to Larry."

"Do you like him?"

Apollonia groaned. "Am I twelve? I'm not some infatuated girl who falls in love with every idiot who hires her. He's weak, ineffective, and foolish. Without a doubt, the worst mastermind I have ever worked for, but I'm paid to protect him while he's in charge."

"It's a job thing? Sacred calling of the henchagent? That's all?"

"I'm not here to bare my soul. We both know that it'd be stupid to expose any vulnerability to the other. We both know things are likely to become troublesome between us. Looking after Larry is my job, and I don't want you screwing with him. He deserves better than that."

"I'm confused. Do you like him or not?"

Apollonia put her glasses on. Her face remained unreadable.

"None of your fucking business."

She marched out of the room, and Connie sat on the bed. She didn't need this. She was just trying to help a friend, do some good. This particular adventure was getting more complicated than she cared for.

She called Byron. It was late, and she was an hour behind. He'd probably be in bed by now. He answered groggily.

"I didn't wake you, did I?" she asked, even though she obviously had.

"No," he lied. "I was up. What's wrong?"

"Nothing," she said. "I just wanted to call."

"You never call on your adventures. Is something wrong? Are you in danger? More danger? Like extra levels of danger?"

"No, I'm okay. I swear. Nothing to worry about. It's just . . . It's just I wanted to talk to you. It's stupid."

He laughed, and she felt embarrassed.

"It's not stupid. It's good."

"I'm sorry," she said. "Sorry about treating you like some delicate flower I have to keep in the dark."

"Are you certain you're not about to die?"

"Certain?" She glanced around the tastefully decorated guest bedroom. "No, but I think I'm okay. I'm trying to acknowledge your feelings. That's all."

"Feelings acknowledged. How are things going, then?"

"Weird. Extra levels of weird."

"Want to talk about it?"

"It's late. You need your sleep."

"I can talk," he said.

She almost told him to forget it. She didn't want him to worry, but that wasn't up to her. But she also didn't want to unpack all the problems she was dealing with now.

"Let's talk about your day," she said.

"Oh, the usual. Defeated a paper jam. Had an interoffice-memo typo emergency. Had a good lunch. Defused an unlabeled-yogurt-cup crisis started by Gayle."

"Sounds like Gayle."

"You've never even met Gayle."

"I know the type."

She lay back in bed, feeling a million times better as he shared his trials and tribulations with her.

16

The death of Lady Peril, genuine or not, had left Siege Perilous with dozens of pressing problems. Larry had a corkboard on his office wall, filled with index cards. Each was a possible bomb in need of defusing. Information wasn't always clear. The organization was large and compartmentalized. It was the way Lady Peril ran things. Schemes within schemes, some of those schemes working in direct opposition to each other so that no matter which one succeeded, Peril would win.

Larry decided Connie's next bomb by throwing a dart at the corkboard, which was how she ended up dispatched over the Indian Ocean, investigating a forbidden aquatic archeology mission being held captive by giant starfish.

The helicopter hovered over the largest tugboat, and Connie, Tia, and their soldiers rappelled to the deck.

The captain exited the bridge. Behind him, a massive echinoderm flopped forward on six thick legs. Its suckers popped with each ponderous step. The blue and yellow spines along its back bristled.

"What seems to be the problem?" asked Connie.

"These goddamned things have been keeping us prisoner," said the captain. "Destroyed our engines. Won't let us leave."

"Anyone hurt?"

"Not yet," he said.

The giant starfish raised up, and its circular mouth gnashed. It didn't have any teeth. When necessary, it would evert its stomach to digest its meals outside its body. Connie had a book on starfish as a kid. They were truly terrifying monsters of the deep, and this one, weighing nine hundred pounds conservatively, was a thing born of nightmares.

It lurched on two legs, threatening to topple over onto her and the two soldiers behind her. From there, it could dissolve them at its leisure. The soldiers raised their weapons, but Connie gestured for them to hold fire.

The monster flapped its top tentacle back and forth and whistled in the ancient language of the echinoderms. "Hello, Constance Verity of the land things."

"Tweep of the deep dwellers, is that you?" asked Connie with a melodious whistle. "You're looking good. Is that a new arm?"

Tweep wiggled the limb. "Yes, thank you for noticing. But you, Constance Verity, possess the same number of limbs as the last time we met. Have you been ill?"

"No, it's a land-thing thing."

Tweep fell on his back and folded in on himself in a traditional gesture of apology. "Excuse me if I offended."

"It's fine. No apologies necessary."

The giant starfish flipped over. "It is good to see you again, Constance Verity of the land things. Fortuitous, as well. We have been attempting to communicate with your fellow land things, but our efforts have met with no success. Now that you are here, there is hope.

"Long ago, my people waged a terrible war to see that the god of the depths would never rise. Until your fellow land things discovered the lost city under which the god dreams of the light above. As he stirs, the universe itself shall unbecome. The disturbances of its resting place threaten us all."

The ocean rumbled beneath them, churning and bubbling. White sand muddied the waters.

"And why didn't you just scare them off?" asked Connie.

"If we'd caught the desecration in time, we would have done so. But the god already stirs, and we need help to return it to its slumber. Help only a land thing can offer."

Tweep of the deep dwellers briefed Connie. It was all so much whistles and squeals. At one point, Connie had to make a farting nose with her armpit. The alien linguistics and inhuman body language were impossible to follow.

"She does this all the time," said Tia to a soldier. "I barely passed conversational Spanish."

More starfish creatures climbed up from the water and onto the deck as they talked. All of them were smaller than Tweep, but their alien otherness put everyone on edge. Everyone but Connie.

Maybe Tia had been wrong to worry. Connie wasn't invincible, but she wasn't stupid. A sidekick was handy to have around but not required. Connie had been saving the day for decades, and despite it all, she was still alive. She knew what she was doing.

Tweep vomited up an asymmetrical tube of black and purple. Connie picked up the slimy thing and bowed, flapping her arms. Tweep repeated the gesture. They both blew raspberries.

Connie said, "Here's the deal. There's this monster or god or something under the ocean. The sun might be a figment of its imagination. Or it's just a giant monster. Either way, these guys want to put it back to sleep. Unfortunately, they needed a human to play this flute to do it, and they couldn't get anyone to understand."

"Sounds simple," said Tia as she handed Connie a cloth to wipe the juices off the instrument.

Connie cleaned the slime and goop off and offered the cloth back.

"Keep it," said Tia.

Connie put the flute to her lips. "You're going to want to cover your ears."

She played a soft, discordant tune, both terrible and hypnotic. Even with her ears covered, Tia felt the urge, almost irresistible, to hurl herself into the welcoming icy depths, to fill her lungs with water and rest forever on the ocean floor.

One soldier surrendered to the siren song. He ran toward the edge, but a pair of starfish tackled him before he could do it. He laughed and cried as he struggled to free himself, but they kept him pinned to the deck.

The song was only thirty-one seconds long. Tia counted those long seconds. If it'd been thirty-four or -five, she'd have probably needed restraining herself. By the end, she was crying, pining for the primordial depths that her ancestors, buried under millions of generations of DNA, had once called home. In the blackness, there was peace. In the darkness, the world was as perfect as it ever could be.

Connie gave the all clear, and Tia uncovered her ears.

"How did you not jump in the ocean?" asked Tia.

"I like pizza too much. There's no pizza down there."

"Sometimes, it's really hard to tell when you're joking."

A deep rumble below whipped the waters.

"Probably just rolling over to go back to sleep," said Connie.

The waves roiled, and the ship rocked to one side.

"Damn it."

Connie whistled at Tweep who gurgled back.

"I might have a shot if I can get closer. Captain, where do you keep your diving gear?"

A tentacle slapped over the railing as a giant nautilus dragged itself onto the main deck. The horrendous thing sloshed toward them.

"That's not so scary," said Tia. "Not *monster god of the deep* scary."

"That's not the god," said Connie. "It's just one of its children."

More nautiluses pulled themselves onto the ship. Soldiers fired their weapons. The bullets bounced off their shells or splattered against their exposed squishy bodies. A few of the creatures withdrew into their shells with squeals. Others charged with impossible speed for giant invertebrates. A soldier was grabbed by the ankles and dragged, screaming, overboard.

A tentacle wrapped around Tia's waist, but before she could meet the same fate, Connie hacked the appendage with a knife. The nautilus howled, releasing Tia and sliding into its shell.

The ocean tossed the ship around. An angry wave crested over the deck, carrying several more people into the merciless depths. Tia was knocked over but somehow managed to stay on deck. Funny word, *somehow*. It meant she had no clue how, but she'd take whatever small miracles she could.

A howling nautilus flailed its many tentacles as it rushed at her. Even if she'd had the sense to spring into action, she'd have no chance of escaping across the rocking, slippery deck. But she didn't spring. She stared into the thing's white eye, and amid its hundred writhing tentacles, she caught a glimpse of its snapping beak. This was how she died, eaten by a giant bivalve.

Were nautiluses bivalves? And was that really going to be her last thought?

Tweep pounced on the nautilus. He wrapped his arms

around the monster, which whipped its tentacles in an attempt to escape. Tweep shrieked.

Connie grabbed Tia's arm. "His people are buying us some time."

They ran through the chaos of monsters and humans and monsters. It was all indecipherable to Tia. Just water and howls and gunfire. Somehow, Connie guided them through it, and they ended up in a radio room. Or a room full of electronics that Tia assumed was the radio room. She didn't know enough about ships. Connie shut the door and locked it.

The angry sea lurched, and Tia felt like she was going to throw up. Then she threw up.

She wiped her mouth. "Are nautiluses bivalves?"

"Cephalopods," said Connie.

The ship bobbed. Tia threw up again.

She didn't wipe her mouth this time. She could sense another bout of nausea punching her in the gut.

"Stay here," said Connie.

"Yeah, okay."

Tia considered arguing, saying something about belonging by Connie's side. It was right there in the word *sidekick*. The very first syllable said it all. But Tia wasn't going to do anybody any good.

Connie exited, slamming the hatch shut behind her. Tia dragged herself over to the small window and watched as Connie jumped overboard without any diving gear. Just a flute in her hand.

A huge white eye appeared in the window. Tia ducked against the wall. With some luck, she hadn't been seen.

Funny word, *luck*.

The monster pounded on the door. The hinges buckled. Tia looked around for a weapon. Anything. All she found was an old mop. She struck it against a console, breaking off the tip. It was shorter than she would've liked, but it was better than nothing.

The door fell in with a clang. The doorway was too small for the nautilus's shell. It flailed with dozens of tentacles, and Tia pressed against the far wall. She wished she knew the vulnerable parts of a sea monster.

A shotgun blast chipped away at the nautilus's shell. It screeched and withdrew.

Tia struck. She shoved her spear into its eye. It burst, spraying goo everywhere. The monster retreated, hurling itself into the ocean.

She threw up again, though she had nothing left to vomit. The retching dry heave nearly caused her to drop to her knees.

Hiro steadied her. "It's okay. You're okay."

She leaned against him. She nodded toward the weapon in his hand.

"What kind of ninja uses a shotgun?" she asked, her throat dry and raw.

"Whatever gets the job done." He patted her back. "Sit down."

She walked to the railing. It wasn't smart. Not with the

monsters and the waves and the very real possibility the ship might capsize at any moment.

"She's down there," said Tia, but there was too much noise from the ocean and the shrieking and the groaning ship. She pointed.

Hiro nodded, holding her tight. She hoped he was holding tight to something else.

He'd seen Connie jump and hadn't tried to stop her. Tia elbowed him rather than waste her time yelling.

He shrugged, and that said it all.

If Connie was determined to do something, she'd do it. No matter how stupid. Tia had seen it a hundred times. Somehow, Connie always came out okay.

Somehow.

Something massive stirred in the depths. A bright red eye opened, and Tia realized how much she'd underestimated its size. It was huge. An island on fins, perhaps. It would rise and swallow this ship like popcorn before sending devastating tidal waves across the globe simply by swimming. Then it'd stomp whatever was left in its wake, crushing humanity beneath it without thought or mercy.

The sun flickered as if it might extinguish.

"Come on, Connie."

The flute's song drifted from the raging ocean. Tia and Hiro stepped back from the railing and covered their ears. Despite the noise, despite the impossibility of it, the flute played in their heads. The frozen, wet darkness beckoned. Tia and Hiro edged toward the siren's song. They couldn't stop. They could only slow their progress, taking one hesitant step at a time.

Tia tried thinking about pizza. It didn't work.

The song stopped suddenly, and she found herself poised half over the railing. Hiro had one of his legs over. She pulled him back.

The ship rocked with the dying waves. The sun stabilized, seeming brighter than usual, but that was only because of its previous dimness. The dreaming god of the depths closed its eye and sank quietly into the dark to rest until the end of time. The nautiluses skittered overboard, and Tia's shaky legs wanted to give out. She pulled herself along the edge, scanning for any sign of Connie.

"She's all right," said Tia. "She's always all right."

"Yeah," said Hiro.

Neither of them admitted that maybe she wasn't. This might be the last time she saved the day. There had to be a last time. Debra had said so. The law of averages said so.

A starfish splashed to the surface. It rolled over, holding Connie in its arms. She whistled a thanks and swam to the boat. Hiro helped her aboard.

"Oh, thank God," said Tia. "I thought . . . I just thought . . ."

She didn't know what she'd thought. Of course Connie was fine. Connie was always fine.

Tweep lumbered over. He uttered a disquieting series of squeaks and fart-like noises.

"Couldn't have done it without you." Connie gave the cursed flute to Tweep, who swallowed it. He belched.

"I'll see that the god is left undisturbed," she said.

He blurted out a slobbery good-bye, and Tweep and the other starfish went overboard.

The boat rocked with the lingering waves as they watched the starfish swim away.

"How the hell do you play a flute underwater?" asked Tia.

"Practice. So, do you want to tell me what Hiro is doing here?"

He stepped behind Tia. "It was her idea."

Tia considered surrendering to the lingering impulse calling her to the ocean depths.

While repairs for the boats began, Connie, Tia, and Hiro changed out of their wet clothes. They had to borrow some new clothes and neither Connie's nor Tia's fit very well. Hiro's looked like they'd been made for him. Tia was trying to remember a time he'd ever looked less than perfect. Even when saving her from the giant nautilus aboard a supernatural storm, he'd only looked mussed. He didn't even have bedhead in the mornings.

Her hair was all over the place. She really should cut it shorter if she was going to keep this up. Sidekicking demanded certain practical choices.

They sat in the small dining area of the tugboat, had some coffee to warm up.

"I'm sorry," said Tia. "I was just worried about you, so I came up with this stupid plan to have Hiro follow us around. Like secret backup."

Connie took a drink of her coffee but didn't say anything.

"I should've asked," said Tia. "I didn't because I was afraid you'd say no."

"You didn't know that," said Connie, more into her coffee cup than to Tia. "It's true, but you didn't know."

"It was a stupid idea. I admitted that."

"Not that stupid," said Hiro. "I did save you."

Tia didn't need reminding.

"I shouldn't have done it," said Tia. "But, Connie, even you have to admit that things have felt a bit off lately. Like there's something different happening out there. Like maybe the universe has it out for you."

"The universe always has it out for me," said Connie.

"I know." Tia slumped across the table. "And you handled everything. You always do. The world was blowing up around you, and not only did you stop it from ending, you saved me while doing it. I'm the sidekick. I'm supposed to make things easier. Not get in the way."

"You weren't in the way."

"If you weren't looking out for me, it would've been easier."

Connie chuckled. "It's never easy, Tia. I just make it look easy."

"You're not mad, then?" asked Tia.

"Why would I be mad? You and Hiro were looking out for

me. I'm not happy that you thought you needed to lie about it, but it came from a good place. I'm glad he was here to save you."

He leaned in and kissed Tia. "So am I."

"You're not getting rid of me?" asked Tia.

"Hell, you're my sidekick, my friend, not my mindless lackey. I don't need your unquestioning obedience."

Connie poured herself another cup. She didn't like coffee, but she was still cold. A few minutes of meditation and biofeedback could shake the chill, but she didn't feel like interrupting the conversation.

"When I was down there, staring into the eye of that monster sea god, I thought it might finally be it. I'd thought it before, but not like that. And I wondered if things have changed. Maybe I broke the caretaker destiny. Maybe my luck is finally running out. Maybe I'm getting slow."

Hiro threw his empty mug at her. She caught it in her free hand before it hit her in the face.

"Are you nuts?" asked Tia.

"Reflexes look fine to me," said Hiro.

Connie set his cup down and went on deck. Tia tried to follow.

He took her arm. "Give her some time to figure it out on her own."

Connie stood on the deck of the ship, leaning on the railing, staring into the ocean depths. The waves lapped against the ship with rhythmic beats, and she imagined all the wonders lurking beneath the surface. Wonders and horrors she'd seen up close and personal plenty of times. Possibly too many times. There had to be a limit of how much adventure could be crammed into one life. She might've hit hers.

She'd been at peace with the caretaker mantle for most of her life. As a kid, she'd loved it. Back then, foiling international spy rings and thwarting alien invasions had seemed like endless fun. In her twenties, it'd become second nature, just the way life was. Now, in her thirties, she'd had her ups and downs, but she'd managed to find a balance.

Maybe that'd all been a lie she told herself. She might have only been delaying the inevitable. Assuming she could stop, hand off the job to someone else, she wasn't sure she wanted to. She'd been so eager to get rid of the responsibility not that long before, and now she dreaded the idea. She'd been saving the day so long, what would she do if she didn't have to?

Who the hell was she if not Constance Danger Verity?

The beautiful, awful song of the deep dwellers echoed in her head. She was immune to mind control, but it didn't prevent the tune from lingering, whispering in the back of her head. It was too bad she couldn't be hypnotized. Jumping into the ocean was a way of solving all her problems. Beneath the depths, there'd be nothing to worry about.

"Connie, what are you doing?" asked Tia.

Connie noticed she'd climbed halfway over the railing. It was difficult to hear anything as the song whistled sweetly in her ears.

Tia and Hiro were running over. They shouted something. "It's all right," said Connie with a smile. "I've got it figured out."

She wasn't stupid. She couldn't hold her breath forever, but she could hold it long enough to figure something else out. A little thing like air wasn't something to fret over.

Hiro shouted something about mind control, but that was silly. Connie was immune to mind control.

She jumped, but hands caught her, pulling her back onto the ship. They said something, but the song of the deep dwellers swallowed their useless chatter. She slipped free. Tia and Hiro stood between her and salvation.

Hiro moved forward, hands held out to her. She couldn't hear him, but she could read his lips. "You're not in control of yourself. You need to come inside."

She laughed. The sound echoed faintly in her ears. Mad and desperate. "Get out of my way, Hiro."

He tried to tackle her. She sidestepped and, on autopilot, broke his arm. She felt his radius snap, heard his soft scream from some distant place. To ensure he was out of commission, she broke his tibia in two places. He fell to the side, clutching his shattered leg, no longer a concern.

"Jesus, Connie."

Tia's voice was louder. The song was fading. Once it was gone, only uncertainty would remain. Connie pushed her way past Tia, but Tia grabbed Connie by the shirt.

Connie whirled, ready to unleash the dreaded seven-headed dragon strike. Tia flinched but didn't let go.

Connie pulled the blow at the last moment. What should've exploded Tia's heart and lungs only knocked her off her feet. She rolled around on the deck, gasping for air.

"Oh god." The song of the deep dwellers disappeared. Connie checked on Tia. "Oh god. I'm sorry. It must've been a side effect of the psycho-amplifier," said Connie. "Must've weakened my psychic defenses enough for the flute to affect me."

"Ya think?" asked Tia breathlessly.

"Are you okay? Do any of your internal organs feel . . . squished?"

"I'm okay. I think." Tia sat up, groaning. "Damn. It was one punch. Why do my toes hurt?"

"You're lucky. Another pound or two of pressure and . . ." Connie didn't want to finish that sentence. "You should be fine in an hour or two."

"Yeah, terrific," grunted Hiro, cradling his twisted arm. His leg bent at an ugly angle. "Oh, and you broke my fucking limbs over here. Just in case you should care."

"Sorry, Hiro. I just acted by reflex."

"Reflex." He shrugged and yelped. "Cool. Not like I needed my arm or leg as an international ninja-slash-thief."

Crew carried Hiro away, and Connie took a few minutes to clear her head on deck. Tia, despite the wobble in her legs from Connie's strike, stayed beside her. There wasn't much Tia could do if Connie surrendered to the impulse to take another swim, but Connie was fine now. The urge had passed.

She still stayed away from the railings as a precaution.

"Maybe I do need to slow down," said Connie.

"Maybe that's not such a bad thing," replied Tia.

Connie hated the idea. She was barely getting a handle on her life. She'd found the right balance. But here she was again, trying to figure it all out. That was how it worked. Life wasn't something you pinned down. It was always shifting. The thing you wanted wasn't the thing you thought you wanted. Except when it was, and then you couldn't have it.

Connie took a step toward the ocean. Tia put a hand on her shoulder.

"Maybe we should go inside and have a cup of coffee or something," she said.

Connie nodded. "Sounds good."

They turned away from the gentle lapping of the welcoming depths.

17

Although she would never have admitted it to anyone, Connie didn't feel safe until she reached dry land. It was only when she was a few hours from the ocean that her head finally cleared.

Larry suggested she take a break after the ordeal of her last mission, and she almost refused. That instinct to hurl herself into the fray was so strong, even knowing he was right. But some rest wouldn't hurt, and Siege Perilous would be fine for a couple of days. If things got really bad, they had her number.

Neither Byron or Connie felt like cooking. They went to an Italian place with soft lighting and a fair amount of authenticity, which was to say that the piped music was operatic and there was a mural of a gondolier on one wall. There was also another of a bullfighter from when the place was an authentic Mexican restaurant, which did challenge the tenuous illusion. But Byron had heard good things, so Connie gave it the benefit of the doubt.

So far, Connie and Byron had talked about nothing

important—the weather, her flight, his job. They smiled and laughed and pretended they weren't avoiding the subject of her latest adventure. It might have worked, but Connie's life was mostly adventure. She didn't have a lot to talk about beyond that.

She scanned the menu, listening as Byron went into the latest bit of office politics. ". . . so, Barbara says to Gene that she doesn't appreciate him getting extra breaks just because he smokes. And Gene shoots back that he gets his job done and what does it matter how many breaks he takes? You can imagine how she took that."

Connie nodded. "Sure, sure."

Although she couldn't. She had a hell of an imagination, but she'd never had an office job. Byron's stories made her increasingly glad she hadn't. Navigating a nine-to-five job seemed every bit as perilous as jumping into mysterious transdimensional vortices but with none of the satisfaction of saving the day.

"Sorry, I know it's boring," said Byron.

"It's your life. I'm not bored by it."

He closed his menu, folded his hands under his chin, and smiled skeptically.

"Okay, so it's a little boring," she admitted, "but I like boring."

He stared into her eyes with that slight smile.

"Not that I'm calling you boring," she said with a nervous laugh. "Just your job. Not that it's bad that your job is boring. Not that you think it's boring."

"It's a little boring," he said.

She exhaled with relief. "Oh, thank God. I love you, Byron, but I don't know if I could do it."

"I'm pretty sure you can do anything."

"Everybody has their limits."

She took his hand. She needed these moments, few and far between recently, where the world wasn't on the verge of exploding. The siren song of the ocean depths couldn't compete with this.

She needed Byron. Not because he was ordinary, though that was a nice perk. She needed his stability, his steady intelligence, his reassuring hand on hers.

The server appeared with drinks.

"One iced tea, one diet cola," he said curtly.

He set them on the table with hard thuds, spilling a bit over the top.

"We didn't order these," said Byron.

"Are you sure?" The server sounded disgusted by the very idea.

"We haven't ordered anything yet."

"My mistake."

The server took the drinks back. Connie noticed the scars on his knuckles, his ever-present snarl that was unusual for someone who made a living based on tips. "I'll be right back."

He walked to another table, and the shaking heads of the customers there indicated he had the wrong one again.

There were bad servers in this world. It didn't have to mean anything. Not everything was suspicious.

"How was your adventure?" asked Byron.

She'd been dreading the question, considering what she'd say. He had a right to know things, but she didn't want him worrying.

"Oh, fine. The usual."

It was a clumsy dodge. One he wouldn't fall for.

"That's good," he said, squeezing her hand.

It wasn't that easy.

It couldn't be that easy.

"There was this sea monster god, but I put it to sleep with a magic flute," she said.

"Uh-hmm." He opened his menu again. "I'm thinking about the spaghetti, but it feels like such a wasted opportunity. You can get spaghetti anywhere, but I really love spaghetti." He glanced around. "Is it just me or is this place really slow?"

"It's not you."

A server in a red vest walked briskly by. Byron tried to get her attention.

"Sorry. Not my table, sir," she said.

Her accent smacked of the Mishar Tatar dialect, possibly from Nizhegorod Oblast. There was no law saying everyone in the restaurant had to be Italian. It wasn't suspicious.

And the scar on the woman's neck, it was just a scar.

Russian people with bullet scars were allowed jobs as servers. It didn't mean anything.

"Maybe we should go somewhere else," said Byron.

Connie wanted to, but all the not-suspicious things

happening there had her curious. She was probably only imagining things. It was a hazard of her life. But she might not be
imagining things. That was also a hazard of her life.

"Let's give it a minute," she said.

He shrugged. "Maybe if I set down the menu, they'll get
the idea."

"You know, you can ask about my adventures," she said.
"More details, if you like. I don't want you to be afraid to do that."

"I know."

There was an edge in his voice. She almost missed it because
she was busy watching the serving staff moving among the
tables without doing anything, just going through the motions.

"I'm just not sure what the rules are, Connie," said Byron.
"One day, you don't want to talk about it. The next, you do."

"I want you to be comfortable with what I do."

"I am. Mostly. And maybe that's the best we can expect."

A smartly dressed dark woman flanked by several bodyguards entered the restaurant.

"Ah, damn it," said Connie.

"Know her?" asked Byron.

"The Rajmata of Chirayam. I didn't know she was in town."

The Rajmata was led to her table.

Connie signaled a server. "Not my table," he said, adjusting
the cloth napkin hanging over his arm. She glimpsed the barest
hint of a knife in his hand under the napkin as he wandered
away. It might have been the traditional sacrificial dagger of
the Cult of Mot. It might have been a butter knife.

"I just want some goddamn water," she mumbled.

"I think we should go," said Byron, dropping his napkin on his plate. "I'll settle for a cheeseburger right now."

"Sounds like a plan," she said, "but I might need a minute here to take care of this."

He glanced at the Rajmata. "Is something happening?" He hunched over the table and whispered, "Is this a thing? Are you about to do a thing?"

"Yeah, probably. Just act natural."

"Yeah, okay. Natural." He straightened, folded his hands on the table, and looked directly at her. It was like his neck was stuck facing forward, and he didn't blink. "Is this why the service is so lousy?" he asked, barely moving his lips from the fake smile plastered across his face.

She nodded as she caught the attention of a lanky, swarthy server of indeterminate ethnicity with an immaculately trimmed a la souvarov mustache.

"Not my—"

"Can we just get some breadsticks?" she interrupted.

He tried to stare her down, but when that didn't work, he grunted. "Yes, ma'am. One moment." He cast a glance over his shoulder at the Rajmata and rushed to the kitchen.

"We should do something this weekend. Maybe get out of town," she said.

Byron nodded stiffly as if afraid his head might fall off. "Will that interfere with your work at Siege Dangerous?"

"Perilous. And they can get on without me for a few days.

And if they can't, not really my problem. Benefit of being my own boss."

It'd do her good to not worry about that stuff. If she was slowing down, it wouldn't be so bad with Byron around. Her dilemma with normality wasn't rooted in fear of boredom. It was the great unknown of not being an adventurer. A quiet weekend with Byron would be just the thing to remind her there was more to living than derring-do.

"There's this cottage in the mountains I sometimes rent. It's beautiful. Nothing around for miles."

"Miles away from civilization? I have bad luck with the great outdoors. The last time I went camping, I had to keep the peace between a tribe of bigfoots and leprechauns."

"Leprechauns are real? I'm only sort of surprised that bigfoots exist, but leprechauns, that's weird."

"It's even weirder when you consider I was in North Dakota at the time. Tons of leprechauns in North Dakota. Don't know why."

The steward presented the Rajmata a selection of wines, all probably poisoned. The maître d' watched with burning intensity. He clutched a pistol under his pile of menus.

"How about a trip to the beach?" said Byron.

"I hate the beach," she replied. "Shark attacks."

"I thought those were exceedingly rare."

"Oh, they are," she said. "Sometimes, it's giant squids. The warriors of Atlantis. A phantom U-boat where the ghostly crew are just smugglers in cosplay. And another where the ghosts are actually ghosts."

"I don't know. A bed and breakfast, then?"

She smiled. "That sounds good. That might work."

"No bad experiences with those?" he asked.

"Some, but how many B&Bs can there be that are run by vampires? Not more than two, I have to assume. Now that I think about it, Tia and Hiro went to this place a couple of months ago. She called it charming."

The Rajmata sniffed her glass and nodded approvingly.

The server returned with a basket of breadsticks and tossed it unceremoniously on the table.

"Thanks," said Connie. "Oh, one more thing."

Connie grabbed his wrist and twisted it around his back. With her free hand, she threw her plate across the table to knock the glass of wine from the Rajmata's hand.

Her server broke out of her wrist lock. He ignored Connie, charging the Rajmata with a horrible scream. Connie stuck out her foot and tripped him. She snatched his dagger as he fell and hurled it into the hand of the maître d', who dropped his gun with a yelp.

The neck-scarred assassin leapt at Connie, who sidestepped and whipped the tablecloth around her opponent, spilling breadsticks in the air. She used the assassin's momentum against her and slammed her head into a table, breaking it in two and knocking her senseless.

The Rajmata's bodyguards sprang into action. The fight was mostly over, but they managed the cleanup, dragging the assassins away.

Connie found the real staff tied up in the back of the kitchen.

"It seems, Ms. Verity, that once again I owe you my life," said the Rajmata.

"Don't mention it."

Byron offered Connie a breadstick. "I managed to save this one for you."

"My hero." She took a bite of the cold, stale breadstick, chewed twice, and swallowed. "So, that burger place down the street, huh?"

"I've heard adequate things," he said.

She threw the breadstick away. "Sounds like heaven."

The next day, Tia came over to help Connie pack. Although her help consisted of watching while sitting on the bed. "I think this is a great idea," she said.

"Of course it's a good idea," said Connie.

"I said great. Not good." Tia pointed to Connie's half-filled suitcase. "Is that all you're taking with you?"

"It's only the weekend," said Connie.

"I thought you might pack some surprises. You know? Sexy surprises."

"Oh, please. Like a lacy nighty? A French maid's outfit? Does that sound like me? And Byron's not really into that kind of thing."

"That's what they all say," replied Tia. "But you should see Hiro's face light up when I become the Black Tigress, naughty assassin queen."

"No, I shouldn't," said Connie. "And Black Tigress sounds vaguely racist. And doesn't that border on cultural appropriation?"

"I'm black and my boyfriend's a ninja. I'm allowed. You really never did anything like that with Hiro?"

"What I did and didn't do with Hiro isn't a conversation I'm interested in having right now. Or ever."

"Fair enough." Tia smiled to herself.

"What?" asked Connie.

"It's just funny. I'm not used to thinking of you as boring."

"I've made love in the Amazon jungle," said Connie. "On the moons of alien worlds. In palaces of gold and aboard pirate galleons. I don't think my sex life could be described as boring."

"That explains it, then. You've never had to spice things up before. Correct me if I'm wrong, but Byron is your longest relationship."

"Yeah."

"And so far, you've only had sex in bedrooms and ordinary places like that?"

"I've studied the secrets of the pleasure priests of Aphros. I know what I'm doing."

"I'm not talking about technique. I'm sure your technique is as flawless as everything you do. But it never hurts to expand your repertoire."

"The pleasure priests believe the best sex eschews props, relying on the infinite pleasures available through pure physical contact," said Connie.

"Sound like a fun bunch. Far be it from me to disagree with esteemed masters of sex, but I'm just suggesting that if you come to the bedroom wearing a naughty explorer's outfit, you probably won't hear any complaints from Byron."

"They make naughty explorer costumes?"

"They do not," said Tia, "but fortunately, you have a side-kick who knows the right places to shop to throw one together." She left the room, returning with a shopping bag. "The pith helmet was the trickiest part."

Connie glanced in the bag. "The bullwhip is a bit much."

"Didn't feel complete without it."

Connie said, "And this isn't demeaning?"

"It's fun, Connie. You know, fun, right? It'll be a nice surprise. And didn't you spend three days dressed as a half-naked harem girl, as I recall?"

"I was undercover. It's not the same thing. And I don't hear you suggesting that Byron dress up in a costume."

"Funny you should mention it." Tia stepped out and returned with another bag. She handed it to Connie. "Don't look in it. It'll ruin the surprise."

"Since when did you get interested in my sex life?"

"I'm just doing my job as a friend and a sidekick. I want this trip to go well. Don't make it creepy."

"Yes, I'm the one who is making it creepy."

Connie thought about the pleasure priests of Aphros. Their secrets of sexual bliss were renowned throughout the universe. So much so that visitors agreed to be executed after a single night with a priest in order to keep the secrets of the order.

But there was probably a place between boring and execution sex, and Tia might be onto something. Connie tossed the bags into her suitcase.

"There. Happy?"

"Delighted. You can thank me later."

Connie's cell buzzed in her pocket. She didn't recognize the number. If the world was trying to drag her into another adventure, she wasn't interested. She denied the call.

"How's Hiro doing?" asked Connie. "He's not still mad at me, I hope."

"Oh, he's gone past mad to bored now. Mostly. He's actually more mad at me than you. It was my idea that he tag along in the first place. Get this. He accused me of wanting it to happen. Not you breaking his arm and leg, but just something like it to get him to stay home more. Like I want him around more. The bloom's off that rose."

"Trouble between you two?"

"No. He's just getting stir-crazy, and I'm having to listen to him complain about it. And I can't tell him to get over it, because he is right. It is because of me."

"Or us," said Connie.

"Oh, you're not to blame. You were mesmerized."

Connie didn't disagree aloud, but she imagined what she might have done with her impossible martial arts skills, unchecked by her better judgment. Hiro was lucky to walk away with only a few broken bones, but she was luckier. She didn't need to live with those regrets.

Her cell buzzed again. This was so much easier before cell phones. Ringing phone booths could be walked away from. Pagers could be ignored. But this thing, carried in her pocket, was a direct line from destiny that hated to be ignored.

And yet, if she hadn't answered a misplaced call once, the entire Eastern Seaboard would be an irradiated zombie-plagued wasteland.

But not today. The world could save itself. She was entitled to some me time.

The phone dinged as it received a text.

"Maybe you should leave that home this weekend," said Tia.

Connie, despite herself, glanced at the text.

We need to talk-Bonita

"Anybody you know?" asked Tia.

"Nobody important." Connie silenced the phone and tossed it on the bed. "Do you want to grab some lunch?"

The cell jumped into the air, spinning like a top. An electrical crackle filled the air. The phone exploded in a shower of sparks as Bonita Alvarado materialized in insectoid form. Her arrival was off by a few feet, and Bonita fell onto the bed. Her feet slipped with the blanket, and she tumbled to the floor with a sharp chirp.

"I'm not interested, Bonita," said Connie.

"Friend of yours?" asked Tia.

"I wouldn't say friend. Bonita was our old schoolteacher who was really part of a grand conspiracy to manipulate my life. She's also a shapeshifting alien from an ancient progenitor race."

"I thought she looked familiar."

From the other side of the bed, a long, thin exoskeletal arm reached up, and Bonita pulled herself to her feet. Her large black eyes blinked as she hacked and retched. "Goddamn digital teleport. You'd think someone would have perfected the technology by now."

"You owe me a new phone," said Connie.

Bonita straightened and dusted herself off. Her antennae twitched. She transformed into a shorter, Latina woman.

"Mrs. Alvarado?" asked Tia.

"Hello, Tia. Good to see you again. I hope I didn't freak you out."

Tia said, "I've seen weirder things."

"You must hear me out, Connie," said Bonita.

"I'm taking the weekend off. Look me up Monday," said Connie.

"No, I'm not here to ask for your help. Or your forgiveness. I'm here to help you." She squeaked shrilly. "Could I trouble you for a glass of water? Getting beamed across the galaxy through primitive receptive devices has left my throat dry."

Bonita drank three tall glasses of water, one right after the other, and wiped her mouth. After, they adjourned to the living room to talk.

"You can beam out of here." Connie took Bonita by the arm. "Or I'll beam you out of here myself."

In a blink, Bonita transformed into a nine-foot-tall giant

vaguely humanoid beetle. She lifted her arm, and Connie, still holding onto it, was hoisted off the floor.

"I'll leave after you listen to me." Bonita's voice remained the same.

Connie gazed into Bonita's dozen eyes. It was hard to gauge sincerity in the shiny green disks, but if Bonita was going to be difficult about this, it would probably just be easier to hear her out.

The wall burst as Luke and Vance's boxy security robot smashed its way into the condo. It tromped forward, beeping, its buzz saw spinning. Luke and Vance, in battlesuits, came rushing in behind it.

"Don't worry, Connie! We've got your back!" shouted Luke.

They leveled their blasters at Bonita. "Drop the human!" said Vance.

Connie let go of Bonita's arm and held up her hands. "Guys, what the hell are you doing?"

"We detected an intergalactic matter transmission from across the hall, and we're here to rescue you."

"Aw, that's kind of sweet of them," said Tia.

"Guys, you can't come busting in every time something weird happens," said Connie.

"You don't need us to rescue you?" asked Luke.

"What I need is for you to stop smashing my wall the second you get jumpy. There's a door right there."

The security robot's saw arm slowed to an awkward halt,

and it clicked its pincer arms with a fair bit of shame.

"We'll pay for the damage," said Vance.

Bonita changed back into her human form and waved a device over the hole. The pieces of wall reformed. "Temporal recursivator. Great for all those little messes around the house."

Luke, Vance, and their security robot left through the door this time.

"You've got five minutes," said Connie to Bonita.

Bonita said, "It's about the caretaker spell you host. We've been monitoring it, and we've come across some troubling readings."

"Who has been monitoring it?" asked Connie.

"I'd rather not get into that just yet. It's not important. I can only promise you that our motives are not nefarious. After you destroyed the Engine and ensured free will remains in the universe—"

"We," said Tia.

"What?"

"After *we* destroyed the Engine." Tia pointed to herself and Connie. "We were both there."

"Yes, I'm sure your contribution was very important," Bonita said in an offhand manner. "That's not relevant. We're talking about forces beyond your—"

"I pushed the self-destruct button," said Tia.

"Good for you," said Bonita flatly.

"I'm just saying that was kind of a big thing."

"Do you mind? I'm here to explain aspects of reality your

species has yet to even detect. I'd like to stick to the subject."

"Sorry. Go on."

"The thing I need you to understand about the spell or destiny or whatever else someone wants to call it that influences your life is that it isn't really any of those things. Those are just labels we use for convenience. No one knows how the thing works, what it wants, who made it, and for what purpose. Or if it was even made at all. Perhaps it's simply something that exists. The only thing we know for certain is that it empowers those who host it, placing them at the center of important events. How the host deals with those events is up to them. Not every host has been as benevolent as our Constance here.

"That was a long time ago. Almost before the records of my own race. But there are whispers of a terrible savage age before the caretaker role was finally properly harnessed for the greater good of the universe."

"*Greater good* by whose definition?" asked Connie.

"Whether you approve or not, the system worked. Hundreds of interlocking conspiracies, appearing and disappearing throughout the eons, each of them convinced they control the fate of the most important person in the universe. A delicate system of checks and balances, but one in the end that makes sure that whoever that person is, they aren't a megalomaniacal fiend."

"You flatter me."

"Imagine it, Connie. Imagine someone like you, but not you. Someone who finds themselves steadily nudging the line between triumph and tragedy as they wish. Imagine if that person didn't care. Worse, imagine if they sought to use that power for their own gain."

"And how would they do that?" asked Tia. "How does being the person who saves the day allow someone to be evil?"

"That's just it. We call it the caretaker role, but it's more versatile than that. Life is a complex equation, beyond anyone's ability to understand, but one thing that can make all the difference is a little luck at just the right moment. That's what the caretaker destiny does. It gives its bearer that slight advantage. It gives them the power to save or destroy.

"Picture yourself, Connie. Now picture yourself devoted to enslaving the universe. With everything you've done, can you say it's impossible?"

"An evil version of myself did conquer the Earth on the other side of the sun," said Connie.

"Evil Connie," agreed Tia. "That is a scary thought."

Automatica, robot bride of Doctor Malady, smashed her way through the wall.

"Have no fear, Constance," said Doctor Malady. "We have detected the unauthorized matter transmission and are here to help."

Connie put her face in her hands. "There's a goddamn door."

Explanations were offered to Doctor Malady and his robot bride. Bonita fixed the wall again, though she warned that using the recursivator too often might lead to minor disruptions to the space-time continuum. Nothing earth-shattering, but a small thing like Connie suddenly retroactively owning a cat or a different color paint in the condo.

"We've always assumed the caretaker destiny was indestructible, but we think something's gone wrong with it," said Bonita. "We don't know if it's because you are the first person to ever have the spell removed and then reclaim part of it. We don't know if it has to do with the part of it that was lost when you destroyed the Engine. It might just be natural wear and tear. But for whatever reason, it's unraveling, falling apart."

"Connie's going to become normal again?" asked Tia.

"She might, if she doesn't die in the process," said Bonita. "The function of the caretaker mantle is the manipulation of probability itself. It's why Connie finds herself in such unlikely situations. It's also what gives her that extra bit of luck when she needs it."

Connie said, "Hold on. I'm not just lucky. I'm good at what I do."

"Yes, you are, but with so many close calls and improbable escapes, you must have suspected that there were forces granting you an advantage when you most needed it. It's not all luck, but you must admit that throughout your adventures, fortune kept you alive with fair reliability."

Connie had never been fond of the idea of luck. Taken to its extreme, it made every action irrelevant.

"This isn't about your ego," said Bonita. "The caretaker destiny is part of who you are, has been even before it manifested on your seventh birthday. You've come to expect a certain amount of probabilistic fudging in your favor. You probably don't even think about it."

Connie grunted her displeasure at the idea, not quite able to disagree.

"She's right," said Tia. "You take risks that would scare the piss out of ordinary people, and they usually pay off for you."

Connie folded her arms, pursed her lips, and grunted again.

"Connie, three days ago I watched you jump into a raging ocean full of sea monsters with nothing but a magic flute."

"I'm an excellent swimmer, and I can hold my breath for six minutes. So, it wasn't as dangerous as it looked."

Tia said, "You have the skills to reduce the risks, but they're still there. But you didn't hesitate. You just did it."

"The mantle doesn't guarantee success," said Bonita. "But it does mitigate the chances of failure. Its influence is forever part of how you operate, and that's how it's meant to be. But now it's dwindling. Fortune will be more fickle than before. Worse, we suspect that it might have a negative effect on your luck. Probability abhors a vacuum."

"Oh my god." Tia snapped her fingers. "That explains it!"

Connie snorted. "There's nothing to explain."

"Have there been signs?" asked Bonita, leaning forward.

"No," said Connie.

"Yes," said Tia. "She's just too stubborn to admit it."

Bonita paced the room and thought aloud. "Ideally, we'd simply extract the spell, but in its damaged state, any attempt could prove disastrous. We could end up destroying the spell itself, which could have incalculable ramifications on the universe."

Connie stood. "And who says I'd let you, anyway?"

"Wasn't it just a year ago you couldn't wait to be rid of it?" asked Bonita.

"Things change."

"We are not your enemy, Connie. We're not going to take it from you without permission."

"And that's why you won't tell me who *we* are."

"That's irrelevant. Can I borrow your phone?"

"You destroyed my phone," said Connie.

"Yours, then?" Bonita asked of Tia. "I promise it won't be damaged. It's only the arrival that tends to break the system."

Tia tossed Bonita her cell. "I need an upgrade, anyway."

"We can fix this, Connie," said Bonita. "We'll need some more time to figure it out. Until then, my advice is to avoid adventure. If you play it safe, you should be okay. Ignore the caretaker destiny, and it will likely return the favor. Push your luck, and things will go wrong, sooner rather than later."

"You don't have to worry," said Connie. "I'm taking the weekend off."

Bonita attached an oblong doodad to Tia's phone. It vibrated loud enough to be heard throughout the room. She started dialing. The area code for the other side of the galaxy was shorter than one might expect but still fairly long. "We will fix things, Connie. If you want to carry the destiny all the way to the end, we won't stand in your way. But those instincts that have served you so well, you have to ignore them for the time being. For your sake, and perhaps the universe itself."

She pressed SEND and disappeared in a crackle of electricity. The phone fell to the floor. Tia picked it up. She couldn't detach the alien doodad.

"What a load of bullshit," said Connie with a derisive chuckle. "The universe is out to get me? Can you believe that crap?"

"What?" Tia pivoted at various angles, checking to see if the doodad on her phone ruined the line of her pants. "How many warnings do you need?"

Connie opened her mouth, but Tia cut her off.

"And, yes, I know. There's always danger. But maybe things really are different now. Maybe just this once, a bit of caution isn't out of order. Remember how you said you run toward danger? This time, try not doing that. Just for a few days."

Connie tried placating Tia with a curt nod, but Tia wasn't fooled.

"Goddamn it, Connie. You don't have to be so goddamn stubborn all the time."

Connie sneered, not at Tia but at the universe. "If I'm afraid, I can't live my life."

"No one's asking you to be afraid," said Tia. "Just not reckless. There's a difference between the two. Most people know that. I don't know why we're arguing. You've already agreed to take a few days off. It's only your bullheaded resistance to doing the sensible thing that's pissing you off. Forget that. Enjoy a few days with Byron."

Connie smiled. "I can do that."

"I know you can."

Tia's cell rang. She struggled to pull it from her pocket.

"I need to speak with Connie," said Apollonia on the other end. "She's not answering her phone. Is she with you?"

"No, thanks," said Tia. "We're not interested right now." She disconnected.

"Now how about some lunch?" she asked Connie.

"Who was that?"

"Nobody important. I'm feeling burgers." Tia's cell started ringing. "Wrong number."

"You didn't look at it."

Tia glanced at the phone. "Yeah, wrong number." She ignored the call.

Connie held out her hand. "It's for me, isn't it?"

"What? No. It's just Hiro."

"I thought you said it was a wrong number."

The phone rang again. "It was a wrong number before. Now it's Hiro."

"You didn't even look at it."

Tia repressed a scowl. She wasn't a great liar. Connie didn't have to be a master detective to see through Tia's clumsy dishonesty. But Connie was a master detective, which just made it worse. But Tia kept trying via sheer stubbornness rather than any sensible reason.

"Ever since Hiro broke his leg, he's been acting like an invalid. He probably needs me to rush home to fluff his pillow or find the TV remote. It'll be good for him if I don't answer. Teach him some self-reliance."

The cell rang again. Tia turned her back to Connie as she answered it. "Stop being a big baby and take care of yourself. Stop calling me." She silenced the phone, disabled the vibrate function.

"Hiro's ring tone on your phone is 'Kung Fu Fighting,'" said Connie.

"I changed it. It was racist. And not even appropriately racist."

"I'm going to need to see that phone, Tia."

Tia stiffened defiantly. "No."

"No?"

"You heard me." Tia stomped her foot down because it felt appropriate, realizing immediately that it seemed like a child's futile defiance of authority. "No. It's my phone. If I don't want you to see it, I don't have to show it to you."

"I can always take it from you," said Connie.

Tia clutched the phone tighter.

"You could, but you won't."

Connie didn't move, didn't twitch. She only stood there, relaxed. Tia had once seen Connie, while sitting and without getting up, take out a sumo wrestler, so her posture didn't mean much.

Connie held up her hands, and Tia flinched. There were

dozens of ways for Tia to be incapacitated without hurting her. Some of them made the victim wake up more refreshed. There was a nerve pinch that put someone to sleep for thirty seconds and cured migraines and did wonders for lower-back pain.

"Fine. It's your phone," she said. "Let's get some lunch."

They walked to a nearby sidewalk café. While they waited for their food, they talked about nothing important. All the while, Tia's phone sat quietly in her pocket. Maybe getting calls. Maybe not. She didn't check.

"The call was for you," said Tia finally.

"No shit." Connie stirred the ice in her soda and smiled knowingly.

"I hate when you do that," said Tia.

"Do what?"

"Smile knowingly."

"Is that a thing I do?" asked Connie without dropping her smirk. "I had no idea."

"People who smirk come across as obnoxious."

Connie sipped her drink with a slight grin and a raised eyebrow. "Do tell."

"I'm trying to protect you, you idiot!" said Tia.

Their server, walking toward their table, abruptly changed direction and headed back to the kitchen.

"Oh, you're clever," said Tia. "Bringing me out in public so I won't make a scene. Well, I'll make a goddamn scene if I goddamn feel like it!"

She raised her voice. She didn't care.

"It's my job to look out for you. Not just my job. I'm your best friend. You heard what I heard. You can't adventure. All you need to do is take it easy for a few days. You've already made plans with Byron. What about him? He might have the patience of a saint, but it's not fair to him."

"No, it isn't." Connie's smile dropped.

"With everything you do, I get that you think you're invincible, but—"

"Tia, I'm not an idiot. I know it'll end one way or another, probably violently, but I also know that since weakening the spell or destiny or curse or whatever, I've had more choice in the matter. I can ignore adventure's call more than I could before, but it's still out there. It's still waiting. Sometimes, I can ignore it. Sometimes, I can't."

"And what makes you think you can't ignore this one?"

"I don't know. It's just an instinct. I can't quantify it."

The sudden steady thump of helicopter blades beat the air as the UH-1Y Venom descended.

"I just know."

The wind kicked up by the rotors tipped a few nearby tables, sent dishes and tablecloths flying. Connie, having heard the helicopter approaching a minute before, had the presence of mind to cover her salad with a spare plate. Tia saved her burger, but her fries were lost.

The copter set down in the middle of the street, between two cars, and a pair of agents in gray suits approached.

"Ms. Verity, we have a call for you." The agent reached

into his jacket pocket and held out a cell phone for her to take.

She didn't.

"You're my advisor here," said Connie to Tia. "Tell me. What do you think I should do?"

Tia relented with a wave of her hand as she ate the one fry she had managed to save.

Connie took the phone. "Please, state the nature of your emergency."

Apollonia spoke up from the other end of the line.

"Larry's missing."

19

The day was winding down when Wilcox stopped by Byron's office.

Wilcox never just stopped by. He might act as if he wanted to say hello or share the latest joke making the rounds around the floor. He might ask you about your problems, and he might listen just enough to fake interest if he ran into you at the break room later. "Hey, Steve, how are little Brenda's braces coming along?" "Oh, Vera, don't tell me Travis is still having trouble with his back." And you'd reply because it would be rude not to while staring into his vacant wide eyes, waiting for him to ask for his favor, sometimes reasonable, sometimes not.

Wilcox kept his feet in the hall while leaning forward, bracing himself on the doorjamb and knob. "Hey, Byron. That's a great tie, buddy."

Byron didn't glance up from his computer. "Thanks."

"I've always admired your style." Wilcox eased a foot into the room, as if testing for a pit trap.

Byron squinted at the screen, hoping to convey a sense of urgency and concentration. There were very few accounting emergencies, but Wilcox sometimes got the hint and went in search of easier prey.

He stepped in with his other foot. Once breaking the seal, he sauntered over to the chair across the desk and had a seat. "Hey, man, where do you get those shirts, anyway? I have to get the name of your tailor."

Byron, having failed to avoid this interaction through indifference, looked directly into Wilcox's eyes. It was another desperate tactic. Like a mouse staring into the eyes of a cobra, hoping to scare it away through sheer bravado.

"Sears," said Byron. "They have tables full of them. Ties, too. And pants. The whole ensemble."

Wilcox kept Byron's gaze, and in that primal moment, the mental struggle between the two men might have been the stuff of legends if anyone wrote legends about interoffice politics. Byron had fought this battle before, and this was always a risky tactic. If Wilcox was successfully repelled, he'd offer mumbled thoughts about the weather or sports or some other inanity before beating a hasty retreat. If it failed, it would only extend the conversation.

Wilcox grabbed a photo off Byron's desk and whistled. "Say, is this your girlfriend?"

"Yes." Byron's reply was curt, emotionless. The final gambit would be to answer all questions with only one word to avoid being lured into a conversation. It didn't work often, but desperate measures and all that.

"That's a pretty lady," said Wilcox.

"Thanks," said Byron with the cold response of a voice synthesizer simulating human speech but not giving a damn enough to really try.

"How'd she end up with a loser like you?" Wilcox chuckled with a smarmy grin. "Hey, I'm just kidding you, buddy. You know I love you, right? I always tell everybody. Byron's my guy. The guy I can always count on around here."

Byron replied with a nonspecific noise that he invented on the spot.

Wilcox asked, "She looks familiar. Is she famous or something?"

"Something."

"How's the live-in situation? Getting it regular now?" He stood, reached across the desk, and slapped Byron on the shoulder. "I'm just kidding you, buddy."

Byron admitted defeat. "Something I can do for you, Wilcox?"

"See? That's what I mean. You're a stand-up guy. Always ready to help out." He stood, repeated the entire routine just to slap Byron's shoulder again. "That's why you're my guy."

"What do you need?"

"I'm having some trouble with the Ramsey account. I was

hoping you'd stick around tonight and maybe help me sort it out."

"Can't do it," said Byron. "Connie and I are going out of town this weekend."

"I get it. I get it. Gotta keep the girlfriend happy, right? A little alone time. A little romance." He winked and then he winked again, in case Byron missed the first time. "But seriously, dude, it'll only be an hour or two. I swear."

"Can't do it," said Byron.

"Okay, I guess it isn't an emergency. We can always untangle the whole mess on Monday. I'll drop the files by your desk tonight so that when you come in Monday, fresh from your"— he paused, winked yet again, and made a kissy face—"alone time, you can just get right to it."

It was classic Wilcox maneuvering. He was okay at his job, but he was great at getting other people to do it. Byron couldn't recall agreeing to anything, but somehow, promises had been made. It was all lost in the fog of battle.

"Monday. Sure, whatever," said Byron, his will to fight fading. Anything to end this conversation.

Wilcox jumped to his feet and waltzed out the door. "That's a relief. Can't tell you how much better I feel knowing you're on the case. Later, buddy."

He snapped his fingers and made a clicking noise and bumped right into Connie.

"Oh, hey. Connie, right? Great to see you!" He gave her an unsolicited hug. "Take special care of my guy here, would you? Enjoy your"—wink—"alone time."

He walked away, off to hide in whatever hole he squirreled away in around forty-five minutes before quitting time to avoid getting any more work.

"Am I wrong or is that guy a real asshole?" she asked.

"You're not wrong. What's up?"

Connie entered the office, hands in pockets. "You're going to hate this."

Byron leaned forward. "Let me guess. Aliens are invading Greenland."

"Something like that." She crossed around the desk and hugged him from behind his chair, wrapping her arms around his shoulders. "I wouldn't if it wasn't an extra-big emergency."

"I know."

She kissed his head. "It's okay to be mad."

"I'm not mad, Connie." He turned the chair to face her and hugged her, resting his head on her chest while she stroked his hair. "It goes with the territory, right? We can always get away next weekend."

"Sure. Next weekend."

"You could've just called if it was an emergency."

"My phone was destroyed by a . . . Never mind. I would've, but since I was passing through the neighborhood, I thought I'd do the polite thing and tell you in person."

"Just passing through?" he asked.

She pointed up. "I've got a helicopter waiting for me on the roof."

"Of course you do."

She took his hands, and he stood. He wasn't upset. He really wasn't. He was annoyed, irked, irritated, but not angry. He didn't hide it. She would've seen through him if he had.

"I know I've been crazy busy lately," she said, "but once I get this wrapped up, things will be more manageable. I swear."

She kissed him, and he couldn't stay mad at her. Not that he had been mad. But she was a good person, out there saving the world. He couldn't even be irked with her.

"Sounds great," he said.

"Thanks, Byron. You're the best. Really."

He nodded. "I know. Now get out of here and go keep the universe from exploding. I'll be here when you get back."

Barely four seconds after she'd walked out of his office, Wilcox poked his head in.

"Trouble in paradise, buddy? My ex-wife kept making excuses to cancel plans on me. Turned out she was having an affair with our gardener. But I'm sure that's not happening to you. Forget I said anything."

"What do you want, Wilcox?"

Wilcox stepped into the office, carrying an armload of ledgers. "Couldn't help but overhear. So, if you're free, you'd be doing me a solid if you got these sorted out ASAP. Falcone has been riding my ass for a week about it."

He was about to throw the ledgers on the desk when Byron held up his hand.

"Do it yourself."

"But, Byron, buddy—"

"Do it yourself."

"Hey, I get it, dude. I do. You're pissed because your lady is blowing you off, but that's no reason to take it out on me."

Byron switched off his computer. "First of all, I love that lady. But you I barely tolerate. And maybe if you just did your fucking job instead of working so hard to avoid doing your fucking job, you wouldn't be so far behind."

Wilcox whimpered.

"The rest of us do our jobs," said Byron. "Even my girlfriend is off doing her job, even when it gets in the way of our relationship. But you, Wilcox, can't be bothered. You, Wilcox, are the special office exception. Nobody's allowed to say anything to Wilcox. Heaven forbid Wilcox do his goddamn job!"

Outside the office, the heads of various midlevel employees popped out of their cubicles.

Byron said, "So, do your job, buddy! Or don't do it, pal! Either way, I don't give a shit."

He got up and pushed his way past Wilcox, who dropped a few papers. When he bent to pick them up, more went spilling across the floor.

"I'm going home early!" shouted Byron to the office as he stabbed the elevator button.

It was a long eleven seconds before the doors finally opened. Another long four before they started to close.

"And I am not upset," he grunted to the empty elevator.

C onnie boarded the helicopter. From there, she and Tia
were flown to the airport, where they were ushered onto
an experimental supersonic jet. The total trip took only
an hour from leaving Byron's office to touching down and being
driven to Larry's last known location, a secret base hidden
outside Helena, Montana.

Tia only asked how Byron took the news once.

"He was fine with it," replied Connie while sipping a Coke
on the jet. "He gets how it is."

"Sure. He gets it," said Tia, but there was something in her
voice. A tone. A lilt. A cadence. Whatever it was, Connie
elected not to read anything into it.

"I can't just abandon Larry," said Connie.

"No, you can't." The *something* was now accompanied by
a sardonic eyebrow raise.

"This is life-and-death," said Connie.

"Yes, it is." Nothing accompanied the words. Nothing but a shrug.

"What about Hiro?" asked Connie. "Aren't you worried about him?"

"Hiro can take care of himself," said Tia.

Connie leaned forward. "Yeah, but what if something happens to you? Did you think about that?"

"Oh, sure. We've talked about it."

Connie had blundered into booby traps and ambushes before, but she was usually smart enough to not be caught completely unawares.

"Hiro knows sidekicking is dangerous," said Tia, "but going full-time was his suggestion in the first place. And it's not as if he's new to this lifestyle. Before he moved in, we set the ground rules."

"How practical." Connie noticed something in her voice. A tone. A lilt. A cadence. Whatever it was, she didn't like it.

"It helps to know where you stand," said Tia.

"He's still stealing," said Connie, and immediately felt bad about that.

"Well, no shit," said Tia.

"You know?"

"I'm not a moron. He's the world's greatest ninja-slash-thief. He steals. I willingly follow an adventurer into dangerous situations, and tacos make me gassy. Nobody's perfect."

Connie wished there was a window to gaze out of. Something to pretend to distract her.

Tia said, "If I don't make it back from one of these adventures, he's already agreed to mourn for two months before moving on."

"Two? It must be love."

"It's Hiro. I'll take it as a win."

Damned if Connie wouldn't too. Hiro wasn't a bad guy, but he always had himself in mind. As far as Connie knew, he'd never cheated on her. Betrayed her, yes, and left her in the lurch. But even at his worst, he'd never broken his word, never went back on a deal. Unless a significantly better deal came along. Somehow, it never seemed dishonest when he did it. Maybe because he was consistently upfront about it.

She'd been upfront with Byron. She'd never lied about how things worked. She might have omitted some things. She might not have mentioned the glorious death she was supposed to have or Bonita's warnings about waning luck. But those were all details. He didn't need to know everything.

Tia busied herself flipping through an inflight magazine.

"Oh, shut up," said Connie.

"I didn't say anything."

"Yeah, but you were thinking it."

"What I was thinking was how the hell does a cutting-edge supersonic aircraft not have a single magazine published within this decade?"

Connie let the subject drop, and Tia didn't press. They passed the rest of the flight in silence, reading dusty celebrity gossip and irrelevant fashion tips.

Once the aircraft set down, they were whisked away to the base, where they were greeted by Apollonia, who wasted no time escorting them to Larry's last known location. They passed through several security checkpoints, three blast doors, dozens of cameras, armed patrols, and a small army of flying monitor drones.

"How the hell did you lose him?" asked Connie.

"We don't know," said Apollonia.

"You have to have some idea."

"We've recorded no breaches. It's impossible for him to exit the compound without leaving some record. We know everything. We could tell you how many rats are in this facility right now."

"How many?" asked Tia.

Apollonia nodded to an administrative minion in a green jumpsuit.

"Four, ma'am. Although one of them is pregnant and about to give birth to eleven in two days," said the assistant.

"Wow. I thought you were exaggerating for effect," said Tia.

"No, ma'am. The rats currently have a nest in the heating system of subfloor B, where the males scavenge food from the garbage chutes. The female has fashioned a nest made of sixty percent newspaper scraps, thirteen percent foam insulation, with the remaining twenty-seven percent comprised of indiscriminate refuse. The female weighs somewhere between—"

"That's more than enough," said Apollonia. "As you can see, we run a very tight operation here."

"And yet you still lost him," said Connie. "Congratulations. Aren't you supposed to be his bodyguard?"

"Aren't you supposed to be his friend?" replied Apollonia coldly. "If you are so concerned about Lord Peril's safety, then where were you?"

"I thought you could handle keeping an eye on him. My mistake."

Apollonia stopped, whirled around, and glared down at Connie. "You can criticize or you can help us find him." She pointed toward a door. "This is his room. It's the last place anyone saw him."

"What am I supposed to be looking for?"

"You're the master detective." Apollonia pushed a button, and the door swished open. She folded her arms. "You tell us."

Larry's quarters were out of place among the sterile steel functionality of everywhere else. Framed posters of classic movies decorated the walls. Larry had always loved screwball comedies. Cary Grant and Irene Dunne had always been particular favorites. That hadn't changed over the years, apparently.

The living area was messier than she would've expected. Larry had always been a tidy guy, a habit he'd picked up from his mother, who had a pathological distaste for disorder. Lady Peril once executed a minion for failing to button his jumpsuit properly.

Connie pointed to a beer on the end table. "Have that analyzed."

"Already did, ma'am," said the clipboard minion. "Nothing

peculiar. Just beer. We returned it after analysis to help with your investigation. There is a margin of error of two milliliters, if that should matter."

They went to the sleeping area. The bed was unmade, but Connie was assured that Larry never made it. She picked up a framed photo of Larry, Connie, and Tia, barely twenty, taken inside Base-13, the secret outpost on the dark side of the moon. She handed the photo to Tia.

"I can't believe we were ever that young," said Tia. "Where does the time go?"

"It gets eaten by the chronovore," said Connie, "the giant maw that consumes old time to keep the universe running."

"You know what I mean."

"I know."

Connie took back the photo. They were just kids. It seemed like it would go on forever then, just like that. But it never did. Everything ended. She'd met more than one immortal who'd shared that truth. There was no such thing as forever. There were just the moments in time.

"Remember how pissed Lady Peril was when Larry helped us escape?" asked Tia.

Connie smiled. He'd always been a good kid. Considering his mother, that was saying something.

And now he was missing.

She set the photo down and studied the others on the wall. There was one of Lady Peril, a tall, thin, pale woman in a black lab coat standing beside her five-year-old son, glaring down at him disapprovingly, though she disapproved of most everything, so it didn't mean much. A smiling Larry held Lady Peril's hand, which she tolerated. A family portrait that summarized their relationship nicely.

There was a photo of Larry with Connie, taken as they hid out at a seedy hotel in Moscow. Another photo of Connie alone, her profile staring off into the distance, lit by the fading light of a dying neutron bomb in the horizon.

"There are a lot of photos of you," said Tia, waving at a few others.

"Not that many," replied Connie. "These are probably old, anyway."

"Actually, Lord Peril asked that these particular photos be placed at all his places of abode," said the clipboard minion.

"Thank you," said Connie through clenched teeth.

It didn't mean anything. They were only memories of the good ol' days. That's what she told herself.

"How do we know he wasn't just teleported out of here?" asked Tia. "It's not like that's outside the realm of possibility. Or disintegrated? Or fell into a wormhole?"

"Our analysis shows no sign of any of that," said the clipboard.

"You can scan for that?"

"Yes, ma'am. There are always traces left behind. A sweep showed the normal amount of lingering genetic particulate, no tachyon or other meta-particle readings, no residual waveform disturbances in the local space-time field. There's always the possibility we could've missed something, but statistically, if Lord Peril left this room, he did so via conventional methods."

"He walked," said Tia.

"Yes, ma'am."

"Or he was carried," said Connie. "But there's no sign of a struggle, and if he was subdued and taken against his will, they'd still have to get past security."

She sat on the bed, took in the room. It wasn't much. The furnishings were simple, and aside from the photos and posters, there wasn't much to make it a home. Barely a home away from home.

"Why is he in here?" she asked. "He is Mastermind of Siege Perilous. This can't be where he's supposed to be."

"Lady Peril's quarters were offered to him," said Apollonia. "He insisted he stay here."

"And that didn't strike you as suspicious?"

"It's Larry. He's not a traditional Mastermind, and I assumed he didn't want to mess anything up when Lady Peril . . ."

Apollonia's voice trailed off.

Connie completed the thought. "When Lady Peril returned."

Apollonia shrugged.

"Is she alive or dead?" asked Connie.

"Could anyone reasonably be expected to guess?" said Apollonia.

"So, you don't know?" asked Connie.

Apollonia said, "I can't answer that."

"So, you do know?" said Tia.

"Can we stick to Larry? Have you figured out what happened to him yet?"

Connie went to the bookshelf and ran her fingers along the spines. "It's not like it's a switch I can flip. I'm not some cartoon detective who says *Elementary* and then solves the whole thing."

She paused at a copy of *A Wrinkle in Time*. It'd been her favorite book for a long time, possibly because it seemed so easy to relate to as a kid.

She pulled a book from the shelf. It caught halfway with a soft click as the shelf swung aside to reveal a secret room.

"Well, shit." She shook her head. "That doesn't negate my point."

"That shouldn't be there," said clipboard.

The secret room was big enough for a person. A ladder leading upward. Connie knelt down and picked up a lake-monster magnet sitting on the floor. She pocketed the magnet before anyone else noticed. They climbed the ladder that led to a tunnel that zigzagged below the ground, exiting well away from the secret compound and prying eyes. Tire tracks behind a bush that led to the nearby road.

"Mystery solved."

"Someone sneaked into a secret tunnel that nobody knew was there, drugged Larry or something, and hauled him back out of that same tunnel?" said Tia. "Why would anyone do that?"

"They didn't," replied Connie. "Larry left on his own."

"Impossible," said Apollonia. "Lord Peril knows the importance of his work. He wouldn't abandon it."

Connie knew where all the evidence pointed, and until some new facts presented themselves, she didn't see any point in arguing.

"I don't know what you're upset about," said Connie. "With Larry jumping ship, you're free to go back to henchagenting for someone more to your liking."

Apollonia, surprisingly, did not look happy. She never looked happy, but she looked less happy than she ever had before. "The damned idiot should know better than to run off on his own. His mother is going to kill me," grumbled Apollonia. "If she's still alive," she added.

"Well, good luck with all that," said Connie.

"We're not going to help them find Larry?" asked Tia.

"Yes, you must have some unique insight into Larry's state of mind," said Apollonia.

Connie said, "I really don't know the guy that well. No idea where he'd go after this."

"Bull," said Apollonia. "You just don't want to help."

"No, I really don't." Connie balled her hands into fists. "And I don't have to. I promised to help Larry, not you. If Larry wants to be on his own, I'm going to respect that."

Apollonia raised a hand as if to poke a finger in Connie's chest. Tia stepped back, expecting it to come to blows any moment now, but Apollonia stopped short of the poke.

"Do you know how many people want Larry dead now? Are you willing to leave him out there unprotected?"

"His choice," replied Connie. "I've got a life of my own. Come on, Tia. We're leaving."

Apollonia stood in Connie's way.

"All right, here's the deal," said Connie. "As much as I'd love to shove those glasses down your throat, you're probably the only person in Siege Perilous who seems to have Larry's back. With all the resources at your disposal, you should be able to find him before anything bad happens. If you can't, then it's a good bet no one else will either, and I'm not about to screw up his clean getaway."

"You know where he is," said Apollonia.

Connie folded her arms and stared down the towering Amazon. "I can't answer that, but I sure as hell can kick your ass if you really need me to."

Scowling, Apollonia stepped aside and started issuing orders to the administrator. Connie and Tia walked away.

"But you do know where he is?" whispered Tia.

Connie pulled the lake-monster magnet from her pocket. "I might have an idea."

21

S tanding on Hiro's doorstep, Byron held up a pair of paper bags with a smiling cow on them. "I brought burgers."

Hiro gestured for Byron to come inside.

"I didn't know if you liked yours any special way," said Byron.

"Extra pickles, no mustard." Hiro grabbed a bag. "But I'll take it."

He loped across the room on a crutch and a broken leg. Somehow, he still moved more smoothly than Byron ever had in his life. Hiro sat on the sofa, rifled through the bag with his fully functioning arm, and ate a handful of fries.

"Grab a beer from the fridge, would you? And one for yourself while you're at it."

Byron found a pair of imported beers and sat in a recliner as Hiro peeled back the wrapper and took a bite. Smiling, he chewed.

"I know I'm supposed to be a sophisticated man of the world, but damn it, there's nothing like a good fast food burger."

Byron's burger sat unopened on his lap.

"Aren't you eating?" asked Hiro.

"Not really hungry." Byron set the burger on the coffee table.

Hiro nodded. "You look like a man with a lot on his mind. I was surprised when you called. Pleasantly surprised. How'd you get my number?"

"Tia gave it to me. In case of emergencies."

"And is this an emergency?" asked Hiro with a slight grin.

"I don't know. I just wanted to talk to somebody about this thing with me and Connie, and I figured you'd be the best guy for that."

Hiro's face dropped. "Why would you figure that?"

"I'm not an idiot. I know you and Connie have a history. She's never said so, but it's obvious by watching the two of you. And she changes the subject whenever you come up."

"Does she, now?" Hiro tossed a fry in the air and caught it in his mouth. "Am I the topic of conversation often?"

"So, you were a thing," asked Byron.

"If this comes up, I want you to tell Connie, for the record, that you figured it out all on your own, but yes, we were a thing. Several on-again, off-again things. More than just a thing, I'd like to think."

Byron said, "Isn't that a bit weird now that you're dating her best friend?"

"Sometimes, but whatever Connie and I had was a long time ago, before Tia. It does confuse things now and then. But I'd like to think we're mature enough to deal with it."

"You and Tia never fight about it?"

Hiro cracked open a beer and propped his broken leg on the chair. "You didn't come here to talk about my relationship with Tia."

"No, I didn't." Byron grabbed a knickknack off the end table and tossed it back and forth with nervous energy. "But if it's strange to talk to you about this—"

"It's not strange. Connie is an unusual woman. You're hoping I might offer some insight into her recent behavior."

Byron clutched the knickknack in tight fingers. It snapped in two. "Oh, shit. I'm sorry."

"Don't worry about it. Just a little souvenir I picked up at the British Museum."

Byron examined the broken image of Nekhbet, the vulture goddess. "You might be able to glue it back together."

"Hardly worth the trouble. It's not as if it's irreplaceable. There are at least six or seven left in the world."

"I could pay for it."

Hiro chuckled. "No, you couldn't, but these things happen. If there's one thing you learn in my profession, it's that people place way too much value on material objects. Not that I'm complaining. It's been a lucrative flaw to exploit. But back to Connie. I assume she's become distant, distracted of late?"

"Yes."

"Always away? Always finding excuses to run off and save the world?"

"Yes."

"Classic Connie. Could practically set your watch to it."

"Is that why things never worked out between you two?" asked Byron.

"First of all, what Connie and I had was different than what you and she have. Our relationship was daring escapades and thrilling exotic locations. I'm the greatest ninja-slash-thief in the world. You're . . . What are you again?"

Byron lowered his head and mumbled. "Accountant."

"Really?"

Hiro took a drink of beer and contemplated Byron.

"An accountant? Really?"

Hiro rubbed his chin as his brow wrinkled.

"You wouldn't happen to be an accountant for the mob or a shadow government agency?"

"No."

Hiro shrugged. "Takes all kinds, I suppose."

"This was a dumb idea."

"We don't know each other well, so I'll just apologize for being me. But I like you, and I do want to help. Drink your beer. We'll figure this out. So, what's happening?"

"It's like you said. It feels like Connie is finding excuses to not be around. I can't be certain. Her job has always made her schedule unpredictable."

Hiro said, "I had the same problem when I dated a ninja-slash-assassin. She'd disappear for weeks at a time, only to show up unannounced in the middle of night for a quickie. Then she started leaving stuff in my bathroom, toothbrush, curare extract, tampons. Poked myself in the ass sitting on her favorite yanmaodao, but heaven forbid we talk about what we're doing."

His face twisted in a mocking expression. "Why do you have to put a label on everything, Hiro?"

He downed his beer and, despite his broken leg, jumped off and over the couch to limp to the kitchen and grab a new one. He returned, grumbling.

"Sorry. This isn't about me. Go on."

"Maybe I'm being paranoid," said Byron.

"Maybe," agreed Hiro. "Except you're not. I've seen it. Hell, I've lived it, buddy. Do you want to know why Connie and I never worked?"

"We're talking about you again?"

"No, we're talking about me *and* Connie. If you ask Connie why it didn't work, she'll tell you it's because of my betrayals, but that's bullshit, just an excuse."

"I would imagine betrayals would usually be a deal-breaker," said Byron.

"Maybe in the circles of accountancy-slash-human resources manager, but not in our world. See, the thing that Connie never admits is that she always betrayed me first."

"That doesn't sound like Connie," said Byron.

Hiro shook his head. "Why? Just because she saves the day all the time? Just because I'm a thief? She's still human, even if she likes to ignore that fact now and then. But heaven forbid our little Connie ever take a moment to acknowledge her own failings. Oh, no, she's too busy keeping the universe from exploding, too busy being little miss amazing to ever reflect on her own mistakes."

He guzzled his beer and burped.

"You can't put her on a pedestal, Byron. That's no way to build a relationship."

"I don't do that." Byron considered it for a moment. "Do I?"

"How could you not? She's like Batman and Wonder Woman and MacGyver and a grown-up Nancy Drew who also knows karate and how to fly spaceships. And you're, my god, man, you're an accountant. Sorry to keep hitting that, but it's hard to get over."

"You're not really helping."

"Sorry. Sorry."

"How did Connie betray you?" asked Byron.

"How do you think? The same way she's acting with you. She always checked out emotionally long before my own betrayals."

"Didn't you leave her trapped in a death labyrinth twice?"

"Only once." Hiro waved his hand. "Oh, wait, wait. Does she call the Temple of Airmid a death labyrinth? It had maybe four or five decent booby traps at best. But that's just like Connie. Always pointing the finger at somebody else when it comes to relationship problems. And can you honestly say which is worse, emotional dishonesty or a spring-loaded guillotine?"

"The guillotine is worse," said Byron.

"Is it, though?"

"Yes, it is."

"But is it, though?" asked Hiro, leaving the question to hang in the air with all its uncertainty.

"Yes, it is," said Byron.

Hiro put his chin on his chest and chewed on his lip.

"Is it—"

"It's much worse," interrupted Byron.

"Forget the guillotine," said Hiro. "Forget the booby traps and the betrayals, justified or not. I like you, Byron, but if you want my honest opinion—"

"I don't think I want that anymore."

"If you want my honest opinion," continued Hiro, "then it isn't going to work between you. It's not your fault. You're a good guy, and it's obvious you care about Connie, and she cares about you. But at the end of the day, she's used to adventure, and, buddy, I know I'm not the guy to break this to you, but you aren't adventurous."

"She says that's one of the things she likes about me."

"You're a novelty. Once that wears off, what are you left with? What do you have in common? In another year, if she's still around, if you're both still trying your damnedest to make it work, and you're staring at each other across the dinner table, trying to feign a conversation, you'll realize that she's Connie. And you're an accountant."

Every counterpoint running through Byron's head came up hollow.

"Ah, shit," said Hiro. "I know that's harsh. But Connie isn't meant to have what you have to offer. My advice is just relax and enjoy the ride. There's an ancient ninja parable about a guy in a sinking boat surrounded by sharks. I don't remember it, but it fits your situation, I think. Are you going to eat that?"

He reached for Byron's burger, but Byron snatched it off the table. He wasn't hungry, but guys like Hiro, smooth and good-looking and confident, just thought they could have everything.

Byron could never be a guy like that. He could never be the guy Connie needed.

But he'd be damned if he let Hiro have this.

The burger had pickles.

He didn't like pickles.

"Something wrong, buddy?" asked Hiro.

Grumbling, Byron took another bite.

22

Decades before, Lake Lake Monster had been nothing more than an unremarkable body of water, just picturesque enough to encourage real estate developers to make it into a campground, complete with prefabricated log cabins and carefully calculated folksy-themed restaurants and shops.

Connie's family had vacationed there then, and by the end of the week, she had foiled a plot to drive down the property value by scaring away visitors with a mechanical lake creature. At the time, it'd made sense, though later, she would wonder why anyone capable of building a functional sea monster robot would waste time on real estate scams.

The lake was uncreatively renamed and turned into a different sort of tourist trap. The monster robot was repurposed, performing two shows a day, three on Saturdays. She hadn't kept up with the place over the years, but she was disappointed to see it financially floundering now.

The Lake Lake Monster lake monster's head sat in a display

case in the cabin rental office. It was a ghastly thing, a metal skull with a few bits of plastic flesh clinging to it. Its once-terrifying glowing crimson eyes, now just two lifeless orbs. Its jaw hung open, leaning to one side, like it was aghast with embarrassment to be seen this way.

The clerk caught Connie and Tia studying the artifact.

"You can touch it for ten bucks," he said. "We aren't supposed to allow that, but I won't tell if you don't."

"Thanks. We're good." Connie lowered her head on the off chance he might recognize the girl in the yellowing photographs as her. "Where's the rest of it?"

He sucked on a lollipop, flipping through a muscle car magazine. "I think it's out back somewhere, under a tarp. They tell me it broke down beyond repair ten years ago. Tried to keep the show going, but nobody was interested in a lake monster that could only swim in irregular circles."

"Shame. It was impressive," she said.

"That's what they say." He glanced up from his magazine, at Connie, at the photos in the case. He chewed on his lollipop and grunted. "So, do you want a cabin?"

"I might have a reservation."

"Well, I might be able to check that for you." He pushed the magazine aside and typed on the old keyboard. He had to smack the aging computer a couple of times to get it to turn on. "Name?"

"Constance Verity."

"Sounds familiar. Are you famous or something?"

"Or something," said Connie.

The green screen went black. He jammed a few keys persistently with his fingers and shook the monitor.

"Why would Larry come here?" asked Tia. "This place is a shithole."

The clerk paused in his battle with the computer.

"No offense," added Tia.

"None taken, miss. It isn't the Ritz, but the lake is nice, even without the monster show. Got some decent fishing."

He resumed his struggle.

Connie pointed to one of the photos. A familiar boy stood to one side.

"Is that Larry?" asked Tia.

Connie nodded. "Helped me catch a fake monster. Didn't have anything to do with Lady Peril. Just happened to be staying here at the same time." She held up the lake-monster magnet. "It was a clue only I'd figure out."

A portly older woman poked her head from the other room. "Just check the manual system." She paused on Connie's face. "You look familiar."

"I have one of those faces," said Connie.

The clerk grumbled as he reached under the desk and deposited a ledger with a heavy *thunk*. "Why the hell do we even have a computer if we have a manual system?"

"The march of progress?" said Tia.

He glared at her attempt at humor, ran his finger down the page.

"Here it is. Verity, Constance. Must be why I remembered your name."

"Must be," said Connie.

"Some of your party has already arrived."

He handed her a key and directed her to Cabin Six with a working fireplace and a good view of the water. Connie and Tia followed the trail.

In the light of day, Lake Lake Monster had its charms. The cabins themselves were falling apart. The picnic tables were all broken, and even Connie would've feared for her life using any of the rusted grills scattered throughout. But the woods themselves were lovely, and the afternoon sun reflected off the water in a cascade of shimmering blues.

"Is this a trap?" asked Tia. "Should we be on guard?"

"Why would you think that?" replied Connie. "Am I acting like it's a trap?"

"Waiting for you to act nervous is a waste of time."

"No, I don't think it's a trap."

"You don't think?"

They stepped onto the cabin's porch, and Connie knocked on the door. "I've been wrong before."

Tia stepped behind Connie as the door opened, but it was only Larry.

"That was faster than expected," he said. "I wasn't sure you'd remember."

"I remembered." She tossed him the lake-monster magnet. "Are you going to invite us in?"

He moved aside and gestured toward the sofa. "Please."

The cabin's interior was tastefully decorated in generic outdoorsy kitsch. Paintings of wilderness scenes decorated the walls. A stuffed deer head hung over the fireplace. A threadbare imitation bearskin rug and assembly-line "handmade" furniture rounded out the look. The place smelled faintly of mold and pot. Lots and lots of pot, infused throughout, a ghost of the general clientele.

"Can I get you anything?" he asked. "I've got some beers and stuff for sandwiches."

"You can tell us what's going on." Tia sat on the lumpy sofa, having to shift to find a spot with support that didn't have pointy springs poking her in the ass. "Why'd you leave?"

"It's complicated. Are you sure I can't get you anything?"

Connie went to the window and parted the curtain slightly. "Just answers, Larry."

He sat in a creaky rocking chair. "You weren't followed, were you?"

"I don't think so," said Connie.

"You don't *think* so? You don't know?"

She shut the soiled curtain. "If it was a successful tail, we wouldn't know, would we? But I'm fairly positive we weren't."

He leaned back in the poorly balanced chair, and it nearly toppled over. "Ah, screw it. Not like it matters. Not like any of it matters. I honestly don't know what I was thinking. Who the hell am I? Larry Peril, mastermind. It's a fucking joke."

"Where's this coming from?" asked Tia. "You seemed okay last time we saw you."

"I was faking it. I do that a lot. Mom taught me. Put up a brave front. That's what she always said. Actually, what she'd always say was 'You're a bitter disappointment to me, Larry, so please shut up and stay out of the way.'"

"She was a supervillain," said Connie.

"Yeah, well, she was still my mom, and she did the best job she could with me. Couldn't have been easy for her, but she tried. And all I ever did was let her down."

"You let her down because you're a good person," said Tia.

"No, I let her down because I wasn't any good at being an evil genius. Never had any aptitude for it. I'm not a commanding presence, a logistical genius, a master manipulator. I never was. Lord knows I tried. I really did. But I wasn't cut out for it."

"Why here, Larry?" asked Connie. "There were plenty of places from our past that you could've picked. Places nicer than this."

"I don't know. Maybe it's because it was where we first met. Thought it might be more memorable."

"That's not why," she said.

"You always did know me better than almost everyone. Even after all these years." He smiled. "I've been thinking about it, and the best times of my life were with you, Connie. Stupid, I know. They probably didn't mean the same thing to you. Why would they? You're always off doing amazing stuff, meeting amazing people. The only thing special about me is Mom. I've always been in her shadow. Admit it. If I wasn't Larry Peril, you'd probably not even remember my name."

He scraped paint off the armrest with his fingernail.

"When Mom died, if she died, I wasn't interested in taking her place. Then I thought I might be able to do some good. And have an excuse to see you again."

He looked away, blushing.

"You could've just called."

"I know, but I thought if you saw me doing something extraordinary . . ." He glanced at Tia. "Never mind what I thought."

"Hey, I saw some cool knickknacks at the gift shop," said Tia. "I'll just pop out and take another look."

"Yeah, you do that," said Connie.

Tia grabbed a beer and headed out, and Connie had a seat across from Larry.

"I'm flattered, Larry, but I'm in a relationship."

"I know. I knew before I contacted you. I'm not a great mastermind, but I did some checking. This Byron guy, he's nothing special. And I thought if you could go for a guy like that, maybe you could go for me."

"Byron is special," she said. "He's a good guy."

"I'm a good guy."

"Larry—"

"It's not that crazy. We have a history, at least."

"Larry—"

He jumped out of his chair and poked the logs in the fireplace, even though there was no fire. "And how long do you think you'll be able to juggle your relationship and your adventures? He's bound to get sick of it sooner or later."

"Don't make this about Byron. Or me. It's about you. Are you seriously nursing a twenty-year-old crush? We were just kids."

"Oh, god. It's pathetic, isn't it? I'm pathetic."

"I never said that."

"But it is." He kicked a log and cursed as he bruised his toe. "Shit, it sounds so fucking stupid when I say it out loud. Putting my life at risk to impress some old flame. I can hear Mom now. *Nice job, Larry. You have the resources and power to do anything, and you chose to woo my greatest foe.*"

"I wasn't her greatest foe," said Connie.

"You were up there. She really hated you, but she respected you. She never respected me." He limped over to the couch and sat beside her. "I'm a joke. And not even a funny one."

She considered her next move carefully, as if defusing a bomb. She put her hand on his shoulder.

"Larry, you were raised by a supervillain. That comes with some baggage. Not becoming a megalomaniacal madman is a triumph in itself."

"You're just saying that."

"No, I mean it. You can say it was lack of aptitude, but there's more to that. I've run across plenty of lousy masterminds. There was this one guy who wanted to crash the moon into the Earth. And when I asked him how he planned on achieving world domination like that, he had to finally admit he didn't know. It was just the first thing that came to his mind when his scientists invented a gravity ray."

He laughed. "That's pretty stupid."

"Or this other idiot. He wanted to melt the polar ice caps, but his secret base was built right on the coast. We're ankle-deep in water, and he's screaming at his engineers about waterproofing."

They chuckled.

"You can claim it's a lack of aptitude, but you had the resources and background for it. You didn't take it up, and that's a good thing. It says you're a good guy."

"Yeah. Maybe." Larry took her hand. "Connie, if things had been different, do you think we could've been something?"

"We were kids," she said. "When does that ever work out? But who knows? If there's one thing I've learned, it's that anything's possible."

She couldn't decide if that was true or not, but it didn't matter. She said it to make him feel better.

"What are you going to do now?" she asked.

"I don't know. What do you think I should do?"

"Oh, no. You don't want to take life advice from me. We can head back to Siege Perilous and continue what you started. Or I can walk away, and you can stay hidden. It's your call."

He lay back, put his feet on the coffee table. "If I go back, I'm destroying my mother's legacy. If I walk away, I'm leaving it in the hands of nefarious individuals who will use it for evil."

"That doesn't have to be your problem."

"But it is. Doing nothing is the same as allowing it to happen." He covered his face with his hands. "I guess the only way to get out of her shadow is to follow it through. Funny thing, I can't shake the feeling that this is all part of some master plan, that she faked her death and I'm playing right into her hands. I don't know how dismantling Siege would do that, but I never could predict her plans."

"She was one of the best," admitted Connie. "And one of the worst."

"But you always managed to stop her," said Larry with a smile. "It's why I called you. Well, one of the reasons."

"I've got your back, Larry."

He went to pack, and she walked out on the porch, where Tia was standing by the lake, waiting for the conversation to end.

"How'd it go?" Tia asked.

"Good. We're taking him back."

"Cool, but that wasn't what I was asking."

Connie grabbed a stone and sent it skipping across the water. "We straightened it out."

"That's good." Tia threw a stone of her own. It landed in the lake with a loud *plunk*.

"You can say *I told you so*," said Connie, "about Larry."

"Wouldn't dream of it," said Tia.

Connie threw another stone. This one bounced across the water to land on the other side of the lake.

Tia managed to get a single skip out of her next toss. "You don't have to be great at everything."

"It's all in the wrist," replied Connie.

Tia said, "Poor guy. Guess having an evil genius for a mom can really screw with your head. But I suppose we all have to deal with our parents' efforts one way or another. I'm still waging a brussels-sprout war with mine from when I was five. Every Thanksgiving, there's a big plate of them and an expectant look from my mother. And every year, we have the same stupid argument about it."

Most of Connie's childhood had been off adventuring, far from parental influence, but she still compulsively made her bed, a habit drilled into her by her mother. And she couldn't throw away pennies because of her father. She'd carried fifty-eight cents halfway across the galaxy once, which worked out in the end when she found the blueprints for the cosmic decimator station array in a universal vending machine on Betelgeuse 7. She'd never gotten around to thanking him for helping her save seven inhabited worlds. She'd have to remember next time they had lunch.

"Larry isn't wrong," said Tia. "On paper, you two have a lot more in common than you and Byron."

"That's why it would never work," said Connie. "I get in enough trouble as it is without having a sinister mastermind as a mother-in-law. It would make for some awkward holidays. *Sorry about smashing your plans for world domination, Ms. Peril. Pass the potatoes, please.*"

"At least nothing dangerous happened this time. We don't have to worry about you straining your luck."

"I wouldn't say that just yet."

A shadow moved in the nearby trees. Two more skulked from the woods on the opposite of the cabin. Connie kept them in her peripheral vision. Tia couldn't see them, but she knew that look on Connie's face.

"How many?" asked Tia.

"At least three. Probably more."

Tia had enough experience to act casual. She threw another rock. "Three what?"

"I can't get a good look, but their tactics are standard special ops. Soldiers of some sort, moving into position before striking. I'd say we have a few minutes before things go down."

"Do we have a plan?"

"Working on it."

They walked inside as nonchalantly as possible. Tia resisted the urge to cast a glance around. She wouldn't have seen them.

Larry stood by the fireplace. The deer head had slid aside to reveal a monitor with a virtual map of the area surrounding the cabin. Red dots closed in.

"We might have a problem," said Larry.

"What is that?" asked Tia.

"I might have taken some precautions." He pushed the coffee table aside and lifted the bearskin rug. From there, he removed a secret panel and typed in a code on a hidden keypad. A rack of high-tech tools rose up from the floor.

"And you said you were no good as a mastermind," said Connie, looking through the weapons.

"I am my mother's son."

"Wait a minute," said Tia. "We don't know if they're bad guys. I mean, Siege Perilous is full of bad guys, but those bad guys are on your side. Some of them. How do we know these guys aren't just here to take you back home?"

"Then why are they sneaking around?" asked Larry.

"They might think we're bad guys. They could be under the impression this is a rescue mission. Damn, this is confusing."

Connie took a misshapen weapon from the rack. "Where did you get a Rigellian stun rifle?"

Larry shrugged. "Does it matter? We could never figure out how to turn it on."

She pushed a series of buttons on the device, and it hummed to life. "This should work."

"You didn't answer my question," said Tia. "How do we know they're hostile?"

"We don't," said Connie. "We're going to play it safe and assume so. You two stay here. I'll go take them out. We'll sort this mess out later."

"Connie, you can't go out there," said Tia.

"It's just a few commandoes."

Connie sounded as if she were talking about a spot of inconvenient weather. Under normal circumstances, she probably would've been right.

"Nine." Larry pointed to the advancing blips on the monitor. "Also, looks like a BX12 power-armor operator."

"Ninja or rhino class?" asked Connie.

"Ninja."

"Don't worry. I've got this."

She attempted to slip out a window, but Tia grabbed Connie by the shirt, pulling her back in.

"Are you serious?" asked Tia. "After Bonita's warning, after all the stuff that's happened to you over the last few days, you're doing this?"

"It's not that dangerous," said Connie.

Tia didn't let go. "I can't let you go out there."

"You can't *let* me? I don't recall asking you for permission."

"Is something wrong?" asked Larry. "Estimating thirty seconds until enemy engagement."

The blips on the monitor had spread around the cabin, with the big red blip representing the power armor bringing up the rear.

"The only way I'm letting go is if you make me," said Tia. "And the only way—"

Tia didn't see it happen, but somehow, she was thrown across the room to land gently on the sofa. It might not have hurt at all aside from a few springs poking her here and there. Cursing, she jumped to her feet, but Connie was already out the window, followed by the sound of gunfire and stun-rifle discharges.

The monitor played out the battle as the many blips shifted and zipped around from a bird's eye view. It was like a video game but with her friend's life at stake. She punched the sofa, just to hit something. The soft *thump* was unsatisfying.

"She's going to get herself killed."

Larry pushed another secret button and the couch tipped over as a cylinder extended from the floor. It held a black-and-silver suit of power armor. It stood nine feet tall. Mini-missile racks sat on its shoulders and chain guns were mounted on its gauntlets. The helmet was fashioned in the likeness of a grinning demon with oversized tusks and two horns spiraling from the sides.

"Not because of me, she won't."

He put his hand on the suit's chest, and with a beep, it opened up so he could step inside.

"Why do you have that?" asked Tia.

"Mom gave it to me. It's custom. She always said I could never defend myself, so she'd have to do it for me."

Outside, a grenade exploded close enough to rattle the windows.

"Do you even know how to use that thing?" she asked.

"I've logged about a dozen simulator hours."

She helped him into the armor. It shut him inside with a loud hiss as everything locked into place. He took one tentative step forward on its giant metal boots, clomping with the force of a minor earth tremor. He tilted forward, and she jumped back to avoid being crushed if he toppled over.

"Maybe you shouldn't," she said. "You're likely to be a liability to Connie in that thing."

His normal voice spat out of the monstrous skull. "I have it under control." He moved his arms, knocking over a lamp with the barrel of his chain gun. "And I'm through relying on other people to protect me."

On the monitor, the green dot that was Connie wove between the red dots of the enemy. Gunfire filled the air, and Tia waited for Connie's blip to stop moving. Instead, it ran up to a red dot and did something that caused the red dot to blink off.

But the blinking red blip of the enemy power armor was closing in.

"Just promise me you'll be careful," said Tia.

He turned, nearly knocking her over. He clomped forward on uneasy legs, like a toddler who had only learned the art of walking a few days before. He tried to go around the rocking chair but ended up smashing it to pieces with a swing of his arm.

"I might be out of practice."

Outside, something exploded. Most of the enemy blips were out of commission, but the big red one was following Connie, who weaved in serpentine fashion as machine gun fire echoed through the forest.

"Screw it."

Larry moved forward, plowing through the cabin wall without slowing. Tia stood at the hole he'd left, watching as he tromped his way into the woods. He uprooted a few trees unfortunate enough to get in his way.

She'd learned to stay out of the way when things went down. She'd spent years mastering keeping her head down while Connie saved the day. Sometimes Tia helped, but mostly she survived on the sidelines.

She was a sidekick now. Officially. And Connie was living on borrowed luck. Tia shouldn't just wait this one out.

There was a weird screeching sound, like a buzz saw made out of shrieking demons, followed by a bright silent flash. A plume of red flame shot into the sky over the tree line, and clouds of black smoke drifted toward the cabin.

Tia glanced back at the monitor. Whatever was happening out there had blown the sensor grid. It was only a blank, blue screen.

She went to the rack and grabbed an AK-47. Or maybe it was some other brand of assault rifle. She didn't know. Connie would've known, would've known how to load it, how to fire effectively. She didn't like guns, but she knew how to use the damned things. Tia had some time at the firing range. As Connie's friend, it was common sense, but it'd been a few years.

She put it aside because common sense also said she'd be a liability. She picked out an automatic pistol. A Glock or a Smith & Wesson or something. Damn it, she needed to learn more about guns.

Outside, the sharp *zap* of lasers and weird science-fiction weapons pierced the air. She wouldn't be much good against anything going out there. She'd only shoot herself. Or worse, she'd shoot Connie. There was a perfect irony to that, and if luck was out to get Connie, Tia walking around with a gun was probably tempting fate.

Power armor smashed through the wall. It wasn't Larry's but the BX12 Ninja. It was grossly misnamed, large and blocky, like a sumo wrestler with snapping pincer claws and an improbable number of guns mounted on its back, shoulders, and chest.

Larry charged in and unleashed a haymaker that sent the Ninja flying through the chimney and back outside. He tromped after his opponent, and the cabin rattled with the clang of clashing steel. The roof creaked, and Tia picked her way through the debris toward the door, just in case the roof fell in.

Then the roof fell in.

She wasn't crushed, but she couldn't move. Bits of light streamed through the rubble. She could only wait for rescue in the dark, dusty hole. She'd never felt more useless. It was only a few minutes before Connie threw aside a piece of roof.

"Are you okay?"

"I've been better," replied Tia, more annoyed than anything. "How's Larry?"

"Still fighting."

A series of small explosions raised dust, and Tia sneezed.

Connie started clearing the rubble.

"Don't worry about me," said Tia. "You have to help Larry."

"Larry can hold out for a minute or two without me," said Connie.

With some effort and some makeshift levers, Tia was extracted from the wreckage. Connie pulled her free.

"Anything broken?" asked Connie.

"Don't think so."

"You might have internal injuries. We'll have to get you looked at."

A blast sent nearby trees flying as the Ninja battlesuit came crashing out of the forest, shattering a crumbling picnic table. The power suit's dented armor sparked at the joints. The operator struggled to stand, flailing ineffectively.

Larry stepped from the woods. His suit had its share of dings but it was mobile. The left leg was sticking, and he limped forward.

He said, "Oh, jeez, Tia. I'm sorry. I didn't even think—"

"It's fine," said Tia. "I'm fine. Is that the last of them?"

He swept the area with the sophisticated sensor array built into his power armor. "I think so."

"Are we still certain these were bad guys we're dealing with?" asked Tia.

The Ninja power armor managed to rise to his feet. He flew forward via rocketpack toward Connie.

Tia pushed Connie out of the way.

Larry pushed Tia out of the way.

The Ninja tackled Larry, roaring across the lake. They skipped like stones across the water as they struggled. Larry fired his own jump jets and the pair flew high into the sky. They spiraled in midair combat for a few seconds.

And then they exploded.

"Oh shit," whispered Tia. "Oh shit."

The flaming debris of the power armors arced through the blue sky like a terrible firework. Connie and Tia ran toward the lake, like there was anything they could do. "Look out!" shouted Tia, although she was already pushing Connie to the ground, more from reflex than anything. Larry's demon helmet rocketed like a cannonball and bounced off the ground at their feet, barely missing their heads, embedding itself in a tree trunk.

Larry and the Ninja hit the water with a splash.

"Oh shit," said Tia. She was aware she was repeating herself, but it was the only thing that came to mind.

Connie jumped in the lake. She swam to the center and dove beneath the depths. Tia could only watch from the shore.

A pair of soldiers came up behind her. They pointed their weapons at her, and she raised her hands. This was the part where the bad guys took her hostage. Or maybe Connie would rescue her before that happened.

The soldiers lowered their guns, nodded to one another, and retreated into the forest.

C onnie spent half an hour dredging the lake for any signs
of Larry. She only found pieces of his battlesuit.

Agent Ellington was called, and she brought in divers
to carry on the search. Connie put on a wetsuit herself and
joined them.

The sun had set hours earlier. Tia and Ellington stood on
the shore, watching the boat spotlights dance across the water.

"We don't have a lot on this Larry Peril," said Ellington.
"Last we'd heard, he'd given up on being an evil mastermind."

"He had," replied Tia. "And he wasn't evil."

"Then what the hell happened here?"

"He was trying to reform Siege Perilous. Guess not everyone
liked the idea."

An agent approached. "Our divers haven't found anything
yet, ma'am. The explosion might have disintegrated the bodies
beyond recovery."

"Pack it up," said Ellington.

"You aren't going to keep looking?" asked Tia.

"What for? It's not important enough to waste more resources on."

"He was our friend."

Ellington nodded to the agent, who walked away.

"My condolences, but this is done. I'm not Verity's personal government valet. Don't see a reason to spend taxpayer money recovering a finger or two. If Connie wants to keep looking, she can hold on to the wetsuit and diving gear. I'll send along a bill."

Ellington and her agents left. Tia sat on the shore, staring across the lonely lake lit by the stars and moon, waiting for Connie. It was around nine thirty that she emerged from the water. Exhausted, she dragged herself up the shore and sat beside Tia.

"Where's your air tank?" asked Tia.

"Ran empty hours ago," said Connie. "I ditched it. It was only slowing me down."

"Find anything?" It was a dumb question, but Tia asked it anyway.

"Just pieces of armor."

"That's good, right?" asked Tia. "Larry was a mastermind, right? No body means he might not be dead. Right? Like his mom?"

Connie rested her arms across her knees, her head against her arms. "Larry wasn't much of a mastermind."

"But he could've faked his death."

"Why would he do that?"

"Maybe he was in over his head and thought this was the best way to get out from under it."

"Maybe. Or maybe he was in over his head and paid the price for it."

Tia put her arm around Connie. "It's not your fault."

"I was right here, and I didn't save him."

"You can't save everyone."

"I was right here."

"Connie—"

"Screw this. Let's go home."

"What about Larry?"

"What about him? He's either dead or he's not. Either way, it's not our problem anymore."

"But Siege Perilous—"

"Don't give a damn."

Connie removed her flippers and stood. Her body language was different. For the first time ever, Constance Verity looked defeated. Not simply tired or discouraged. Not disinterested in the good fight. Not annoyed by it. But beaten by it. As if the weight of every previous adventure was too much to bear.

"Let somebody else save the world. I just want some sleep." She trudged away.

Tia cast one glance at the lake before turning away and following.

24

The last time Connie remembered crying was when Frankenstein's creature had died in her arms. She'd been twenty-three.

She'd cried since from physical pain, but when it came to emotional turmoil, she made it a practice to shove that crap aside. She didn't have time for it.

She didn't cry as she shared the news with Byron, but her eyes watered a little. She wiped them. "He's dead. I screwed up, and now Larry's dead."

Byron hugged her. "I'm sorry, but I'm sure you did everything you could."

"No, I could've done more. I could've done something. The right thing. Whatever that was." She moved to the couch and sat, grabbing a throw pillow and smacking it with her fist. "Why don't I know what that is? I always know the right thing."

He sat beside her. "Connie, nobody expects you to be perfect."

"That's just it. I don't need to be perfect, Byron. But I need to be good enough, and I wasn't."

"You can't tell me you've saved everyone every time," he said.

"No, but I always felt like I did everything I could when I didn't. This time feels different."

"You knew Larry a long time, didn't you?" asked Byron.

She nodded. "We were close-ish once."

"It's only natural that it'd hit you harder than usual, then."

"That's just it. I've lost people before. People I was much closer to, that meant more to me. It might sound terrible to say, but . . ." She sighed. "Never mind."

He pulled her toward him and took her in his arms. "It's okay."

She nestled her head under his chin. "I think I'm done. The caretaker spell might be broken. It might disappear entirely."

"Which means?"

"Which means I could become ordinary."

"I don't think anyone who has done everything you've done could ever be ordinary."

"It could mean no more adventures."

"That's not so bad, is it? Wasn't it only a year ago that you wanted that?"

"I got over that. When the spell's influence diminished, I was grateful for the quiet it gave me. I love those moments, but I love saving the day. It's a chance to make the world a better place, and I'm good at it."

"Maybe you can't have your cake and eat it too."

Connie pushed away from him. "I'm Constance Verity. I can do that."

Byron looked away. "Uh-huh."

She said, "What does that mean?"

"Why does it have to mean anything?" he asked.

"That's a weird way to say that. It means that it does mean something."

Byron pondered whether they should have this conversation now. He decided they shouldn't but knew the time he'd spent pondering made it likely unavoidable.

"We can talk about it later."

It was, he realized, the exact wrong thing to say.

"So, there is something to talk about, then." She sounded accusatory, like a prosecutor getting a witness to bumble into a verbal trap.

"You're having a bad day," he said. "It's not important."

"Not important enough to talk about *now*," she said. "But important enough to talk about *eventually*."

"Goddamn it, Connie," he said. "You're like a dog with a bone. Can't you just let it go for a bit?"

A scowl passed over her face before softening. "You're right. I'm not in the mood for a fight, and I just want to not think about stuff for a while."

She moved closer, and her hand ran up his leg. He pulled her close and kissed her. She did that thing that she'd learned somewhere in her adventures (he didn't ask where) that drove him wild even though it had nothing to do with naughty bits and they were still both fully clothed.

She straddled him, unbuttoning his shirt. She needed this. Everything else could wait. No talking. No adventures. No thoughts about tomorrow.

He put his hand on her cheek, and she kissed his palm.

"It's going to be a fight, though?" she asked softly.

His hand moved down her neck and along her shoulder. "Not necessarily."

She rolled off him.

"You've just lost a friend," he said. "You're dealing with an identity crisis. We don't need to talk about this now. It's not fair to either of us."

She knew he was right, but she couldn't help herself. "What's wrong?" She wasn't happy about how annoyed she sounded.

"I'm just wondering how much you want to be here."

"I'm here," she said.

"Physically. But you're not really here. You're out there, somewhere." He waved in the general direction of the world. "Thinking about your next adventure."

"I just told you, there might not be any more adventures."

"So, I'm your consolation prize?" he asked. "You can't be off fighting spider soldiers at the center of the Earth, so you'll settle for this?"

"I never said anything about settling," she said.

"You didn't have to."

"Christ, don't tell me you're getting insecure on me. I love you, you stupid asshole."

He lowered his head. "I love you, too."

Connie wanted to let it go at that. She couldn't.

"I'm sorry if my mixed feelings about being the savior of the universe are screwing things up for you."

"Damn it, you're impossible to talk to sometimes. I need some air."

He left the condo. He didn't slam the door, at least.

She sulked for a few moments. He'd been right. She didn't need this. It was better for both of them if she let him go, giving them both time to cool off. And if he never came back, it might be better. Period.

She went to the window and waited for him to appear on the street below. He appeared, glanced up at her. She wanted to be angry at him, for him to be angry at her. He looked annoyed, sad, tired. But not angry.

She should've known the right thing to do. Why didn't she?

She opened the window and jumped out of it. An awning below broke the two-story fall, and she slid gracefully to the sidewalk.

"Just something I learned from a trapeze artist," she said with a playful smile.

He didn't smile back.

"Why are you here?" he asked.

"Because I love you."

"That's not an answer."

"It's not?"

"We're two fundamentally different people. What happens when the novelty wears off and we can't deny that any longer?"

"But you're the one who wanted this," she said.

"And you didn't?"

"Of course I did." She caught herself. "I do. Okay, I get it. Adventuring has been crazy lately, and maybe I let it get crazy because I wasn't sure how I felt about us. I've had some of the same doubts, even if I didn't admit it to myself until now. But, Byron, I might be an ordinary person soon. Then we won't have anything to fight over."

"That's just it," he said. "It's not about *ordinary* and *extraordinary*. It's about compatibility. If tomorrow, the adventures stopped, can you see yourself happy being with me?"

"Sure."

He held up his hand. "Don't just say it. Think about it. No adventures. Just you and me, doing regular stuff regular people do. Dinners and movies, watching TV together, maybe having kids. Do you even want kids?"

"Sure. Unless you don't want kids. I mean, it's no big deal either way."

He didn't reply. He looked tired. She only wanted to stop fighting.

"I don't know what you want to hear," she said.

"That's just it. I don't want you to tell me what you think I want to hear. I want you to tell me what you think."

"I think this is stupid. I have enough hassles without trying to manage a relationship."

It took her a moment to hear herself.

"God, Byron, I didn't mean that."

"Yes, you did, and it's good that it's out in the open. Like I said, we're just too different. You don't belong in my world, and I don't belong in yours. That's not because of some spell. It's who we are."

She wanted to argue. So many times in the past, she'd assumed things were ending between them. He was always the one who convinced her otherwise. Now that their roles were reversed, she couldn't find the right words. She'd stopped wars with diplomacy, but this wasn't a war. And it wasn't about finding a workable compromise. Sometimes, there wasn't one.

"So, are we done?" she asked. "Is that it?"

"I don't know. Maybe."

"Well, this has been a really shitty week," she said.

He laughed without humor. "Tell me about it."

Her cell rang. She answered, grateful for the distraction. She'd never wished so much for the world to be imperiled. Anything to take her mind off all this.

Tia's voice broke through with urgency. "Don't talk to Byron."

"Too late," said Connie.

"Shit."

Connie turned away from Byron. "Wait. How did you know?"

Hiro's distant voice mumbled indecipherably.

"Oh, she's going to figure it out eventually," Tia said to him.

Connie put a few more feet of sidewalk between her and Byron. "What the hell did he do?"

More of Hiro's mumbling.

"No, I'm not going to lie to her," said Tia. "It wouldn't work, anyway."

"What the hell did he do?" asked Connie, louder this time.

"He might have sabotaged your relationship," said Tia.

Hiro mumbled.

"*Accidentally* sabotaged," clarified Tia.

"I'm going to kill him," said Connie.

"He says he's really sorry."

"I'm going to fucking kill him."

"In his defense, he meant well," said Tia. "He's just a dumbass."

A dark calm fell over Connie. "You tell Hiro that he's a dead man, and I promise, it'll be an ugly death."

"You were right," said Tia to Hiro. "She's promising to kill you."

"Put him on the phone," said Connie.

"I would, but he's already disappeared. Probably halfway to the airport by now."

Connie mentally ran through a list of contacts that would enable her to track a wayward ninja across the globe. Hiro was the best. It'd take a long time. There'd be dead ends.

He'd make sure of that. And when she did find him, he'd probably give her the slip, but she could be patient. It wasn't like she'd have anything else to do now that neither Byron nor adventuring appeared to be part of her future. Having something to keep her busy sounded like a relief. She'd have to figure out what to do after she accomplished the task, but that was a ways off.

"I know he's your boyfriend, but—"

"No, he's earned it," said Tia. "You do what you have to do."

Connie's phone cut out as a low thrum vibrated the air. A shadow fell over the street as a high-tech aircraft hovered overhead. It was shaped not unlike a giant flying broadsword, and it bore the Siege Perilous logo on its underside.

"I am not in the mood for this!" shouted Connie as the craft descended.

It launched several drones from its top. They orbited her condo, creating a glowing blue forcefield around the entire building.

The aircraft hovered low over the street. It must've been powered by antigravity technology because she saw no engines. It had wings, but they were mostly there to give the resemblance of a hilt, and its tail was rudderless. The thrum was what clued her in. Antigravity drives always thrummed like that in an atmosphere.

She returned to Byron's side. "Don't worry. I'll handle this."

A ramp lowered, and two women stepped off it: Apollonia,

tall and dark with her black glasses, wearing her black suit, and looking very bored, and Lady Peril.

Some evil geniuses liked to taunt and cackle, viewing world domination as a cool idea, less interested in ruling the world than in dreaming up schemes to do so and getting the satisfaction of watching humanity quake in fear for a few hours every now and then.

Lady Peril wasn't that kind of evil genius.

She was nearly as tall as Apollonia and twice as humorless. She never smiled. She never laughed. For her, world domination was merely the inevitable result of her own innate superiority.

Her hair had some gray. There were a few more lines under her eyes, and a bend in her lips made her ever-present disapproving frown more disapproving than ever. She must've been pushing sixty-five at this point, but it didn't stop her from rocking that sleek white bodysuit and long black lab coat, a look that shouldn't have worked but did if you were a mastermind with the skills to back it up.

"You killed my son," she said.

Connie said, "That's how we're going to play it? Nobody's going to pretend they're shocked you're still alive?"

Lady Peril raised an eyebrow. Her eyebrows were perfectly shaped for raising. "Are you shocked?"

"No. Why would I be?"

"Then let's skip that, shall we? Instead, let's talk about my plans, which you, in your ever-predictable fashion, have screwed up once again. It was useful to me for certain people to think I was dead. Or to at least be uncertain if I was alive. And now you've forced me to reveal myself."

"Forced you? You're the self-professed genius who left her son in charge of an evil secret society. You're the one who sent goons with guns and power armor after him."

"That wasn't me," said Peril.

"It wasn't?"

"No, but rest assured whoever it was shall be dealt with accordingly."

"So, deal with them," said Connie. "I have my own problems to deal with."

Police sirens could be heard in the distance. Lady Peril remained unconcerned. "You must understand, Constance, that I was never particularly fond of Larry. He was, by any measure, a disappointment. Yet I could never deny a primal attachment to the boy. I knew that it was only a trick of nature, a survival instinct forged into the genetic code, a leftover from when such things mattered."

"This is some guy's mom?" asked Byron. "Poor kid."

"You have no idea," said Connie.

"Yes, do judge me by the outdated standards of foolish primitive cultures." Lady Peril turned her nose up at them and smoothed her coat. "I'll admit that motherhood was never my passion, though I do sometimes think that was my mistake. I shunted Larry's childhood off on robotic caregivers. They kept him alive and offered him stimulation, and I assumed he'd follow in my footsteps naturally. Alas, we know how that turned out. It might have been different had I taken a more direct hand in things. Larry's failings were perhaps a product of my own oversights."

"I think they have a Mother's Day card that says something like that," said Connie.

Lady Peril disapproved. She was always disapproving, but her tightened lips and narrowed eyes meant she especially disapproved.

"It was my assumption that Larry would take after me. It was my assumption that he could manage Siege Perilous for the short time I needed. And when Larry contacted you, it was my assumption that you could prevent any harm from coming to him."

"If you're blaming me," said Connie, "why aren't you blaming Apollonia? She was his official bodyguard."

Apollonia, blank-faced, step forward, but Lady Peril stopped her with a casually raised hand. "Apollonia and I will have that discussion at some point in the future, but she remains useful to me. You, however, do not. Under other circumstances, I'd be content to leave you alone. But these are not normal circumstances."

A police car came screaming on the scene. A drone hovered over the car and sliced through its engine block with a high-powered laser. The cops stepped out, guns drawn, but the drone blasted the weapons out of their hands and circled the helpless officers.

"Revenge, Peril?" asked Connie. "That's not like you."

"And yet here we are." Peril's face pinched so tight, it threatened to split in two and allow her skull to come out. "Damned genetic imperative."

She waved her hand, and Apollonia stepped forward.

"Now we fight. Finally." Connie adopted a fighting stance. "Fine with me. I've been having a lousy couple of days, and maybe kicking your ass will make me feel better."

She dashed forward, debating on going for a knockout roundhouse kick to Apollonia's head. It'd be a shame to end the fight so quickly, but Lady Peril couldn't be ignored for long. Three steps into the attack, Connie realized Apollonia wasn't making any move to defend herself. A moment later, a drone carved a line before Connie with a bright red laser, stopping her in her tracks.

The drones circled her, whirring menacingly, their weapons glowing for no other reason than to remind her of the threat.

"Pretty cowardly," said Connie. "Is this how you want it to go down?"

"No," said Apollonia, "but I'm only an employee."

She walked past Connie and grabbed Byron. He struggled, but she chopped him on a pressure point. He crumpled in her arms, and she threw him over her shoulder.

Connie moved to intercept. Drones fired at her feet, missing by scant inches.

"Your problem's with me, Peril. Leave him out of it. You want revenge. I'm right here."

Lady Peril said, "Pardon the cliché, but you have taken something precious from me. Now I shall return the favor."

"We're not even together anymore!" shouted Connie. "We just broke up, I think."

"More's the pity, then." Lady Peril ascended the ramp with Apollonia and Byron behind.

Connie had only moments to come up with a plan. She hastily calculated angles of trajectory, figuring the series of steps that could lead the drones to catch each other in the crossfire.

Another drone was almost within arm's reach. She could grab it, use it as a shield, use its lasers.

She could do something. She might not be the caretaker anymore, but there had to be something left in her. Some remnant of bravado, some spark of luck that'd turn things around.

The ramp started to close.

"Goddamn it." Connie bolted forward. It wasn't a plan. It wasn't anything but pure stupid desperation. The kind of stupid plan that shouldn't work but had gotten her out of tighter spots.

A drone grazed her calf. Another burned her shoulder. Neither blast was at full power, but they hurt like hell and broke her stride. She fell to her knees as the ramp sealed and the aircraft rose in the air. There was still time to do something.

The drones hovering over her suddenly shorted out and crashed to the ground. The forcefield around her condo building collapsed, and her neighbors rushed out. Duke Warlock and Nim helped her up.

"I was able to send out a focused EMP burst that shorted out the drones," said Doctor Malady. "Are you all right, Connie?"

"No."

The aircraft disappeared over the skyline, and there wasn't a damned thing she could do to stop it.

C onnie threw the pistol in her suitcase.

"A gun?" asked Tia. "That's not like you."

"I'm not like me lately," replied Connie.

"What about all that stuff about trying not to kill people?"

"Desperate circumstances. And, let's face it, I talk a good game, but I've killed a lot of people. And people-like things." She tossed a pair of short swords in the case and rifled through her closet. "I know my infiltration gear is in here somewhere."

"Connie, you can't do this," said Tia. "I know you're worried about Byron, and still dealing with Larry's death, which wasn't your fault, by the way. But this is stupid."

Connie started throwing clothes on the floor. "What would you have me do? Just leave Byron to Lady Peril's mercies?"

"No, but this isn't the way to save him."

Connie found both her black and camouflage ninja suits. She decided to pack both for good measure.

"Will you stop and think about this for a minute?" asked Tia.

Connie went to the bathroom and found the plastic explosives left over from a previous adventure that she'd stored under the sink. "Can you do me a favor and check the kitchen for detonators? There might be one or two in the junk drawer. And I think there's a pen that shoots poison darts in there too. That might be useful."

Tia found one detonator and a whole bunch of pens. She grabbed the detonator and a handful of pens and returned. She threw the pens on the bed, and Connie sorted through them, clicking them one by one. Most were just pens, although one did start beeping until she clicked it again. She stuffed that one in her pocket and held out her hand for the detonator.

Tia folded her arms tightly, tucking the detonator under her armpit. "Not until we talk about this."

"What's there to talk about?" asked Connie. "He's my boyfriend. Or he was. I don't know really. But he's only in this mess because of me. I knew this relationship was a bad idea. I thought I could make it work. I really did. But he's right. We really are from two different worlds. But I'll be damned if anything happens to him because of me."

"It's not always about you."

Connie said, "If he'd never met me, he'd probably be married by now with a couple of kids, living in the suburbs with a pretty wife, living a normal life."

"You've only been together a little over a year."

"You know what I mean. He doesn't deserve to get caught in the crossfire."

"Absolutely, but you don't have to do this on your own," said Tia. "Call Agent Ellington. Call some friends of yours. Call somebody."

"No, I need to do this on my own."

"Damn it, Connie. This isn't about your ego."

"No, it isn't. It's about Byron. And Lady Peril's plan to use him against me. She doesn't care about him. She wants to lure me into a trap. So, I'm going to oblige her and hope like hell that it's enough to get her to release him."

"That doesn't make any sense. If she wanted you, she could've just taken you. Why bother with Byron?"

"Because she's an evil genius. They love overly complicated plans, and she blames me for Larry's death, so this is her way of making me suffer. It's not enough to just kill me."

"That doesn't sound like her."

"She's lost her son. Grief makes people do funny things."

"She didn't even like Larry, and she's a sinister mastermind," said Tia. "Have you considered perhaps she has a hidden agenda?"

"Of course she does," said Connie, "but that doesn't change anything. Can you check the hall closet for my night-vision goggles?"

Tia stepped between Connie and her suitcase.

"You're doing it again. You can't run off half-cocked anymore. The spell is failing."

"So, that's all I am?" Connie glowered. "Just some dancing puppet? And now that it's fading, I'm supposed to give up?"

"No, but it's not unreasonable to take some time to think about it. I've been in Byron's shoes a hundred times before. Getting kidnapped by an evil genius isn't fun, but most of them are civil enough about it. Most of them even have pleasant prisoner facilities. There was this hidden base under New Orleans that served the best crab bisque, and once when I was abducted by aliens, there was a six-armed masseuse who was a miracle worker. I'm not saying getting used as bait is a spa day, but in my experience—"

"Experience doesn't count anymore," said Connie. "You said it yourself."

"Which is why we need to be smart about this," said Tia. "We?"

"I am your sidekick. If you insist on doing this, then I'm coming with you."

"Tia, this is dangerous."

"That's what I've been saying, but it's always dangerous. If you want to do something stupid, I can't stop you. But I like Byron. And if you're going to rescue him, you'll need all the help you can get."

"Things are different now," said Connie.

"Exactly, which means you'll need more help than ever." Tia stepped aside. "You finish packing. I'll grab my suitcase from the car."

"You have a suitcase ready?"

"I always have a suitcase ready," said Tia. "I'm a very good sidekick."

"Yes, you are."

Connie jabbed Tia in the chest. Tia stiffened, and Connie caught her before she hit the floor. Connie lay Tia on the bed.

"What did you do?" mumbled Tia, unable to move anything but her mouth and eyes and barely either of those.

"I can't be responsible for Byron and you." Connie tossed four pairs of spare underwear into her suitcase and zipped it up. "You'll be fine in about an hour. You might crap yourself. I apologize for that."

"You aren't getting rid of me that easily," said Tia. "I'll come after you."

"Good luck with that."

Connie saluted and left the room. Tia heard the front door open and close. She lay on the bed, grumbling curses. She closed her eyes and concentrated. Connie would've known some secret technique to kickstart her voluntary nervous system, but Tia could only concentrate on fingers, trying to get them to wiggle. She managed to get her pinkie to move. Then her entire right hand. Then her toes. A tingle ran through her extremities, like her whole body was recognizing itself. She tried sitting up but could only manage a flop.

The front door opened again, and Connie returned.

"I'm glad you came to your senses," said Tia, able to speak mostly normally aside from a slight slur.

"I'm impressed," said Connie. "It takes the monks months to get to that level to shake off the paralyzing touch. But you always were determined."

Connie jabbed Tia in her chest and followed it up with a pinch to her lower back. This time, Tia went rigid as a board.

"What the hell?" asked Tia. Or she tried to ask. Her mouth barely moved, and all that came out was a hiss.

Connie carried Tia to a closet. She threw aside all the clothes and adventurer knickknacks and propped Tia inside.

"Sorry, but I realized that while the odds of you actually being able to follow me are small, you might be stubborn enough to figure it out. Don't be mad."

Tia's right eyebrow bent in a manner not dissimilar to a scowl.

"Okay, so be mad," said Connie, "but just know that, whatever happens, I love you and I'm only doing this for your own good."

"Stupid," hissed Tia faintly.

Connie turned on the closet light and shut the door. She shoved a dresser and her bed in front of the door.

"Excuse me," said Doctor Malady from behind her.

Instinctively, she unleashed a kick that Automatica caught in a metal hand.

"Terribly sorry if we startled you," said Malady. "We knocked, but you must've not heard us while you were moving things."

Automatica released Connie's foot. "The front door was open."

"Doctor, I don't have time to talk," said Connie.

"Yes, yes, I understand," said Malady. "I thought you might like this, though." He handed her a printed map. "I was able to track the graviton emissions from that aircraft, and I assumed you might be interested."

She folded the map. "Doc, you've saved me a lot of trouble. Thanks."

"You're welcome. If you'd like, I could have Automatica accompany you on your rescue mission. She's grown quite fond of Byron."

"Harm to Byron would lower my happiness index to unfavorable levels," said Automatica.

Connie considered the offer, but Automatica, while significantly more powerful than Tia, was still someone else to be responsible for.

"I work best alone," she said, glancing at the closet.

"As you wish."

"One last thing, Doc. If Tia hasn't found her way out of that closet in five hours, I'll need you to come back in and let her out."

"It would be our pleasure, Constance. One thing I feel obliged to mention: I had the technology to track that aircraft across the world, but it wasn't difficult. It wasn't hiding. This is very likely a trap. Do be careful."

She grunted in a way that was neither agreement nor disagreement and walked out the door.

26

Within half an hour, Tia could move a little bit. Her rigid body slumped in the closet as she grumbled.

Within another twenty minutes, she could finally call for help. She shouted and, while she couldn't stand, she could kick the door with her left foot. Not so much a kick as a harsh nudge.

"Hey, I'm in here!" she yelled. Not very loud, but she had to try.

"Please do avoid harming yourself through overexertion," said Automatica from the other side of the door.

"Oh, thank god. Please let me out of here."

When Automatica didn't respond, Tia repeated herself louder.

"Yes, I'm afraid we heard you the first time," said Doctor Malady's voice. "I'm also afraid we can't do that."

"The hell you can't," said Tia. "Connie needs me."

"Connie made us promise to not let you out just yet," said Malady apologetically.

Tia kicked the door, hard this time. "You're a supervillain! You don't have to keep your promises!"

"Reformed supervillain," replied Malady. "Mostly. And I'm sure that Constance knows what she's doing. She always does."

Tia managed to get her legs working enough that she could stand, though her balance failed her, and she needed to lean against the door. She punched it with limp fists. "If you don't let me out—"

"You're upset," said Malady. "It's understandable. We'll come back in a few hours to let you out."

"Please do not attempt to break out," said Automatica. "I am putting several more items of furniture in place to impede any escape attempts."

Tia heard Automatica barricade the door with what sounded like the couch and maybe the refrigerator. Tia shouted and hit the door and cursed for three minutes with nothing to show for it but bruised knuckles.

"Damn it, Connie."

She sat and felt the lump in her pocket, her cell phone, still awkwardly shaped with the doohickey Bonita had left on it. She punched in Hiro's number.

It went to message.

"Goddamn it, Hiro, pick up your fucking phone."

She dialed again. It went to message again.

"Hiro, I'm trapped in Connie's closet, and I need you to come and get me. Now."

She hung up, then dialed again, leaving another message.

"And, no, this isn't a trick to get you to Connie's place so that she can kill you. I swear."

She hung up, dialed again.

"Forget I said anything about tricking you. Just come over here." She stared at the cell and sighed. "Okay, never mind. I know you're not coming. You're not going to even answer. Maybe you were in such a hurry, you left your phone behind. Maybe you're just a wimp. I'll just call the police. Thanks for nothing."

She didn't call the cops. They could let her out of the closet, but she'd never catch up with Connie. She didn't have the resources or skills.

She tried stuffing the cell back into her pocket, but the stupid alien doohickey got in the way. She dropped it on the floor beside her with a frustrated moan.

"Some sidekick."

Tia glowered at the useless device. Connie would've known a dozen numbers that could solve this problem. Tia couldn't even get her ninja boyfriend to call her back, and she was stuck with a stupid phone that didn't even fit comfortably in her pocket because of stupid useless alien technology.

It struck her then.

She picked up the phone and glanced through her call

history until she found a long, long number that wasn't in her contacts. It had to be the number Bonita had used to teleport, but where had she gone, and would it still work? Bonita was an alien cockroach who understood the situation. She might be able to do something, but there was no guarantee she would be wherever Tia ended up. The universe was a big place, and she might end up somewhere hostile to human life, maybe in the cold void of space, maybe just trapped on an indifferent world across the galaxy.

If she'd been Connie, she'd have rolled the dice and assumed she could handle whatever happened.

She wasn't Connie.

There was some irony to that. Connie's impetuous nature was her greatest enemy right now. Tia was the sensible one, the one who kept her head down, the one who lent a hand now and then but left all the dangerous work to Connie. And that was a smart thing to do. Usually.

There was no caretaker mantle on Tia. The universe didn't offer her forgiving odds. The universe's concern for her mattered only so much as it might help draw Connie into adventures.

She didn't exist to rescue Connie. Help out now and then, sure, but the sensible thing was to trust Connie and the universe to sort it out. It always did.

She'd been in this situation so many times before. Helpless. Sitting in a locked closet, metaphorically and, often, literally, waiting for Connie. But Tia wasn't the hostage anymore. She was the sidekick. It was one step below the hero, and she couldn't save the day, but she could save the hero who saved the day. Or she could die on the other side of the galaxy on a strange alien world. It was a toss-up.

"Screw it."

Tia hit the call button and was beamed across the stars. It didn't hurt and was so fast, she didn't realize it until it was over. It did screw with her balance, though, and she fell flat on her face. She rolled to one side and peered out a window at a sprawling alien cityscape of swirling arches and impossibly tall towers and floating buildings. If she'd typed ALIEN CITY into a search engine, she couldn't have been directed to a more perfect, generic picture.

She couldn't breathe, and her eyes, nose, and throat burned with the harsh, caustic air. Everything turned black as something or someone lifted her off the cold floor.

A whoosh of cold air hit Tia in the face, and she drew in a deep gulp of oxygen. It had a tangy sourness to it, like sucking on an intangible lemon drop, but her eyes stopped watering. She wiped away her tears, waiting for her vision to clear and to catch her breath.

An insectoid hand with a glass of brackish liquid appeared before her. The hand led to a long insectoid arm connected to a tall insectoid figure. The figure's mandibles snapped open and shut as it said something in its strange language, except it wasn't that strange. She sort of recognized it.

The alien repeated itself. This time, she caught a little bit of Mandarin.

"English," said Tia. "I speak English."

"Ah, English," said the alien. "I can work with that."

"Was that Swahili before?"

"Yes. Do you know it?"

"My dad made me study, but I didn't get far."

"Then English it is."

"You speak Earth English?"

"I speak over seven million languages. English isn't my best. I can sometimes use the wrong pancake, but I get by. Also, you don't have to say *Earth English*. You can just call it English."

The alien twitched his antennae and held forth the glass. "Drink this. It'll help you acclimate."

Tia took the glass. The brackish fluid reminded her of dirty dishwater. She steeled herself and drank half in one gulp. It didn't taste great, but she could keep it down.

The room was a small space without decoration. There was a window on one side that showed the alien cityscape, and Tia deliberately avoided looking out it to avoid distraction. She'd been in outer space before. Not nearly as many times as Connie, but enough that she could stay on track.

The tall insectoid wore a brown tunic and nothing else. His bright red carapace and brilliant green eyes were beautiful. Some might have found the bug face disconcerting, but Tia had never had a problem with bugs.

"I'm Amzak," said the tall insect. "And who might you be, and why did you beam through my personal matter transporter?"

"Tia." She gulped down the second half of the drink. "It's about Connie."

"I see," said Amzak. "And who is that?"

27

Tia was certain she'd screwed up. She'd beamed herself across the galaxy and ended up in the wrong place. She was in a worse position to save Connie from herself than before.

The room she was in now was a universal guest room with adjustable settings for any unique environmental needs that a visitor might need. Amzak adjusted the oxygen generators and gravity inhibitors. He pushed a button to generate a chair from somewhere for Tia to sit.

"You don't know who Connie is?" she asked.

"Should I? I'm sorry. I don't know many humans. Or any. Except you."

"But you speak Earth . . . You speak English."

"My species picks up language easily." Amzak fluttered the small wings on his back in the manner of a shrug. "Most of us learn them as a hobby."

"I don't get it," said Tia. "This was the number Bonita called."

Amzak summoned his own chair, a tall stool, and sat. "And who is that?"

"She's like you, an alien. I mean, not an alien here, I guess."

"We're all aliens in this universe, in one way or another," said Amzak. "Wait. When you speak of this friend of yours, Connie, she wouldn't be related to the Legendary Snurkab, would she?"

"Yes, the Legendary Snurkab!" exclaimed Tia, louder than she intended.

Amzak twitched. His antennae flattened.

"Sorry," said Tia. "You've heard of her. Of course you've heard of her."

"If something is wrong with the Snurkab, I'm not the one you want to talk to. That's my mate."

"Can I talk to her, uh, him, um . . . I'm sorry if I get this wrong. I don't have tons of experience with aliens."

"Her."

"Sorry. Can I talk to her?"

Amzak pushed a few buttons and a screen floated out of the wall and hovered beside them. A green insect face appeared in it.

"What is it? I'm busy," said Bonita.

Amzak pointed to Tia.

"What are you doing here?" asked Bonita.

"Connie's in trouble," said Tia.

"I'm aware."

"If you'll excuse me," said Amzak flatly as he rose. He

left the room. A few wisps of toxic atmosphere floated past the stabilizers as he exited. The door whooshed shut with a sharp *snap*.

Tia fought away a cough. "Did I do something wrong?"

"No, I did. He doesn't approve of my work," said Bonita.

Amzak popped up on a smaller screen on the larger one. "Hah. Your work. You call screwing with the lives of lesser life-forms work."

"We are the Makers," said Bonita. "If we don't maintain the delicate balance of the universe, who will?"

Amzak's antennae raised. "Who indeed?"

"How many times are we going to have this argument?"

"I don't know. How many times is my home going to be invaded by uninvited lower life-forms? No offense, Tia."

"None taken?" replied Tia, though it came across a question because she wasn't certain if she was offended or not. She had bigger problems at the moment.

"Can we not fight in front of the lower life-form?" asked Bonita.

Amzak said something snarky. Tia couldn't understand the series of clicks and chirps, but she knew the tone. Bonita and Amzak exchanged a few more clicks, none of them sounding very happy with the situation, before Amzak disappeared from the screen.

"He doesn't get it," said Bonita. "He thinks this is all some silly diversion. Just the fate of worlds I'm dealing with here. No big deal or anything."

From somewhere, Tia heard Amzak laugh once, harsh and rough.

"I'm assuming Connie isn't with you," said Bonita. "Otherwise, I'd be speaking to her."

"I used your phone doohickey," said Tia.

"Very clever. Stupid, but clever. You're fortunate Amzak was home. You would've died in roughly forty-five seconds, give or take. And I'm fortunate Amzak was home, because he would've been displeased to find a human corpse in our home. What was so important that you deemed it worth the risk?"

"Connie's in trouble."

"Connie is always in trouble."

"Sure, but that thing you were talking about, I think it's happening. Her luck is running out."

"Yes, about that," said Bonita. "There might have been some miscalculations. Since you've come all this way, I might as well explain it to you in person."

The screen went blank, and shortly, Amzak returned. He threw a miniature flying saucer into the air. It hovered a few inches over Tia's head.

"This way, please," said Amzak, exiting the room.

Tia stepped into the unprotected room, but the saucer generated a breathable atmosphere and relatively comfortable gravity for her. It was a little light, and she kept lifting her feet too high off the floor.

Amzak showed Tia to the transporter device and started dialing.

"I'm sorry for the inconvenience," said Tia.

"It's not your fault," said Amzak. "Though I do wish you wouldn't encourage her. It was a pleasure to meet you." He sounded polite, if not sincere.

He pushed the button, disappearing along with the rest of the house, replaced by Bonita, in human form, and several other aliens, none of which were even vaguely humanoid. One looked like a mass of flatworms stacked precariously atop one another. Another was a squat sextuped with a cat-like face. Yet another was a giant hovering head with a tiny body dangling from its neck like a vestigial organ. Tia stepped from the machine and thought she should say something.

"Hello."

Bonita nodded. "You've come a long way to have your fears assuaged. Let's get on with it."

She turned, and Tia followed. The other aliens brought up the rear, including a hopping tangle of leaves Tia had erroneously assumed was a houseplant.

"Sorry about intruding," said Tia. "Hope I didn't make your mate angry."

"He'll get over it. He doesn't understand. We Makers are nearly ageless, but when the Great Engine went rogue, our civilization vanished as we were forced to scatter to the far corners of the universe. Most of those who survived that dark time have given up on exploring the mysteries of the cosmos."

"Well, you did nearly destroy the universe," said Tia. "I think."

"Mistakes were made," said Bonita. "But I'd like to believe the caretaker management is still functional."

"But why do it on Earth?" asked Tia. "It doesn't seem important in the grand scheme of things."

"It isn't, and it is. Like everything else, it's a matter of scale. I've lived through the rise and fall of a thousand interstellar empires. Once, Noop's people ruled the entire Zakorr Spiral." She gestured toward the houseplant alien. "Now they live on a wretched little planet in Omnicron."

Noop screeched and popped.

"Oh, don't be so sensitive," said Bonita. "You know it's true."

Noop wilted.

"It's always like that," continued Bonita. "Nothing lasts forever. Yet we carry on. Your planet is no more important than any other. No less important, either. But Connie . . . she might be important."

"The spell, you mean."

"If you have water and a bucket to hold it in, would you consider the bucket less important than the water? Without a vessel to contain it, the caretaker destiny isn't anything. Less than nothing. And it has been floating throughout the universe, from one host to another, throughout the eons. So, it's on Earth for the time being. It will go to other places, other worlds, eventually."

"Pardon me, but this all sounds like a bunch of mumbo jumbo."

"Have you ever heard the expression *Sufficiently advanced*

science is indistinguishable from magic? Well, sufficiently advanced magic is indistinguishable from science as well. They are one and the same. You haven't the ability to comprehend either."

The aliens chuckled smugly.

They entered a room brimming with screens. Data in strange alien writing continually scrolled across each of them. Some played scenes from Connie's life. Tia was in some of them. She recognized herself and Connie as kids, running away from a falling boulder. She didn't remember that.

"You're watching her?" asked Tia.

"We're analyzing her," said Bonita. "Purely for scientific reasons."

The screens played out hundreds of different moments, flashing between them in blinks, from different ages and adventures. On this screen, teenage Connie swashbuckled aboard a pirate ship. On that one, she stalked a werewolf in a darkened forest. Or infiltrated a hidden mountain fortress. Or led a ragtag group of rebels against an alien dictator. Or any of a hundred other adventures.

"Where did you get all this? Were you watching the whole time?"

"Someone is always watching," said Bonita, "but most of these scenes are recreations, created via probabilistic analysis. That's all reality is, in truth. A series of potential and actual outcomes. Everything else is merely an expression of this fact."

The floating-head alien hovered before a screen, and the alien language transitioned to English.

He spoke, curiously with a slight Midwestern accent. "The odds that this universe itself would exist in the first place, the odds that it would create an environment receptive to life, the odds that any of this life would become sapient." He floated before Tia. "The odds that the peculiar code of DNA that you call you would come together, the odds that you would run into Constance on the day of her caretaker activation, the odds that you would stick around as her friend. All these are part of a grand equation beyond calculation."

"This sounds a lot like what the Great Engine claimed," said Tia.

"The Engine wasn't incorrect in its assessments. Merely its conclusions," said Bonita. "This universe, all universes, are colliding particles where actions lead to reactions which lead to further reactions, a chain of probabilities from the very beginning to the very end of creation.

"Control that, and you control everything. The Engine failed to realize how large that equation is. Its failure of imagination was its undoing."

"And you'll do better?" asked Tia.

Bonita sighed. "You misunderstand us. We aren't some sinister secret cabal. We've given up on controlling Connie and the caretaker destiny. We've discovered it can't be controlled. The very act of trying to control it is the surest way to fail. We once thought of ourselves as the wise and benevolent overseers of the caretaker, the puppet masters behind the scenes. But it was all a lie. We might push it one way or another, but the force that resides within Connie is greater than us."

"But what about your warnings about bad luck?"

Bonita gestured toward a screen. A jagged graph surrounded by alienese spread across it.

"As I said, we must've miscalculated." A series of blinking dots marked the lowest parts on the graph. "Each of these incidents represents a moment when the caretaker force ceased its influence and the negative probabilities were at their worst. And in each of them, Connie somehow survived. We don't know how. The math checks out, but one can't argue with reality itself. There is something within Connie, perhaps Connie herself, that allows her to thrive even without the caretaker's influence."

"You're saying Connie can't lose?"

"No, we're saying that whether Connie wins or loses, survives or dies, our actions are irrelevant to that outcome. In other words, we're irrelevant."

"You can't argue with the math," said the cat alien in a squeaky falsetto.

Tia studied the graph. "Do you have recreations of all of these recent low points?"

"Yes, but the recreations are unimportant. All that matters are the outcomes."

"Can I see them?" asked Tia.

"It's unnecessary. Just look at the data."

"Show them to me anyway. Humor me as a lowly life-form."

Bonita nodded to Noop, who nodded to the flatworm alien scientist, who nodded to the cat, who gestured toward a screen.

The scene played out from an overhead angle. Alien characters scrolled across the screen as Debra, the telepathic super brain, ordered a commando to shoot Connie. Debra lay there, struggling to regain control of her body. Trying and failing. Tia's shot wounded the commando, and Connie did the rest. The enhancement device exploded, and Tia pulled Connie out of the way of its crumbling wreckage.

On another monitor, the recreation of Connie about to throw herself into the sea played out. Tia didn't understand any of the strange text, but she got the context as a bright red squiggle flashed ominously as Connie climbed the railing. The squiggle faded as Tia and Hiro wrestled Connie back onto the deck.

At the cabin at Lake Lake Monster, the flying helmet from an exploding battle armor nearly took Connie's head off, if not for Tia's last minute push to the ground.

"Oh my god," said Tia. "Don't you see it?"

"See what?" asked Bonita.

"It's me. Every time the universe is going to kill Connie, I'm there to save her."

Bonita laughed. "Don't be absurd. You're not important."

"Hey, screw you. I may not be Connie or an alien super-scientist who claims to know everything about the universe, but I'm not an idiot."

"You're upset," said Bonita. "It's understandable. When

confronted with the inconsequential nature of our own existence, it's only natural to reject—"

"Just shut up and replay them. And watch them. Don't just stare at the data."

"I really don't see the point."

"That's just it. You don't see. You're so busy functioning in the abstract that you're not paying attention to what's actually happening. You're so obsessed with your grand equation that you stopped seeing. These are lives we're talking about. These are people. So screw your calculations and just look."

The alien assembly offered a collective shrug. "If it'll help you come to terms with the inevitable."

The incidents were replayed, and on second viewing, it was even more obvious to Tia. Bonita and her team rushed to various consoles and spent the next half hour analyzing more data until they came to an unavoidable conclusion.

"She's right," said Bonita. "She's the unknown factor."

Noop gurgled.

"Oh, give it up, Noop," said the floating head. "It's obvious. We just missed it."

"It's a touch embarrassing," said Bonita.

"I'm right then," said Tia.

"More than you know. We've been running the numbers, and it appears you've been influencing them for a while now."

"Perhaps it has something to do with proximity?" suggested the cat. "She was there when the mantle first manifested in the Snurkab. There might have been some spillover contamination."

Bonita said, "If so, it would mean a fundamental shift in how we assumed the caretaker paradigm operates."

"I don't give a damn how it works," said Tia. "We don't have time for you to crunch numbers. This isn't a math equation. It's Connie, and she needs me. You have to beam me back."

"Yes, about that," said Bonita. "There might be a problem there."

"Just beam me across the universe to her phone. You did it once before."

"Oh, we can do it, but while the process might appear instantaneous to you, it actually takes several days."

"What? How many?"

"It varies. Anywhere from two to three."

"I've been gone two or three days already? Why didn't you tell me?"

"I didn't think it was relevant."

Tia bristled. She wanted to yell at these egotistical idiots who'd wasted so much of her precious time. But there wasn't any time left.

She grabbed Bonita by the collar. "Get me back to Earth. Now."

28

Byron's first abduction wasn't so bad, all things considered. He ran his finger down tonight's menu. "No chicken?" he asked.

"No, sir," said the concierge in the black jumpsuit. "The chef felt the poultry was below his standards. He sends his apologies." His skull helmet covered his face, but he sounded sincerely put out by the situation. "He recommends the fish."

"Not really a fish guy."

"I'm told it's quite good."

Byron handed back the menu through the bars. "Sure, why not. And a Coke."

"We only offer Pepsi products."

"Right. Keep forgetting. That's fine."

The concierge tucked the menu under his arm and nodded slightly. "Very good, sir." He walked away, past the two posted guards.

Byron's cell was like a nicer version of his first efficiency apartment if he overlooked the guards and the bars. He retrieved a bottled water from the minifridge and turned on the TV. It had only basic cable, but it was better than nothing.

The most vexing thing about being held prisoner was that he could already hear his sister *tsk-tsk*ing. "Well, you dated an adventurer," Dana would say. "What did you think would happen?"

The concierge returned, without food, and opened the cell door.

"Something wrong?" asked Byron.

"Change of plans, sir. You'll be eating with Lady Peril tonight. This way."

Byron followed. The two guards posted at his cell fell in behind him. He wondered if they expected him to make an escape attempt. Connie probably would've. Or she would've played along, eager to talk to Lady Peril and outsmart her in a deadly game of wits. He had no such aspirations.

They traveled the metal halls, passing minions marching off to do their jobs. It wasn't much different from any office. You didn't know what half the people did, but you trusted that they were doing it. You kept your head down and collected your paycheck. The uniforms might be different, but the archetype was always the same.

They led him to a dining room where Lady Peril and Apollonia were waiting. It was surprisingly sparse and tasteful.

No mile-long table or massive chandelier. No live orchestra or giant shark tank. Just a table with a white tablecloth and some chairs. The Siege Perilous logo was printed on the tablecloth.

Lady Peril wore the same style white bodysuit and black lab coat as he'd last seen her in. "Ah, Byron, so good of you to join me. Please, do have a seat."

The concierge pulled out a chair, and Byron thanked him. Apollonia did the same for Lady Peril.

"I trust your stay has been pleasant," said Lady Peril.

"Good. I have to say I thought I'd be tortured or something."

Lady Peril raised an eyebrow.

"Not that I'm complaining," he said. "I just thought with your son dead and you wanting revenge . . ."

She interlaced her long, thin fingers, the black polish on her perfectly manicured nails reminding him of a lioness's claws.

"I'm sorry for your loss," he said.

He tensed. It was a stupid thing to say.

"Forget I brought it up."

She almost smiled. Or so he imagined. Her mouth never so much as twitched, but he picked up a vague sense of amusement from her.

The henchagents served the meal. Byron waited for Peril to cut into her fish, which she inspected for a full minute before taking a bite. She chewed with a cold indifference, swallowed, and nodded. The staff retreated to their corners. Only Apollonia stood within arm's reach of Peril.

"I must say you're taking this all very well," said Peril. "No pleading, no tears, no begging for mercy, no appeals to my better nature."

"Would it make a difference?" he asked.

"It doesn't prevent people from trying."

"I'd be worried, but I know Connie will rescue me."

"Yes, I suppose this is old hat for you, being in a relationship with Verity."

"Actually, no. This is the first time."

"Well, you never forget your first," she said.

He thought it might be a joke, but he doubted she ever made jokes. Even accidentally. She probably didn't approve of accidents in any form.

"Tell me, how does a man like . . . well . . . like you end up in a romantic relationship with a woman like Verity?"

"I don't know," he replied. "It just sort of happened."

Peril pursed her lips. "Very little in this universe just happens."

"Are you going to kill Connie?"

"Most probably."

"Because of your son?"

"Oh, no. Larry was always worthless."

"That's a terrible thing to say about your own family."

Lady Peril set down her fork, then her knife. She wiped the corners of her mouth, set down her napkin, and scowled, showing the smallest glimpse of teeth. "I consider myself a good host, so I'll ignore that. My worldview places no special value on genetic loyalty. I operate across larger spectra." She picked up her fork again and gestured toward his plate. "Do eat before it gets cold."

He took a bite and thought if he should say anything else.

"You want Connie to come and rescue me," he said.

"That is my goal, yes."

"So you can kill her."

She nodded.

"Why didn't you kill her before?"

"I have my reasons."

Lady Peril was impossible to read. He expected her to either ask for another glass of wine or have him shot.

She raised her glass and a guard poured her another drink.

"Tell me, Byron. What is your opinion on fate?"

"I never liked the idea," he replied.

"Ah, so you've thought about it, then. Only idiots find the notion of destiny to be a comfort, and only because they deceive themselves into believing there's some special reward for blindly believing such nonsense. I've never believed in fate, yet there are times when it has seemed that the universe itself has been determined to prevent my greater achievements."

"We all feel like that now and then," he said.

"Yes."

She let the word hang there as she stared into the distance.

"The difference is that most people are stupid little things, occupying themselves with stupid little lives, whereas I am Lady Peril. From a young age, I knew I was smarter, more capable than anyone around me. It was only natural that I should rise to power in such an environment. I built Siege Perilous from the ground up. When I started, I had only a few million dollars gained through political extortion, and a handful of minions. From there, I created one of the most prominent international self-actualizing organizations on the planet. Would you like to talk to the president? I can arrange that."

"Which one?" he asked with a chuckle.

"Take your pick. I have leverage over all the important ones. Several of them answer directly to me. Name a country. I can have it invaded within the hour."

"No, thanks," he said. "I believe you."

She pushed away her plate and frowned at it. "By any metric, I am among the most powerful people in the world. Yet my final plans of world domination continue to be thwarted. By incompetence. By ridiculous circumstances. By heroes. And, most frustratingly, by your girlfriend."

"That's kind of what she does, isn't it?"

"Yes."

She swallowed the word with a hard gulp.

"At first, I thought it best to simply kill Constance Verity. I'm not a vengeful woman, but I noticed that all my best plans were ruined by her. Over and over again. I am not without enemies. There is always some troublesome fool standing in my way. So-called heroes, defenders of the innocent, rival masterminds, ambitious challengers. But it is an evident truth that in those moments when I was undisputably closest to victory, whenever my ascendance was a foregone conclusion, Constance Verity would appear, and somehow, everything would fall apart. It seemed appropriate to remove this obstacle.

"But Constance's interference in my life is no mere coincidence. Loathe as I was to believe it, I came to realize that there was something greater at work. To remove Constance would only cause another to take her place. She's not a person. She's a force of nature. Only worse. I can tame hurricanes, bring about earthquakes, topple governments. But I cannot contain or control Constance Verity."

"She's pretty amazing," he said quietly. "But she's not perfect. She has issues. She's terrible at trusting people. Has to do everything herself. It's like . . . we get it. You won the Twenty-Four Hours Nürburgring, but sometimes I still want to drive."

Byron lowered his head and concentrated on cutting his fish. He probably shouldn't be sharing relationship issues with an evil genius.

Lady Peril pushed away from the table. "Come with me, Byron. I've something to show you."

They walked down several more corridors, rode an elevator, took some stairs. Byron had given up trying to keep any sense of direction. Five minutes later, they arrived at a large domed chamber carved into the mountain. A flat pillar of rock stood in the center. Lady Peril placed her hand on a biometric scanner, and a bridge extended across the gap.

A strange blue-green glow pulsed in the chasm far below. It wasn't magma.

"Raw magic," explained Peril. "You have no idea how hard it was to find an untapped ley-line nexus that fit my needs. All the easy ones were already discovered. This one only remained untapped by virtue of resting far below this mountain. Digging it out took some time, and imagine my irritation to discover it had become inactive."

The glow flared and rumbled. It growled, like a living thing.

They stepped off the bridge onto the plateau. Hundreds of runes were cut into the stone. He knew nothing about magic, but he could feel the arcane powers vibrating under his feet. Standing stones ringed the edges of the plateau, along with dozens of eclectic objects.

"I've never been fond of magic. Too unscientific, but one must work with the tools available. By acquiring magical artifacts, I was able to activate the nexus through proximity. The Standing Stones of Stenness, the Goujian sword of ancient China, the badge of Wyatt Earp, the helm of the lost god." She pointed to the large crystals floating overhead. "The remaining power crystals of Atlantis. Other objects of power and mystery, mostly important for the awakening."

She stopped before a tall vase made of alabaster. Otherworldly light glowed through the cracks running along its sides.

"And this vase which even now gathers every errant spark of Constance Verity's blessed mantle. Here, in this magic circle, I am finally accomplishing what I never could before. I am putting an end to Constance, but more importantly, I am removing the possibility that another will rise in her place. Here, I shall destroy the caretaker destiny once and for all. And when there is no longer one person favored by fate, when there is only a perfect, indifferent universe, I shall claim my rightful place as master of this world."

A few globules of light materialized overhead, sinking into the ancient vase.

"Another few drops," said Lady Peril. "With every strain, with every bit of reckless heroism, with every death-defying escape and minor coincidence, this magic circle drains more of Constance's blessed life. In a matter of another few hours, a day at most, it'll all be contained within. And once she's no longer under the caretaker mantle, I will destroy the mantle once and for all, and then I will kill her. And that will be that."

"If you make her normal, why kill her?" asked Byron. There were probably better questions, but he didn't understand enough of this to find them.

"Why don't I leave your girlfriend alone?" replied Lady Peril. "Why don't I allow you both to walk out of here, to live out the rest of your miserably drab lives? Because Constance has been a thorn in my side for far too long."

She smiled, and the temperature in the room dropped,

the glowing Atlantean power crystals dimmed exposed to such pure malice.

"And she will die by my hand."

She assumed her default expression of equal parts disgust and disinterest and walked away from the circle. Apollonia gestured for Byron to follow, though he didn't need to be told. They walked through more hallways until reaching a place where the carved rock replaced the walls.

They arrived at a new room minutes later, and it was all but indistinguishable from a cave if not for the lights mounted on the wall and the metal floor under their feet. Scratches were gouged in the floor by what Byron could only assume were massive claws. Then the thing in the darkened corner of the chamber lumbered forward, and he no longer had to assume.

The hulking creature stalked back and forth. The chain attached to the collar on its neck belonged to a battleship anchor.

"Beautiful, isn't it?" asked Peril. "Something our genetic experimentation division came up with. A combination of shark, tiger, and ape DNA, along with a few little extra bits here and there. Completely impractical for any useful purpose, but I can't bring myself to destroy it."

The creature bared its sharpened teeth. Muscles bulged under its orange-and-black fur. It raked the floor with its long black claws, causing sparks to fly.

Beautiful wasn't the first word that came to Byron's mind.

"I find I like you, Byron," said Lady Peril. "As much as I

like anyone. I can console you that your death will be quick, if a bit messy."

Apollonia kicked Byron in the leg, and he fell to his knees. While he was recovering, Lady Peril and Apollonia exited. The only way out of the room slid shut with a solid *snap*.

The monster sat on its haunches and focused its green eyes on Byron. Its rasping breath filled the small room.

Panic seized him, and he pounded on the door.

"Oh, you were making such a positive impression," said Peril's voice from somewhere. "Don't ruin it now."

"You're just going to kill me?" he shouted. "Just like that?"

"No, Byron. If I were to kill you *just like that,* I would've had you shot. Weren't you paying attention? You mean nothing to me. Only a means to an end. If my calculations are correct, you'll be improbably saved at the last minute."

A machine in the darkness whirred, and the mutant's chain slackened. It moved forward, only to meet resistance as the chain unfurled slowly. Perhaps to increase dramatic tension. Perhaps because Lady Peril found some sadistic glee in watching him squirm. The creature leaned forward on its knuckles. Bits of saliva dripped from its jaws.

"What if you're wrong?" asked Byron.

"Possible. This isn't an exact science."

"You're a madwoman!"

"Your reaction is understandable. If it should make you feel any better, I do hope you live. Or rather, I don't require you to die and see no harm in your continued living."

The chain engine roared louder. The creature's shark tail flipped in anticipation.

Byron glanced around for something to defend himself. Not that it mattered. She could've left him a bazooka, and it wouldn't have done him any good against this titan of twisted science.

"Connie will rescue me," he said, more to himself.

"I'm beginning to have doubts myself," said Peril. "Are you absolutely certain that she's particularly fond of you?"

He pressed against the wall and tried to control his breathing. His heart thumped in his chest. She would be there. She would make it. She always made it in time.

The mutant pounced on Byron. In two leaps, it was upon him. Lady Peril had been right. It was quick. So quick, he found himself staring at the jaws bearing down on his head before having time to process the information. He would've been dead before even realizing it if the chain hadn't suddenly tightened again.

It growled, clawing at the metal collar around its neck. With a whimper, it fell on its back, writhing as the tether dragged it away.

The door opened. Lady Peril and Apollonia entered. Peril held a small device in her hand with a single button. "Well, that was disappointing. I thought for certain Constance would make an appearance."

Peril handed the device to Apollonia, who used it to drag the mutant into the darkness.

Byron shook with equal parts fear and rage. "Is this some sort of game to you?"

Peril said, "Game implies some manner of frivolous hobby. I assure you that this isn't that."

Byron would never have a better chance. He took a swing at Peril. She grabbed his fist and squeezed. She might've been a wiry older lady, but she had ungodly strength. She twisted his arm, and he fell to his knees. He whimpered. He tried not to but couldn't help it.

"You're out of your depth," she said. "If you wish to survive, I suggest you avoid further foolish bravado."

The mutant, its eyes glowing in the dark, growled.

Peril released Byron. She sneered, not at him but at the idea of him. He wasn't anything to her. Just a thing to be used and discarded when no longer needed.

She turned her back to him. He was beneath her. "Come along, Apollonia. We'll leave Byron to consider his future actions and the consequences of such."

They exited. He sat there, on his knees, feeling powerless. No wonder Connie hadn't wanted him around.

"We'll try again in another hour," said Peril. "Perhaps without the chain. It might encourage things."

The door snapped shut, and Byron leaned against the wall. The mutant crouched in its corner. It scraped the floor with its claws, creating a steady *scrich-scrich-scrich* sound.

Every so often, it would glance at him, and while hunger and rage burned in its eyes, there was something else there. Byron imagined it was sympathy. Neither were master of their destinies.

"Sucks to be us."

The mutant howled long and low and sad, and, heaven help him, Byron was sorely tempted to join in.

29

It was a long plane flight, car ride, and hike to reach the secret mountain lair of Lady Perilous. An isolated locale was ideal for secrecy but lousy for logistics. Most sensible masterminds had long since abandoned these out-of-the way places, and it made Connie's life easier. But Lady Peril was old-school.

The hike wasn't so bad. Even a bit invigorating to be out in the cool forest air. She liked the outdoors, liked testing herself against the elements. It was almost relaxing, aside from one encounter with a grizzly bear that had gone badly because Connie hadn't been paying enough attention. After a few bluff charges, she went her way and the bear went its. She knew enough to handle the situation, and a bear attack wasn't a big deal. But things felt harder now. It might have been paranoia, but as Connie scaled the sheer face of a mountain in the dark with nothing but her experience and determination between her and a thousand-foot drop, she couldn't help but worry.

It was a lousy night for a climb. Clouds obscured the moonlight, and she didn't have any equipment. Not that she would've used it. She didn't want to make the noise. And the dark worked in her favor. If she couldn't see her own hand in front of her face, it was unlikely someone else would. Not that she expected much security. Isolation was the biggest selling point of carving a secret base into a mountain three hundred miles from the closest town, and that town was barely twenty people and a couple of dogs. And if someone made it this far, they'd have to be an idiot to try the climb.

She'd done stupider things. She couldn't count the number of times she'd played a hunch or taken an impossible risk. Often, she'd had no choice. When being chased by a hungry dinosaur, jumping off a cliff into the darkness below wasn't the smart move, but it wasn't especially foolish compared to the alternative.

Other times, experience told her things would pay off. Experience told her that every spaceship had an escape pod. Experience confirmed that every death trap had a failing. Every mystery had an answer. Most, anyway. Every secret base carved inside a mountain had ventilation ducts, and the best place to hide one of those ducts was on the side of an unscalable mountainside.

A handhold crumbled, and she hung by one arm. In the darkness below, there were no mysteries. Only the unforgiving ground. The end of Constance Verity, a broken pile of bones in a forest. It might be weeks before anyone found her. Years.

She was supposed to die a glorious death, but with whatever lingering bits of the caretaker fate remained within her, that might have changed.

She grabbed another fragile ledge and braced her legs against whatever purchase they might find.

"Not today. Not yet."

She wasn't certain if it was her trademark stubborn resolve or if she was trying to convince herself. Either way, she carried on. There would be a vent. Or a wastewater pipe. Or a garbage chute. Something. And it would be big enough for her to get into. There had to be one.

Connie had no time for doubts. Every inch higher was another inch she'd have to climb down, and after a point, up was the only choice.

She found the vent hidden behind an outcropping. It extended just enough that she could prop herself against it for some support, allowing her to use her free hand to pull a portable laser torch from her utility belt. She started cutting through the grate, but the torch died halfway through the job.

She found a spare battery in her belt, but as she pulled it from the pouch, it slipped through her fingers and tumbled into the void.

It was only a bit of bad luck. Not unusual. Even with the full force of the caretaker spell behind her, things never went perfectly. She'd improvise.

She managed to pry open the grating. Its jagged edges bit into her palms, drawing blood. It wasn't hard to bend, aside from the pain, which she ignored, and the leverage issue while dangling. She wiped the sticky blood on her shirt and crawled through the small opening. It was barely big enough and only because of a trick she'd picked up from the Amazing Howard, world's greatest living escape artist. It was just a question of muscle compression, dislocating a shoulder, and being able to hold her breath for the four minutes it took to squeeze her torso through.

She could really use a break, but the vent was a straight drop. She braced herself against the walls and lowered herself one step at a time. Blood smeared the walls, and she could smell it under her nose where she'd wiped her cut hands.

This wasn't going well.

It had been years since she'd had this much trouble infiltrating a secret base, but she wouldn't read too much into it. She would take one step at a time. She'd find Byron. They'd get the hell out of there.

She reached the bottom of the shaft after many long minutes, and in the darkened junction, she took a moment to wrap her bloodied palms and rest. She focused on ancient biomanipulation techniques, numbing the pain in her hand. They'd be less reliable that way, but the distraction wasn't doing her much good.

Connie thought about giving up. Lady Peril had gone to all the trouble of luring her there. The mastermind would be waiting for her. The smart thing might be to simply defuse the situation and walk up to the front door, offering herself in exchange for Byron. At the very least, it'd be an unexpected tactic.

It'd always end up in the same place. Connie in some impossible situation. Lady Peril gloating about Connie's inevitable defeat. Then at the last minute, Connie would figure something out, like she always did. Peril would die in some way that made it impossible to confirm she was really dead. Connie and Byron would flee an exploding secret base. It was all so mundane at this point.

It was what happened after that troubled Connie. Byron would go his way. She'd go hers. Whatever came then, she didn't know. If the caretaker spell disappeared and she became normal, could they make it work then? Did she even care?

Yeah, she cared.

But did he?

And why the hell was she thinking about that when she might be dead in another hour?

She pushed away complicated thoughts and continued her infiltration. She found an outlet in an unoccupied laundry room and kicked out the grate, dropping among dozens of hanging jumpsuits. She rifled through them.

None were her size. None of them were even close to her size.

She resorted to the bins of dirty, wrinkled suits. One of them had to fit. One always did. She didn't think about all the things she took for granted. The universe didn't guarantee her success, but it did cut her a break now and then. Those breaks were coming less and less, but they only needed to hold out for another few hours. Long enough to get this rescue done.

She found a wrinkled suit with a sizeable mustard stain that smelled vaguely of old tuna, but it was her size, so it would have to do. Connie was sticking her leg in when the door opened and two henchagents entered.

"Hey, what are you doing?" asked one.

Connie turned her face down. "Sorry, I tore my old uniform, so I had to grab something."

"All uniform replacement is done through requisitions," said the second henchagent. "You should know that."

"Yes, but I just thought it'd be easier to pick one up myself. It's no big deal."

"What's your designation? I'm afraid we're going to have to report this to your supervisor." A henchagent clasped his hand on her shoulder and turned her toward him. His eyes went wide. "I know you."

Connie punched him in the gut. He doubled over, and she kneed him in the face. She was already planning the series of moves to take out the second henchagent, who would certainly do the dumb thing and try to subdue her.

He turned and ran.

"Damn it." Connie jumped over her prone opponent and tackled the runner. He screamed and flailed like a frightened child, throwing a few clumsy punches until she incapacitated him with a nerve strike.

The first goon grabbed her from behind in a headlock and

pulled her off her feet. He tightened the hold, and the world darkened as she threatened to black out.

She managed to swivel her legs under her and then behind his ankles. She pushed him back. He fell to the floor, scrambling to his feet. She kicked him in the head again, and while he lay there, his face a broken mess, she used ancient secrets of acupressure to render him immobile.

Connie sat beside him and closed her eyes. Two nameless goons. This should've been easy. She expected more henchagents to enter, but the cruel universe allowed her a few more moments undisturbed.

She dragged the henchagents behind some laundry baskets, where they might stay hidden for a while. She rolled them onto their backs and measured the bloodied one.

"Hey, what size are you?"

He gurgled very, very lightly.

"Eh, close enough," she said as she unzipped his uniform.

Three minutes later, she was walking the halls in her borrowed uniform and helmet. The jumpsuit was a little baggy. Its sleeves were an inch too long, but she tucked them into the gloves. Her collar had some blood splatter. She found a skull helmet and put it on. It wasn't quite fitted to her head, cutting off the bottom of her vision, but it hid her face. There wasn't anything she could do about that. If she walked with purpose, people would assume she was doing something important.

She had around an hour before the laundry room henchagents were able to move again, assuming they weren't discovered before that. Depending on protocol, the base could go on lockdown with sirens and security deployed. That would work to her advantage. It was easier to sneak around in a chaotic situation.

It'd be trickier if breach protocol was silent. She could be being hunted right now and not be aware of it. She kept her head down and an eye out and didn't think about it.

Most secret bases were easy to navigate with clear signage, and Siege Perilous bases, due to Lady Peril's fastidious nature, were especially so. Connie slipped into security and found an empty station, where she cycled through video feeds until she found Byron sitting alone in a room with a giant chained mutant. She noted the location scrawled on the lower part of the monitor.

"What are you doing?" asked a henchagent in a brown jumpsuit. "You aren't authorized to operate that equipment."

"Maintenance." She tapped her yellow suit, having figured out the departmental colors on the walk. "Someone reported a malfunctioning system."

He walked past her to check the console. "It doesn't look broken."

"Loose wire," she said as she moved behind him. "I fixed it."

"Yes." His tone said he was already suspicious.

She poked him in a pressure point then caught him as he collapsed in her arms. She dropped him in the chair. A glance around the room confirmed that none of the personnel had noticed the moment of struggle. Or they had and were smart enough not to give Connie any warning.

She left the paralyzed henchagent behind. Another loose end to be discovered. She'd assumed all her success was due to skill and grit, not pure luck. Actually, she'd never assumed much of anything. She'd been too busy saving the world to think much about it either way. But now she could really use some luck, and it was the one thing she couldn't rely on anymore.

Connie had always lived on borrowed time. Even after losing some of the caretaker mantle, she still knew there were obligations out there she couldn't escape. And there was that glorious-death clause, a useless prophecy when her life involved regular brushes with adventure.

She'd never been enamored of the idea of destiny, but it was a comfort to think that her death would be something spectacular. Now she only wanted to live long enough to get Byron out of there. After saving the day, the world, the universe, on a regular basis, it all came down to that one thing. If afterward she tripped on some stairs and broke her neck, she'd be fine with it. Just so long as she got Byron out of there.

Lady Peril had the mutant almost kill Byron once every hour for the next four hours. By the third time, the monster was starting to look more disappointed than Byron. When the fifth time rolled around, the creature didn't bother moving as the chain unwound around its feet. It waited for a minute, pawing the chain with skepticism. When it became clear there was more than enough to give it run of the chamber, it stood and eyed Byron, licking its lips.

Outside the door, Byron heard something thud, followed by something else. A dull pop. Another one. Gunshots, perhaps.

The door remained closed.

The mutant loped forward. Saliva dripped from its maw. Its claws clicked against the floor.

Another bang. A gunshot. Definitely a gunshot.

It had to be Connie. She was there to save him. She'd made it. Just in time. That was what she did. But the door still hadn't opened as the mutant prepared to pounce.

He thought about the whims of fate, the little moments that could change everything. He thought about Lady Peril's magic circle and how the rules had changed. Connie wasn't going to make it on time. Connie had been shot on the other side of that door and was bleeding to death on the other side of that wall. This was how they died.

The door opened, and Connie stood there. He knew it was her, even though she was wearing a henchagent's jump-suit and a face-obscuring helmet. She was alive, but too late. She dashed forward as the mutant pounced. Byron screamed, covered his face with his arms. It wasn't a dignified way to die, but there wasn't a dignified way to be torn to shreds by a freak of science gone wrong.

He didn't die.

He opened his eyes.

Constance stood before the mutant.

The mutant mewed curiously.

Connie stared deep into its eyes, holding one hand out. The mutant's whiskers twitched, and she placed her hand on its nose. It slumped with a purr and rolled over on its back.

"I don't believe it," said Byron. "I mean, I believe it, but I don't."

She rubbed the mutant's chin. Its tail wagged as it rolled on its back. "Just combined two techniques, one I learned from a Cossack tiger tamer, the other an Atlantean shark charmer. Aren't you a sweetie?"

The mutant squeaked contentedly.

"Are you okay?" she asked.

He took in her wrinkled, ill-fitting jumpsuit, the blood on her collar, the blood from her cut hands staining her gloves.

He asked, "Are you?"

"I'm fine," said Connie.

The mutant grumbled, and she scratched its neck.

"I've got everything under control."

"I didn't ask if you had everything in control," said Byron. "I asked about you."

She stopped petting the monster. It rolled over on its belly and snorted.

"Are we really going to fight about this now? Can't we at least wait until we've escaped?"

"Sure."

The mutant growled at Byron, but she smacked it lightly on the nose. It lowered its head submissively.

"This isn't the right place to have this conversation,"

She caught it then. God help Byron and Tia and everyone else, but she *was* using adventure to avoid talking. It was so obvious in that moment. And this wasn't the right time to have this talk. It was undisputably the worst place to have this talk. But though that was true now, it wasn't always. And she'd do the same thing under different circumstances.

"I'm not great," she said.

It was so freeing to admit. The world didn't explode with her admission of vulnerability, but it hadn't ever been about the world. It'd been about convincing everyone, especially herself, that she had everything in hand. Amid all the craziness, she was still in charge and as long as she kept her head, everything would work out.

"Byron, I'm sorry that—"

"I don't get it," said Byron. "Why isn't Lady Peril saying anything? She was watching before."

"We can worry about that later," said Connie. "We have to get you out of here."

They left the mutant behind, but on the other side of the door, two dozen guards surrounded them. The guards parted, and Lady Peril and Apollonia stepped forward.

"So good of you to join us, Constance."

30

Connie couldn't decide if this was more bad luck or merely the expected moment when the villain captured her before her inevitable daring escape. She stepped in front of Byron.

"You have me now. Why don't you let him go?"

Peril put a finger to her lips. "Oh, but I've grown rather fond of him. Also, his continued presence should dissuade you from trying anything clever."

Connie appraised the situation. Dozens of guards, all with their rifles at the ready. Lady Peril and Apollonia, both dangerous combatants on their own. Her luck running out, if not already completely gone. And Byron.

"Okay, so you've got me. What I don't get is why you went to such lengths to get me. You've never been sadistic, Peril. If you wanted me dead, why not just kill me?"

"Oh, Constance, I could've killed you ages ago. And believe

me, I was tempted over the years, but . . . well, it's a bit of a cliché to spell out my plans, isn't it? How many times have we been here? You, at my mercy. Myself, confident in my inevitable triumph but eager to explain everything so that you might appreciate my genius."

"You know you want to," said Connie.

Lady Peril smiled. It barely qualified with an upward turn of the right corner of her mouth. That scared the hell out of Connie. It meant things were worse than she thought.

"Oh, I suppose it can't hurt to explain a few things—" said Peril.

Apollonia cleared her throat.

"But I went to so much trouble," said Peril. "Seems a shame that Constance should die not knowing how expertly she's been manipulated."

"You instructed me to warn you against doing this," said Apollonia.

"I won't tell her everything. Certainly not enough to foil my scheme this time."

"That's what you said you would say."

Peril's smile faded, and her disinterested expression returned. "Yes, old habits, I suppose. Come along, Constance."

Connie and Byron were led down the hall. Peril was taking no chances, staying behind a wall of guards.

"I'm sorry, Byron," said Connie.

"It's okay, Connie."

"This is all my fault."

"It's not always about you. You have this tendency to take all the responsibility on yourself."

"You're right," she said.

Byron paused, but he'd already prepared himself for this battle and couldn't stop the momentum. "We all make choices. And, despite what you might think, I chose to be your boyfriend. It wasn't forced upon me."

A nearby guard averted his gaze from their conversation.

"Can we not fight in front of the evil mastermind?" she asked.

"Please, don't stop on our account," said Lady Peril. "This is your last chance to iron out your little lover's spat. I'd hate for Constance to go to her grave with unfinished business. Probably come back as a ghost, given her bothersome nature."

"Okay, why the hell not?" said Connie. "I don't know what you want from me, Byron. First, you're upset that I try to keep you out of this part of my life. Then you're mad because you're worried about me. Then you're upset that I'm trying to rescue you."

"No, I'm upset because you keep treating me like a prop," he said. "You keep acting like I'm not part of this, like I have no say in it, like I'm something you have to worry about all the time."

"Didn't I just rescue you from a mutant monster?"

"Maybe I'm starting to wish you hadn't."

"Maybe I'm starting to agree with you."

They stopped, and their escort came to a halt.

"Byron, I'm sorry. I didn't mean that."

"I know, but you can't do everything yourself. It's all right to rely on others now and then."

"I do. I have Tia." Connie hoped he wouldn't ask the logical follow-up.

"Where is Tia?"

"I locked her in a closet," said Connie apologetically. "For her own protection."

"For hers? Or yours? I know you're used to carrying the weight of the world, but it's a lot easier with help. You make things harder on yourself by pretending you're protecting everyone. But I think it's bull. You keep waiting for me to leave, so you're using your life, using this" —he waved at the henchagents around them— "as an excuse to avoid getting close to me."

The agents turned to Connie, awaiting her reply.

"Okay, there might be something to that," she admitted. "But you have to admit you freaked out when you realized just how crazy my life is."

The agents swiveled toward Byron.

"I didn't handle it well," he said, "but I still think we can make this work."

"You forget. We're broken up." She took his hand, tentatively. "Aren't we?"

"I don't know. Are we?" He squeezed her hand.

"Yes," said Lady Peril. "Very cathartic, indeed. If Connie

was going to live past the hour, I believe you two might have a chance." She clapped her hands. "Now, if we might continue on to your destruction."

At her nod, an agent prodded Connie with his weapon, and they started walking again.

"Don't worry, Byron," said Connie. "I will get us out of here."

"I believe you," he said.

She held his hand tighter.

The lights flickered and shut off. Connie was ready to spring, taking advantage of the sudden darkness, but she heard a hard *whoosh* and the hallway vibrated with a strong *thud*. The lights snapped back on. Two emergency lockdown doors had slammed down from the ceiling. Several henchagents had been caught between them and the floor. They groaned and squirmed under the pressure.

Three guards remained on Connie's side of the walls. She dealt with them efficiently, almost entirely by reflex. One guard, the door pressing down on his chest, had the presence of mind to attempt to aim his weapon in Connie's direction, but she snatched the rifle.

"Thanks."

Lady Peril barked muffled orders. Guards attempted to squirm through gaps left by the other henchagents and the floor. Connie kicked one in the face and pointed the rifle at another, who retreated with a squeak.

"Is this your plan?" asked Byron.

"Not mine."

The lights flicked off and on in a pattern, leading down a hallway. They followed. Five times, they were face-to-face with armed guards, only to have more security walls fall in place. A secret door opened in a smooth wall, and they entered.

"Hello, Connie," greeted the very much alive Larry Peril.

31

Very little surprised Connie.

This surprised her. Sort of. Though she had to admit she'd kind of seen it coming, too.

"Larry, you're alive," she said.

"Now, Connie, I know you probably have a lot of questions."

She put her hands on his face to check for telltale plastic surgery scars, signs of cloning, waxy robotic pseudoflesh. When she was reasonably certain he was the real thing, she wrapped him in a hug tight enough to knock the breath out of him.

"I don't care why or how," she said. "I'm not even mad at you, you son of a bitch. I'm just glad you're not dead."

His minions were standard Siege Perilous issue, and Connie kept her weapon at the ready.

"You don't have to worry about them," said Larry. "They're my people."

"You have people?"

"More than you might suspect. Certainly more than Mom

expected." Larry nodded at Byron. "This is him? This is the guy?"

Connie performed quick introductions. Larry and Byron shook hands perfunctorily. They eyed each other with suspicion.

"Larry's an old friend," said Connie.

"Yes. Old friends," said Larry.

He left it at that, and Byron didn't say anything, but he did move closer to Connie.

"Follow me," said Larry. "We have your escape route all prepared."

They walked through the secret passage.

"I saw you die," she said.

"Did you?" he asked with a slight smile.

"You sly bastard."

"I guess I picked up a few tricks from Mom, after all." They turned a corner and came across a monorail tram, which they boarded. "I'm sorry. I knew Mom was up to something, but I needed time to figure out what it was. So I played along, doing what she expected me to do. When I figured it out, I staged my death to draw her out. Unfortunately, she moved faster than I expected. I didn't realize how far along she was."

"Then why are we leaving?" asked Connie. "We should be stopping her."

"Getting you out of here will stop her. Or at least slow her down. It's complicated to explain, but you are what this is all about. Not you specifically but the caretaker mantle that you carry. She's been siphoning it from you slowly, containing it for her own purposes."

Connie said, "Is that all? Well, she's wasting her time. It's broken, fading. I broke it when I sacrificed some of it to stop the Great Engine from destroying free will in the universe."

"You can't break it," said Larry. "The essence scattered, but it will re-form."

"Well, um," said Byron, "her plan is to destroy the caretaker once and for all."

"How do you know that?" asked Larry.

Byron said, "She told me." He sounded apologetic about it, though he didn't know why. "She has this magic ritual that will gather all the spell . . . uh . . . stuff. Once it's all hers, she plans on finally destroying it. I don't really know how, but she seemed certain she could do it."

"Why would she do that?" asked Connie.

"She seems to think that if it's gone, she'll be the inevitable ruler of the universe."

"That sounds like Mom," said Larry.

"We have to go back."

"Are you crazy?" asked Byron. "Haven't you been paying attention these last few weeks? You're in no shape to foil an evil scheme like this. There can't be much caretaker magic left in you."

"It's why we have to stop her now. This isn't a situation that is going to get better by hiding. She'll find me again and force me into some death trap, some no-win situation, drain whatever is left. Then she'll have everything she needs."

"So, we escape and come back with reinforcements before that happens," said Byron.

"It might be too late by then," said Connie. "Right now, we know where Peril is and we know where the caretaker force is being contained."

"I don't remember how to find it," said Byron. "I get all turned around in this place."

"I know where it is," said Larry.

"Can you get us there?" asked Connie.

"I don't know. Probably. Maybe. Hypothetically. But if we turn around, there's every possibility that we'll lose any chance to get you out of here."

"Exactly what Peril wouldn't expect," said Connie.

"No, it's exactly what she would expect," said Byron, "because it's a crazy, reckless thing to do. Don't you get it? That might be why she told me about it. She was betting that you'd rescue me, and then I'd tell you, and then you'd go running into danger out of heroic reflex."

"That does sound like Mom," said Larry. "And if she's right, you'll be at your most vulnerable."

"No, I'll be more vulnerable tomorrow when there's nothing of the caretaker mantle left," said Connie. "And I've been foiling diabolical schemes for decades. It wasn't some magic luck spell that made that happen."

"But what if it was?" asked Byron. "I know you don't like the idea, but what if it was destiny?"

"There are two options. Either the caretaker mantle didn't matter, and this is just another evil genius I have to stop. Or it's all about the caretaker mantle and allowing Lady Peril to destroy it is a crime against the universe. Better to use whatever scraps linger within me to stop that from happening."

"It's crazy, reckless," said Larry.

"Crazy and reckless is what I do best. How many loyal people do you have here?"

"Only about twenty percent, but many of them are in key positions, like the security personnel that overlooked your infiltration. I give the order, and we can sow a hell of a lot of confusion. I can get us there. Probably."

"Wait. So, we're done debating this?" asked Byron. "We're walking back into the lair of an evil genius without any real plan?"

"I've learned there's no point in debating Connie once she's made up her mind," said Larry.

She took Byron's hand. "I know it might be a bad move. I'm not at all sure it's the smart move. I'm winging it here, and I could be making a horrible mistake. But this isn't me rushing ignorantly into danger. I will be careful, I swear. I'll think things through."

"No, you won't," said Byron.

Connie shook her head. "No, I probably won't. But I swear that if there's a way to stop Peril and come out alive, I will find it."

"You can't promise that either," he said.

"No, I can't," she said quietly, more to herself than him. "There are no guarantees. Not in my life. Not in anybody's. But if I make it out of here, I'd like to believe that you'll still be there."

Byron turned to Larry. "When you're right, you're right. And she's right. This is what she does. And we need to help her do it."

"We?" asked Connie.

"I'm coming with you. Even if the magic luck spell that gives you an edge is gone, I believe you can do this. But I also believe you'll need plenty of help. Since Tia's not here, I have to be your backup sidekick."

She took his hand. "Byron, that's sweet but—"

"It's dangerous," he interrupted. "I'll only get in the way. You can't worry about me. It'll be better for everyone if I'm someplace safe. That's what you were going to say, right?"

Connie nodded. "Yes."

"Tough. I'm coming with you. I'm not helpless. I've been studying martial arts, and I still have my Swiss army knife." He pulled it out of his pocket.

"They let you keep that?" she asked.

"Guess they didn't think it would be dangerous enough to confiscate." He flipped out the short, dull knife. "Their mistake."

"You're holding that wrong," said Connie. "You'd cut yourself if you tried to use it."

He adjusted his grip. "I knew that. Just testing you."

"You're still holding it wrong."

He folded the blade and shoved the army knife into his pocket. "I'm not changing my mind, and you don't have time to waste arguing about it. And if this is about the balance of the universe, I'm just as much a part of this as anyone else. I live in the universe too."

"I could always have the henchagents drag him out of here," offered Larry.

She considered it.

"He's right. It's his choice. But I swear to God, Byron, if you get yourself killed, I'll never forgive you for it."

He smiled. "I was about to say the same thing to you."

A ctivate anarchy protocol," said Larry into his radio.

Moments later, a distant series of explosions shook the base. The lights went out for a few moments before flickering on as backup systems kicked in.

"I've knocked out a few vital monitoring systems and jammed the communications systems. Security will be a mess, and emergency will be handling the fires."

"Fires?" asked Byron as he slipped into a spare henchagent jumpsuit. "Is that dangerous?"

"It's all dangerous," said Larry, "but it's more of a distraction than anything life-threatening."

"Those were explosions."

"Some people might have died incidentally," said Larry. "It's regrettable, but . . ."

His voice trailed off.

"Damn, I sound like Mom now."

"You can wrestle with that existential dilemma later."

Connie zipped up her own jumpsuit. "Let's do this."

She caught Byron smiling at her.

"You really are in your element," he said.

She kissed him before putting on his helmet then putting on her own.

"Let's go save the day," she said.

Larry's forces led them through the complex. Once, they were stopped by a security detail, but Larry flashed a secret hand signal and they were allowed to pass. They used a secret tunnel to get around a checkpoint, and he knew the code to punch in to get them through every sealed security door. People ran around, but most were too busy managing the chaos to bother them.

They burst into the magical chamber, expecting trouble, but there weren't any guards.

Only Lady Peril, who stood facing the sacred plateau with her back to them.

"Hello, Larry," she said without looking back. "So good to see you back among the living." The slightest tone of disdain floated under her voice. She always sounded condescending, but there was a touch more this time.

"You knew," said Larry.

"Of course I knew. There is not one thing you've done that I have not expected, not one surprising moment. You always were a predictable boy."

The arcane energies seething in the pit below howled distantly.

"Why go to all this trouble?" asked Connie. "Why fake your own death? Why convince Larry to take the job? Why any of it?"

Peril said, "Ah, yes. Here's the part where I explain everything. I really shouldn't, but it's too delightful. Once I realized that you were never my enemy but the mantle within you, I found myself discouraged. I needed some way to remove the caretaker from the equation, but it's an eternal force. It seemed impossible.

"And then you did the impossible, like you always do. You fractured the force, unraveling it. On its own, it would have fixed itself, but seeing my opportunity, I used these magics to pull at those loose threads, gathering them here. It was only a matter of time before your own adventurous nature would accomplish the task without interference from me. But I saw no reason to wait, so I spurred things along. I created a series of problems within Siege Perilous and, after faking my own death, installed Larry as my successor. Larry would be too weak to solve the problems on his own, and spurred on by his continuing affection for you, he would use the situation as an excuse to call on you for help, which he predictably did."

Larry looked embarrassed. And angry.

"You bitch," he said.

Lady Peril nodded to Apollonia, who punched Larry. He fell to his knees, blood dripping from his mouth, a nasty bruise already forming on his cheek.

"Is that any way to talk to your own mother?" she asked.

"There were backup plans, but I didn't need them. Larry was ever so predictable. As were you, Connie. Always rushing heedless into danger, always saving the world. I need only set things in motion, bait the trap, and watch as you irresistibly walked into it, over and over again.

"Believe it or not, I worried you might exhibit some sense, but sense has never been your strong point. No, you're a care-taker, not just by magic but by nature. It's who you are, and I relished the irony of weaponizing that nature against you."

Lady Peril stood before Connie. "My dear, you look posi-tively exhausted. How does it feel to be so close to normal?" She caressed Connie's cheek. "To know that, soon, the universe will give you no special consideration? To know that you will be no more blessed or cursed than anyone else?"

"You can't destroy the caretaker," said Connie. "The uni-verse needs it."

"Why would I destroy it when I can take it for myself?"

"You're a hypocrite," said Connie. "You're not trying to make the universe fair. You just wanted the power for yourself."

"Am I not worthy of greatness? Whereas you squandered it with your ridiculous adventures, I will harness it to achieve a glorious future for myself. The most powerful force in this universe paired with my superior intellect and ambitious imag-ination." Peril raised an eyebrow. "What could be more fair that that?"

She placed her hand on the biometric scanner. She stepped onto the bridge as it extended across the chasm.

A tremble shook the mountain. Heat rose, followed by a wave of icy cold. A few pieces of stone fell from the roof, tumbling into the void.

"This is too much power," said Connie. "You can't keep it stable."

"I can keep it stable long enough," replied Lady Peril. "Although your presence has stirred up some unexpected agitation."

Lady Peril stepped off the bridge and onto the plateau. The bridge started to retract. Peril paused, waving at Connie.

"Witness the end of an unfair universe."

Connie bolted across the bridge. She didn't think it through. She expected to be shot, but if there was any luck left in her, she prayed it held out.

Byron jumped on a guard. Or he tried to. He ended up with an elbow to the throat and on his back. The guard aimed his weapon at Byron's chest. He might have screamed if he could breathe.

Apollonia punched the guard from behind. He fell over. Another two blows knocked two more to the floor. A fourth minion fired a few rounds, but she grabbed his rifle and thrust it upward. Apollonia yanked the weapon from his hands and struck him across the nose with the butt of the weapon. Another tried to jump her. She pivoted, using his own force against him, and he went sailing over the edge into the abyss. His screams echoed for a long, long time.

She dismantled the remaining minions with surgical

precision. Not a wasted move. Knocking the fight out of them with single, well-aimed strikes. The biggest guard took two kicks, but after she crushed his knee with a blow that made Byron cringe empathically (the visceral crunching sound helped), the goon fell.

Byron stood. "Wait. You're on our side?"

"I'm on Larry's side," she replied as she punched a code into the door access panel that sealed the chamber.

"But you punched him."

"Just following orders."

Larry rubbed his jaw. "You didn't have to follow them so well."

Apollonia smiled. "I am a professional."

Connie had no time to worry about that. She sped toward the edge of the bridge and leapt across the void. The magic below roared, as if hungry for her. She landed with a few inches to spare, rolled forward, and hit a wall that knocked her on her ass.

It was Lady Peril. She towered over Connie.

"So predictable," said Peril.

The circle's magic vibrated the air as the standing stones rang with forgotten druidic chants.

Connie stood as Peril drew a ray gun from her coat. She might get one or two shots off before Connie closed the short distance. A gun this close wasn't a great weapon.

But she hesitated.

Lady Peril read Connie's mind.

"Yes, you might be able to make it. But what if you don't? What if you used the last bit of luck you had crossing that bridge?" Peril backed away, keeping her gun trained on Connie. "Do you feel that hot lump burning in your chest? Does your heart beat faster? Tell me. How long has it been since you've felt fear? Really felt it?"

"What's your game?" asked Connie.

"You asked why I went to so much trouble? It's because in order to take the caretaker mantle from you, I needed for you to come here. Willingly. Magic has all these silly little rules, and one of them is that the transfer ritual can't be forced. The old caretaker and the new must meet on the circle, and here you are. All you had to do was not step on the circle, but I knew you would. I knew I only had to set the trap and let you do the rest. And now, by rite of worthiness, I take the final bits of magic and claim my destiny."

She fired. Connie grabbed the legendary shield of Ajax from the ground and rolled behind it. The heat ray burned against the shield. Connie charged Peril, ramming her with the huge shield. It only staggered Peril, but Connie followed up, kicking the gun out of Peril's hand. It bounced over the edge and into the abyss.

Peril glowered. "Stubborn to the last. I shouldn't be surprised."

Connie said, "You made one mistake, Peril. The same

mistake you always make. You've got me right where you want me. Like you have before. And we both know how it ends. You, presumed dead. Me, stopping you."

"There is one difference this time." Peril pointed to the vase containing magical powers.

"Two differences," said Connie, adopting a combat stance. "This time, you won't be presumed. You'll just be dead."

In a blinding flash, Lady Peril ripped the shield from Connie and threw it to one side. Peril hit Connie with a glancing blow that still sent her tumbling back.

"I'm not a fool, Connie. I know you're a formidable opponent. It's why I made sure you were exhausted. You're slow and clumsy and careless."

"I'm also surrounded by magical artifacts." Connie picked up a cursed black scimitar. It whispered horrible thoughts into her mind, wanting blood. She was happy to oblige.

"If you're so eager to fight to your last breath." Lady Peril knelt down to grab a rune-laden battle axe. "So be it."

On the other side of the chasm, Byron watched helplessly as Connie and Lady Peril clashed. Larry kept an eye on the guards, though Apollonia had knocked most of the fight out of them.

"We have to do something," said Byron.

Apollonia fired a short burst from her rifle. The bullets exploded in tiny sparks at the circle's edge. Nothing outside of it could affect anything inside of it.

"Are you crazy?" he asked. "You could've shot her."

"I could've. I didn't."

She checked the biometric scanner that operated the bridge.

Connie's and Lady Peril's steel met, and each strike sent shockwaves through the chamber. The otherworldly light below flashed with each clash of metal against metal. All the magic warmed the air. Byron wiped the sweat from his brow and looked away from the fight. Connie was doing okay right now, but she was only holding her ground. Just barely, at that.

"I don't get it. If you were on our side, why were you willing to let Lady Peril feed me to that mutant?"

"Larry never mentioned anything about protecting you. Doing so would've been stupid and counterproductive."

"Oh, it would've been counterproductive," said Byron. "Why didn't you say so?"

An ambitious henchagent reached for a gun. Apollonia cast a glance his way, and he changed his mind.

"It was an acceptable risk," said Larry. "Apollonia is the only person I can trust here. She always has my back. I'm sure she was behaving in the best interests of her orders."

"Are you sure you're not an evil genius?" asked Byron.

The room crackled with cosmic power as thunder rumbled. Or something like thunder, since it didn't make any sense for there to be thunder inside a mountain.

Larry said, "Maybe I'm more like Mom than I realized, but you're alive, aren't you? Right now, our priority is to get that bridge working."

Apollonia gave the scanner a few swift kicks. She put a deep dent in the side, but the metal held.

"Don't do that," said Byron. "You might break it."

"It's biometric," she said. "We can't use it."

"Maybe we can rewire it," said Larry. "But we'll need something to open it up."

"It's a long shot." Apollonia ran her fingers along a seam. "I don't suppose anyone has a screwdriver handy."

Byron held up his Swiss army knife. "Flathead or Phillips-head?"

Their weapons locked together, Lady Peril pushed Connie down to one knee.

Peril looked down her nose. "Why do you continue to fight? You've lost. The powers of science have enhanced my strength and speed beyond anything you could match. You're barely standing."

Screaming, summoning every ounce of strength, Connie shoved Peril away. The cavern screamed with her.

Lady Peril lowered her axe, and Connie, exhausted, lowered her scimitar.

"I've beaten stronger and faster," she said. Her hoarse voice surprised her.

"You can't think this will accomplish anything. My victory is inevitable."

Connie smiled. "That's what they always say."

Connie charged forward, bringing her scimitar down against Peril's axe. The enchanted weapons exploded with power, flying away with such force that neither could keep hold of them. The plateau quaked as fissures broke across it.

Connie unleashed a kick that should've broken a rib or two, but Peril barely moved. Connie followed it up with a pair of nerve strikes. Peril's only reaction was a mild grunt. Connie threw a smashing uppercut hard enough to almost break her hand. She swept Peril's legs. It was like uprooting a tree, but Peril fell, giving Connie enough time to put some distance between them.

Laughing, Lady Peril stood.

"Is that it? Is this the glorious death of Constance Verity? Fighting on against impossible odds? How futile. How pathetic."

She advanced, and this was it. Connie couldn't survive another attack. Her legs ached. Her vision blurred. She was slow, clumsy.

She was done.

It only took thirty seconds for Larry to rewire the biometric scanner. The longest thirty seconds of Byron's life as he watched Connie struggle to stay away from Lady Peril.

The bridge extended, one foot at a time, and Byron, Larry, and Apollonia ran to the plateau.

"We should be careful," said Larry. "It might have some sort of—"

Byron jumped onto the plateau. A sharp pain ran through him for a moment, but he made it. Larry and Apollonia hit an invisible barrier. They pressed against it but couldn't cross.

"What's happening?" asked Byron.

"I don't know," said Larry. "I didn't make the spell."

Connie sluggishly dodged Peril's attacks.

"Don't do anything stupid," said Larry. "We'll figure it out. Just give me a minute."

Connie didn't have a minute. Byron grabbed an old book among the scattered relics. There was probably something better, but he didn't have time to figure that out. The book was thick and heavy. It could do some damage. Offer a distraction. Something.

He ran forward, screaming like an idiot. Once he was close enough, he threw the book at Peril's back. It tumbled through the air, falling a few feet short, hitting the ground with a thud.

Lady Peril glanced behind her.

"Really?"

He thought he should say something defiant, but damned if he could figure out what that might be.

"Get away from her."

It sounded stupid.

Peril turned her attention away from him. He was still beneath her, and as much as he hated to admit it, her contempt was justified.

The book had other ideas.

It opened itself and a swarm of smoky batlike things

erupted from its pages. They swirled around Peril. She flailed at the screeching, distracting beasts.

Connie ran to him. "Are you okay?"

"Me?" he asked. "What about you?"

"You have to go back. Let me handle this."

"I'm not going to stand by while a supervillain kills you," he said.

"You're just going to get in the way."

"Maybe I want to be in the way."

She leaned against him. "Byron, this is probably it. If you don't get out of here, you'll die."

"No, I won't," he said. "I'm beside Constance Verity. That has to be the safest place in the world to be."

The chamber surged as the power crystals flared and the standing stones floated a few feet off the plateau. The magic carvings flashed with a rainbow of colors. The abyss howled below as the plateau rocked, tilting at a slight angle.

"I love you," she said.

She kissed him.

The smoke bats dissolved. Peril shook her head. "You've proven even more troublesome than I expected. But you always have."

"You've gathered too much power here," said Connie. "It's all going to come crumbling down. What good is stealing the caretaker mantle if you die moments afterward? You were never this stupid, Peril."

"I don't care." Peril's uncontrolled laughter echoed through the chamber. Connie had never seen Peril like this. She was out of control. All her propriety and decorum gone, replaced by a mad ambition.

"This ends here and now. This is the last adventure of Constance Verity. And your little boyfriend, too."

Byron's cell rang. He pulled it from his pocket, then yelped as the hot plastic burned his hand. The cell bounced off the floor, exploding in a shower of sparks as an alien warrior materialized. She wore alien battle armor made of interlocking, shifting plates that changed color depending on the angle of the light.

The helmet retracted, and Tia, queasy from the interstellar transport, retched. She managed not to vomit and ruin her entrance.

"Oh, thank god," she said. "It worked."

Lady Peril's rage swallowed the last of her composure. She jumped Tia, who blasted her away with a percussive bolt from a gauntlet.

Peril staggered but stayed on her feet. She grabbed a spear that bristled with magical lightning. "You will not—"

A small cannon popped out of Tia's shoulder and fired a mini-missile. It exploded under Peril, launching her into the air. She hit the ground a dozen feet away, lying unmoving on the ground.

"Did I kill her?" asked Tia. "I didn't mean to. I didn't really have time to learn how to use this thing properly."

"Where did you come from?" asked Byron.

"There will be time for explanations later," said Connie. "We have to claim the caretaker mantle before this whole place collapses."

They checked the alabaster vase, glowing with power.

"What do we do?" he asked.

"When in doubt," said Connie, "break something."

They touched it, but before they could shove it over, it shattered on its own. The pieces fell away, and the caretaker destiny flared in all its unharnessed glory. It should've been blinding, but they had no problem looking at it.

A large portion floated up and away, dissolving into nothingness. The bulk of the remaining power settled on Connie. A few stray rays of light passed onto Tia, and one or two glittering particles fell into Byron. They absorbed the magic.

Lady Peril staggered forward. "You cheated."

The influx of magic filled Connie with fresh energy. She still glowed a little.

"I didn't make the rules. And neither did you. You wanted to prove yourself worthy. Well, you blew it."

"You would've never beaten me on your own," said Peril.

"Who ever said I had to?" asked Connie.

The arcane energies in the abyss surged up from below as the standing stones whirled wildly about. An Atlantean power crystal exploded, raining fine powder. Cracks ran up the chamber walls as the edges of the plateau crumbled away.

"It's over, Peril," said Connie.

Every last drop of rage and hate dropped from Lady Peril,

replaced with her normal cold calm. "Yes, it is. Well played, Connie."

A massive chunk of ceiling fell, cracking the plateau in two. Silently, Lady Peril plummeted into the burning energies.

"We really should get out of here," said Larry.

He and Apollonia ran down the bridge, barely avoiding a boulder that smashed the section they'd been standing on. Connie, Tia, and Byron struggled to stay on their feet as the plateau broke apart.

"I got this," shouted Tia. "I think."

She put her arms around Connie and Byron and jumped for it. Wings extended from her back, rockets fired, and they flew in wild circles.

"I didn't have time to train," she said, barely navigating the swirling storm of artifacts. A tentacle springing from a magic mirror almost grabbed her ankle.

"Look where you want to go," yelled Connie. "Not where you're going."

Tia flew to the platform. The landing was hard, but nobody broke anything.

The last of the plateau disappeared into the abyss. The potent magic shook the earth for miles.

"How do you feel?" Byron asked Connie.

"Better," she said. "And you?"

He touched his chest where the lingering warmth of the bits of destiny had settled. "Not different, but sort of different. It's hard to describe."

"It always is," she said.

"So, is anyone else concerned that we're trapped in a base, surrounded by hundreds of enemy henchagents?" asked Byron. "Or is that just normal?"

"You all saw my mom die, right?" asked Larry of the dumbfounded henchagents standing together to one side. "I don't suppose you'd be cool with telling everyone else that I'm back in charge again?"

The mountain roared as it collapsed over their heads.

They blasted out of the self-destructing mountain in one of Siege Perilous's experimental antigravity aircrafts. Ten minutes later, Connie sat alone in the cockpit, watching the landscape whiz by below.

Apollonia stepped into the cockpit. "Larry wanted me to check if you needed relief."

"I'm not really sure how to fly this thing. I was mostly winging it on takeoff, and I think it's been on autopilot for the last six minutes." Connie released the control wheel, and the craft carried on flying. "I was just taking the time to think about things."

"Where is it flying to?" asked Apollonia.

"Don't know. We should probably figure that out. You're welcome to take a crack at it."

Apollonia sat in the copilot chair and scanned dials and buttons.

"You were on Larry's side the whole time?" asked Connie.

"Don't make a big thing about it," said Apollonia. "He pays better than Lady Peril. That's all."

"Sure, sure."

"Also, Larry may be a terrible mastermind, but he isn't likely to kill me to set an example for the other minions."

"I always thought that was a stupid policy," said Connie. "So, you don't like Larry at all."

Apollonia flicked a switch, and they waited for the craft to react. It didn't plunge from the sky or change course.

"He's all right. You know Larry. He's a nice guy. Hard not to like him. But in the end, it's still about the money and the job security."

"Very practical." Connie pushed a button. The craft shuddered, but nothing else happened. "I guess we're not going to fight, then?"

"Doesn't make sense, since we're on the same side. This time."

"This time," said Connie with a smile. "Just promise me you'll look after Larry."

"That's what he pays me for."

"Right."

Connie left Apollonia to figure out the controls. She walked among the other passengers crammed in the cargo hold. They'd picked up two dozen straggling minions and employees they couldn't leave behind to die. Most were technicians or maintenance crew. The few security personnel weren't in the mood to fight. The craft was meant to haul cargo, so it didn't have seats. They sat on the floor in small color-coded groups.

She found Larry and pulled him aside.

"I'm sorry about your mom," she said.

"No body," he replied.

"We saw her die."

"I've seen her die before," he said. "I'm not assuming anything, but if she's dead, she went out the way she would've wanted. Well, actually, no. She would've wanted to take you with her. I'm glad she didn't."

"How much did you know about her master plan?" she asked.

"More than I let on," he said. "Not as much as I should've. I'm sorry that I didn't tell you the truth from the beginning."

"You did what you thought was right. It all worked out in the end."

"I still used you." Larry glanced at his hands. "Not to mention my ulterior motives . . ."

She took his hand and gave it a squeeze. "We all do stupid things. Who knows? In different circumstances, you and I might have worked out. We didn't, and in these circumstances, it was stupid. Incredibly stupid."

"Yes." He shrugged. "Stupid."

"You'll be fine, Larry. You just have to stop looking back. Trust me. I'm learning that lesson myself. What are you planning on doing now?"

"Don't know. If Mom's really dead this time—a big *if*—then I guess I'm still in charge of Siege Perilous. Now that you've defused most of the bombs she left behind, I guess I could give masterminding a chance."

"I've seen worse masterminds," said Connie. "But can you turn a global-extortion and world-domination organization into something good?"

"I can try. And if things go wrong . . ."

She shook his hand and followed it up with a hug.

"You know where to find me."

Tia was in the back with Byron and the shark/tiger hybrid. The giant mutant, lulled by the thrum of the anti-grav engines, lay sleeping in the corner. Tia and Byron were struggling to get her out of her alien power armor, but it wasn't cooperating. Byron tugged at a gauntlet. He placed his foot on her stomach and pulled. The suit zapped him with a jolt, and he jumped back.

"Damn it," he said, "Every time."

"It resembles Grubian technology," said Connie. "That stuff usually bonds to the wearer until death."

"Great," said Tia. "I don't even know how to go to the bathroom while wearing this thing."

Connie borrowed Byron's Swiss army knife and inserted the corkscrew attachment under a plate on Tia's back and gave it a twist. She stepped back as the suit's many plates fell to pieces on the floor.

"Thanks, I've had an itch on my leg that's been driving me crazy for half an hour." Tia scratched at her leg. "Look. I know you're mad—"

"I'm sorry," said Connie. "I kept saying I was protecting you, but I was using that as an excuse to take away your choices. I didn't trust you. Either of you. And it almost cost me my life."

"You were worried," said Byron. "We can't blame you."

"The hell we can't," said Tia. "You should've known better."

"I should've," said Connie. "But it's hard for me sometimes. I've never thought of myself as a loner. I know so many amazing people. But those people just come and go. You've always been there, Tia. That's why you were able to enter the circle. As far as the universe is concerned, you and I are a team. You saved me. You've been saving me since we were kids."

"Damn straight," said Tia. "You'd think you'd have realized that a couple of decades ago."

She held out her fist, and Connie bumped it.

"Now, if you'll excuse me," said Tia, "I'm going to scare up a phone and see if I can reach Hiro. Let him know you aren't planning on killing him anymore. You aren't, right?"

Connie waggled her hand in a *maybe* gesture.

"Eh, close enough." Tia walked away.

Byron embraced Connie, and they shared a long, deep kiss.

"You smell awful," he said.

She laughed. "Adventure does that to a woman."

She put her hands on his cheeks. He was a good guy. She'd always known that, but she'd never truly known it.

"That thing you said about the circle," he asked. "Does that mean we're a team too?"

"Who am I to argue with the universe?"

"But I didn't do anything."

"You saved my life."

"I had a screwdriver. I threw a book. Badly. And I carried a phone. Hardly heroic achievements."

They sat, holding hands. The sleepy mutant woke up and lumbered closer, laying its massive head on Connie's lap before going back to sleep.

"Can we keep him?" asked Byron.

"I'd think you'd be reluctant, seeing as it almost ate you."

"You know what they say. There are no bad abominations of science. Only abominations of science with bad owners. And I've been wanting a pet."

"We could get a cat," said Connie.

"Bit boring, isn't it?" asked Byron as he stroked the mutant on its furry snout, between its jutting tusks.

"I'll talk to Ellington."

She scratched the beast behind its ear, and its tail swished, thumping against the aircraft's fuselage.

Connie said, "People think what I do is amazing and incredible, and it's all very impressive. But saving the day isn't about fighting ninjas or defeating space monsters. Except maybe in the world I live in. But sometimes, being the hero isn't always about being the smartest or the fastest or the strongest."

"Stop. You're embarrassing me."

"Sometimes, being the hero is just being the guy carrying a screwdriver at the right time." She rested her head on his shoulder. "You were that guy for me today. I'd like you to be that guy tomorrow."

"I'd like that too."

She closed her eyes. She'd made a hell of a lot of assumptions about her future, and up to now, she'd never questioned them. She'd been hedging her bets with Byron, even if she'd never admitted it before. She'd stop that now. At least, she'd try.

"Things might be different now," she said. "I'm not sure what happened in that circle with you and me and Tia and the caretaker mantle. I don't know if the balance has changed. I could be back to adventures every day. It could make it harder. More complicated."

"It's always complicated, but I'm willing to fight for us if you are."

He put his arm around her, and a warmth welled in her chest that had nothing to do with cosmic magical forces and everything to do with him. And Tia. And a life she'd been putting off for far too long.

"I can fight," she said. "If there's one thing I can do, it's that."

34

L arry paused at the door.

"You don't have to do this, Lord Peril," said Apollonia. "We can leave."

Their aircraft hovered over the jungle. The only clearing beside the manor was already occupied by a black Siege Perilous experimental jet.

"No, I need to do it." He knocked on the door.

Lady Peril answered. He almost didn't recognize his own mother. Her trademark lab coat and spandex had been replaced by casual cabana wear. The bright colors didn't suit her, but the straw hat, decorated with flowers, was what threw him most.

"Larry," said Peril.

"Mom," he replied.

Peril cast a disapproving glance at Apollonia but didn't address her.

"Can we come in?" asked Larry.

Peril stepped aside. "Please do."

She led them to a sitting room dominated by a statue of Peril holding a sword before her. A few guards stood around, though none of them wore anything from the Siege Perilous uniform. Not even a logo on their suit lapels. She sent one of them off to get some refreshments.

"I suppose you're wondering how I faked my death once again?" asked Peril.

"No," said Larry.

Peril shrugged. "Pity. It was quite clever."

"I'm sure it was, but at this point I don't care."

Peril asked, "Come to bring me to justice then? Vengeance?" She leaned forward. "Have you finally come to kill me, Larry?"

He shook his head. "Holy hell, Mom. You'd love that, wouldn't you? You can see why I've got issues," he said to Apollonia.

The refreshments arrived. Peril helped herself to a butter cookie and some apple juice. "Then why are you here?"

"I'm here to tell you that Siege Perilous is mine now." He leaned back and put his feet on the coffee table because he knew how much it would annoy her. "I'm keeping it."

"Have it then, if you think you can manage it. Frankly, I don't imagine you have the backbone required, and I look forward to your inevitable failure. But don't come crawling back to me when you do."

"Wouldn't dream of it." Larry stood, snapped his fingers. "Let's go."

Apollonia and Peril's guards left the room, leaving Larry and Lady Peril alone.

He said, "I don't know if you have anything planned for the future, if this is all an elaborate scheme, wheels within wheels, but if you stay out of my way, we won't have a problem."

"Am I supposed to believe you'd raise a hand against your own mother? Please, you're far too sentimental for your own good. Always were."

"Maybe," he said. "But I am also my mother's son."

He walked out. A moment later, Lady Peril's manor went dark.

She sat there in the darkness. And she might have been smiling, but there was no one to see it if she was.

"Perhaps you are."

Larry took one last long look at the darkened manor.

"You should've killed her," said Apollonia.

"Probably, but I'm not interested in giving her the satisfaction."

They strolled toward the hovering craft.

"So what now, Lord Peril?" asked Apollonia.

"Don't really know, but we'll figure it out."

He pressed a remote in his pocket and Lady Peril's jet exploded.

"And, please, call me Larry."

35

I can't believe they let us keep her," said Byron.

Cupcake pulled at her leash. The giant mutant could've easily dragged him down the street, but Connie had spent a week training her. She was mostly docile, though there had been an incident with three angry poodles that had got them disinvited to the dog park.

The abomination sniffed at a hydrant.

"We're not keeping her," said Connie. "This is only until Ellington can arrange transport to Monster Island."

"It's not dangerous, is it?" Byron asked.

"It's called Monster Island. What do you think? But it really is the best place for her. She'll be happy there."

Cupcake walked away from the hydrant, leaving a sizzling puddle of acid behind.

"Probably is for the best," admitted Byron.

He put his arm around Connie, and she rested her head against his shoulder as they walked. He kissed the top of her head.

"This is nice," she said.

She said it because it was, because after decades of globe-trotting adventure, she was maybe finally ready for something like this.

They passed Doctor Malady and Automatica walking their dog. The small brown mutt yipped and circled Cupcake play-fully, who danced with equal enthusiasm, until their respective owners carried on their way.

Tia was waiting at the condo entrance. They were meeting for lunch.

"No Hiro?" asked Byron.

"He's still worried Connie is mad at him," replied Tia.

"I'm not mad," said Connie. "I'm really not. He might've been a thoughtless idiot, but he helped us confront some real issues."

"Well, then I guess you might even say I did you a favor," said Hiro from behind her.

Cupcake squealed and bared her fangs. Connie calmed the mutant with a hand on her snout.

"I wouldn't go that far, but I'm not going to kill you." She grinned. "Not today, anyway."

Cupcake growled, licking her maw in Hiro's direction.

"I never doubted you two would work it out." He hobbled to Tia's side. The hobble was for show, to remind Connie that she'd broken his leg in the first place. The transparent appeal to her sympathy wasn't lost on her.

Thunder cracked in the cloudless sky as a green lightning

bolt blasted the middle of the street. An interdimensional rift opened on the spot, grinding traffic to a halt. A minor pileup ensued, with cars smacking each other's bumpers.

A skeleton in black robes stepped through the portal. She raised a gnarled staff sizzling with magic over her head and cackled.

"Behold, mortal fools, your new mistress has arrived! And with my endless undead hordes, I shall sweep across your world extinguishing all cruel life, bringing the beautiful mercy of death!"

"So much for lunch," said Byron.

Connie unhooked Cupcake's leash. "Sic her."

Cupcake pounced on the sorceress, whose shrieks of terror were cut short as her bones were scattered about.

"Maybe we should keep her after all," said Connie.

The skull landed at her feet. The sorceress glared. "I shall see you all fed to my army of death."

A few more skeleton warriors lurched through the portal.

Cupcake loped over and dropped the staff at Connie's feet. She scratched the mutant behind the ear. "Good girl." She picked up the staff and fired a blast of eldritch energies that disintegrated the skeletons.

"You can do magic now?" asked Tia.

"It's mostly the staff," replied Connie, waving it over her head. Red and orange clouds materialized, rumbling in the sky. "Looks like we'll have to close this portal from the other side. Sorry, honey."

"It's fine," Byron said. "Hiro and I will grab something to eat while you ladies do your thing. But don't think an inter-dimensional undead invasion is getting you out of meeting my parents."

"I'll be there." She pulled him close and kissed him. "You're the best."

"I know. Now go save the world."

Connie and Tia and Cupcake stood before the portal. Cupcake slavered, snapping her jaws, growling. Tia held the sorceress's skull under her arm.

"Should we take this with us?"

Connie used the staff to shatter another skeletal invader. "Couldn't hurt."

Tia asked, "This might be a dumb question, but do we have a plan for getting back once the door is closed?"

"I'm sure we'll figure something out. I'm not worried." She slapped Tia on the shoulder. "I've got backup."

Tia grabbed a sword and shook off the skeletal hand still holding it. "Let's do it."

"You shall die, fools," said the sorceress.

"Someday," Connie said with a smile. "But not today."

CONSTANCE VERITY
WILL RETURN.

Communication Failure.

Please hold.

Mechanical Failure.

ase restart your warship.

A NOVEL BY

JOE ZIEJA

A NOVEL BY

JOE ZIEJA

A smooth-talking ex-sergeant, accustomed to an easygoing peacetime military, unexpectedly rejoins the fleet and finds soldiers preparing for the strangest thing: war.

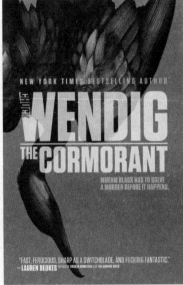

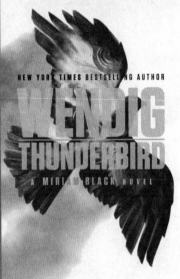

MIRIAM BLACK KNOWS
HOW YOU'RE GOING TO DIE.

She's foreseen hundreds of car crashes, heart attacks, strokes, and suicides. This makes everyday a day from Hell, especially when you can't do anything about it, or stop trying to.

"Exciting, inventive, and brilliantly plotted, this is the sort of urban fantasy I dream about. This book is so damn much fun, it hurts."

—SEANAN McGUIRE,
New York Times bestselling author of the October Daye series

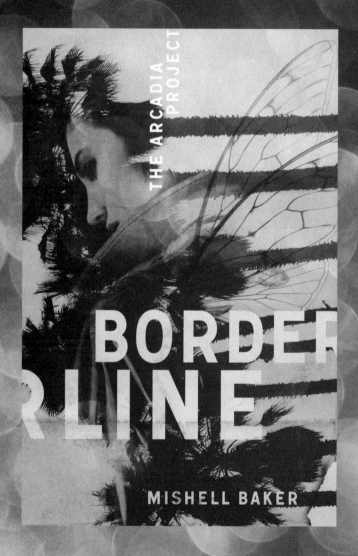

THE ARCADIA PROJECT

BORDERLINE

MISHELL BAKER

PRINT AND EBOOK EDITIONS AVAILABLE
SAGAPRESS.COM